Love through the Seasons

4 Stories from Beloved Author

TRACIE PETERSON

BARBOUR
PUBLISHING

CONTENTS

Celebrating thirty years since first publishing with Barbour Publishing in 1993, Tracie Peterson, most well known for her historical Christian novels, rereleases three novellas along with a newly written story of love in modern times.

Spring

STORMY WEATHER

CHAPTER I

G ina looked at the instructions in her hand for the tenth time. "Official Grand Prix Pinewood Derby Kit," one side read. The other side had "Contains Functional Sharp Points" as its title.

"What in the world are functional sharp points?" she asked, looking down into the questioning eyes of her eight-year-old son. "Do you know what this means, Danny?"

The boy shrugged. "Mr. Cameron didn't say. He just said all the Cub Scouts were going to race them some Saturday."

Gina nodded and turned back to the kit. A block of wood, four nails, and four plastic wheels stared back up at her, along with the confusing instructions. "And we're supposed to make this into a car?"

"A race car," Danny corrected.

"Did your scoutmaster say how you were supposed to make this into a race car?" Gina asked, pushing back limp brown hair.

"You have to cut it into the shape of a car and then paint it. He said to have your dad call if he had questions. I told him I didn't have a dad, and he said moms could call him too."

"I see," Gina said. Three years of widowhood had left a great many holes in her life, including a father to assist Danny in times of crisis. And this was definitely a crisis. The Cub Scout pinewood derby was, according to the date at the top of the page, only a couple of weeks away and she'd not yet gotten up the courage to carve on the chunk of wood, much less produce a finished race car. Looking from the instructions to the kit to her son, Gina felt an overwhelming desire to lock herself in her bedroom until after the pinewood derby race had passed.

"I guess I'll call him," she muttered and went to the list of phone numbers she kept on the refrigerator. Of course, the refrigerator was also covered with a multitude of other papers and pictures, which made her task even more difficult. By Gina's calculations the memorabilia and paperwork added a good twenty pounds to the already well-worn fridge door.

"Cub Scouts," she muttered, fanning through the precariously placed information. Cub Scout letters were always on blue paper. Telaine Applebee, the mother of twin boys who always managed to outperform all of the other Scouts, had created their den's newsletter. She thought by putting it on blue paper it would make parents more organized. She could hear Telaine, even now, her high-pitched voice announcing the newsletter like a prize at one of those home-product parties.

"And look," she'd nearly squealed with pride, "it's blue! You'll always know it's Scout information, because it's blue like their uniforms." Only it wasn't blue like their uniforms but a sugary shade of sky blue that seemed to match Telaine's perfect eyes.

Gina sighed. It wasn't that she didn't like Telaine. She did. Telaine was a wonderful woman and Gina would give just about anything to be as organized. But looking at Telaine and seeing her perfect life was like looking into a mirror and finding all your own inadequacies.

"Here it is!" she declared, forgetting about Telaine and the thought that no doubt her twins had already completed turning their wood blocks into race cars.

"They'll probably be featured on the front of *Great Mechanics*," she muttered and picked up the receiver.

Dialing the phone, Gina noted that Danny seemed oblivious to her feelings of inadequacy, but that was the way she wanted it. To share with her eight-year-old the fears and loneliness of being a widow seemed an injustice of grand proportion. Danny just stood there staring at her with such hope—like he expected her to have some magical formula for changing wood into cars. How could she disappoint him when he believed so strongly in her ability to make things right?

The number she'd dialed began ringing and Gina immediately tensed. What would she say? How could she explain that she'd let the project get away from her and now it was nearly time for the race and she hadn't even begun to help Danny put it together?

"Hello?"

The baritone voice at the other end of the phone immediately commanded Gina's attention. "Yes, is this Mr. Cameron, Cub Scout leader for den four?"

"Among other things," the man replied in a tone that betrayed amusement.

Gina smiled to herself and took a deep breath. "Look, we've never met, but my son is one of your Wolf Cubs. No wait, I think he's a Bear Cub or a Bobcat. Oh, I forget." The man laughed, making Gina feel uncertain whether he was laughing at her in a nice way or because she'd just managed to sound like ditz of the year. "I'm sorry," she muttered and tried again. "This is Gina Bowden, Danny's mother."

"Ah, your son is a Bear."

"Especially in the morning," Gina countered.

The man chuckled. "Well, I can't vouch for that, but on Tuesday night, he's definitely a Bear. What can I do for you?"

Gina looked heavenward and rolled her eyes. *Take me away from the monotony. Give me a reason to put on mascara. Teach me what to do when the sidewalk opens up with cracks big enough to swallow small children or when the dryer won't dry but just dings at you like you should know what that means.*

"Hello?"

The masculine voice broke through Gina's thoughts. "Sorry, it's been a bad week," she said softly, shaking her head. "This is the problem. I'm looking at this pinebox derby stuff—" Hysterical laughter erupted on the end of the line, causing Gina to pause. "Is something wrong?" More laughter. "You are the Cub Scout leader I'm supposed to call if I need help, aren't you?"

The man collected himself. "Yeah, but it's pinewood derby, not pinebox. We aren't racing coffins out there."

"You might as well be," Gina replied, then laughed at her own mistake. "I'm afraid if I start in on this thing that's what it'll resemble. Come to think of it, it already resembles that. And just what are functional sharp points?"

"Would you like me to come over and help you and Danny?"

Gina sighed. "Mr. Cameron."

"Gary. Call me Gary."

"Okay, Gary, I would be very grateful if you would come give us a hand. I'm a widow, and although I've tried to be father, mother, taxi driver, Little League coach, and general all-around good sport, I've yet to master woodwork." She paused for a moment, then remembering that strange "check engine" light in the van, she added, "Or car mechanics."

His chuckles warmed her heart. "I have talents in both areas. Do you have time to work on the car right now?" he asked.

Gina smiled, unable to resist. "Which one?"

"Let's start with the wooden one and work our way up," Gary countered.

Gina breathed a sigh of relief. Just thinking about not having to be responsible for the functional sharp points was making it much easier to face the day. "Sure, come on over. The address is 311 Humboldt."

"Be there in ten minutes."

Gina hung up the phone and looked at her forlorn child. "Mr. Cameron is coming right over." Danny's face brightened. Glancing down at her sweat suit, she added, "I'm going to go change my clothes so I don't look like a bag lady. You let him in when he gets here."

Seven minutes later, while Gina was just pulling a brush through her hair, Gary Cameron was ushered into the house by Danny. She could hear their animated conversation as she came down the stairs.

"Hey, Mr. Cameron, I'm sure glad you could help me make my car."

"No problem, sport. Where's your mom?" It was that wonderful voice. That wonderful masculine voice. Gina paused at the door just to listen, fearful that if she crossed the threshold too soon, she just might break the spell of the moment. She needn't have worried. Danny broke it for her.

"She's upstairs changing her clothes. She didn't want to look like a rag lady."

"A rag lady?" Gary questioned.

Gina stood six feet away in complete mortification. Gone was the feeling of satisfaction that had come in fixing her hair and putting on makeup. Gone were the plans of appearing in total control and confidence.

"That's *bag* lady, and Danny, you really should learn the better part of discretion." The boy shrugged and Gary laughed. Gina felt self-conscious and glanced down at her sweater and jeans.

"You look nothing like a bag lady." He smiled, and Gina noted tiny crow's-feet lined the edges of his eyes. He was obviously a man who liked to laugh. He extended his hand and formally introduced himself. "I'm Gary Cameron."

Holding his gaze a moment longer, Gina felt her pulse quicken. She put her hand in his and felt warm fingers close around hers. "I'm Gina."

For a moment neither one moved, and Gina felt hard-pressed to force herself to be the first to break the companionable silence, but finally she did. "I left the mess on the kitchen table."

"Let's get to it then," Gary said with a smile. "The sky is starting to cloud up and, knowing springtime in Kansas, we could be in for almost anything. Part of our work will need to be done outdoors so as to save you from extra cleanup."

Gina nodded. "It's this way." She walked to the kitchen, Gary following close behind her with Danny at his side. She pointed at the mess. "Nothing like waiting until the last minute," Gina apologized, bending over the pieces, "but I kept thinking sooner or later I would figure out what to do with it." She gazed up mischievously. "I came up with a few ideas, but none of them seemed to benefit Danny or the derby."

Gary held up a small red toolbox. "We'll have you on your way before you know it. We can carve it out today, and if Danny is willing to work hard at sanding it down, I can come back over and we'll work on it some more tomorrow."

"We go to church tomorrow," Danny declared.

"So do I," Gary replied. "But I was thinking maybe the afternoon would work out for us."

"Won't your wife feel neglected?" Gina asked without thinking.

"My wife and son were killed in a car accident four years ago," Gary said matter-of-factly.

"I'm sorry. Danny's father died in an accident three years ago. His car was hit head-on by a drunk driver."

Gary picked up the car kit. "Lot of them out there."

Gina studied the sandy-haired man for a moment, and when he looked up and met her gaze, she suddenly knew that here was a man who understood her pain. Here was a man she could relate to. The look he gave her made Gina tremble at the faded memory of feeling young and loved and happy.

"So would tomorrow work out for you?" Gary asked as though they hadn't just shared a very intimate moment.

"It would be fine with me. What time?"

"How about whenever you're finished with lunch?"

"Why don't you just come for lunch and stay to work on the car?"

Gary smiled. "Sounds great."

"My mom's a good cook," Danny told the man. "'Cept when she burns something."

Gina tousled his hair. "Which is nearly once a day because some eight-year-old demands that I come see what new creation he's built in the backyard."

"She burned the macaroni and cheese, today," Danny announced. "Do you want to see the pan? Mom says it looks like—"

"Danny, I think Mr. Cameron would prefer not to hear about our shortcomings. How about you sit down and let him get started with that…that…thing," she interrupted, looking sadly at all the bits and pieces.

Gary laughed. "Your mom's right. We need to get a move on. We'll want to do our cutting outside, and those clouds are getting darker by the minute." Then he turned to her and flashed a quick smile. "Lunch sounds great. Church is out at noon, so, say I come here directly after?"

"Perfect," Gina replied.

Sitting down at the table, she was relieved when Gary picked up the conversation and began to explain the process of carving out the race car. She felt almost exhausted from their first encounter and needed the neutrality of woodwork. It wasn't long until Danny and Gary settled on a plan and were off to the backyard to start sawing away at the block of wood.

Watching from the kitchen window, Gina couldn't remember the last time she'd had this much fun. She and Danny had remained rather isolated after the accident, but now she honestly felt ready to deal with people again. Oh, it wasn't that she didn't have friends. She had several she felt comfortable enough to spend time with. But for the most part, it was go to church on Sunday, homeschool Danny through the week, and go to Scouts on Tuesday nights. Well, Danny went to Scouts. Gina usually sent him with Telaine and her boys and used the quiet evenings to get personal matters done that she couldn't accomplish with Danny in tow.

Telaine had been sympathetic to her needs and, because of her continual ability to be organized even in the face of adversity, Telaine had honestly helped Gina to get through the last three years. But now, Gina felt it was time to throw off her isolation.

It was funny how spending an afternoon with Gary Cameron had helped her to realize that she was ready to get on with her life again. She felt rather like a flower, opening up to the sun. Hadn't God promised He'd turn her mourning into laughter? At this she heard Danny's giggles and saw that Gary was bent over examining something in Danny's hand.

It was the rain that finally drove them into the house. Lightning flashed and thunder shook the windows, but the storm moved through quickly and the trio seemed perfectly content to ignore it as Gary explained how to sand the wood smooth.

The afternoon passed nearly as quickly as the storm, and Gina was almost ashamed when Danny complained of being hungry. She'd completely forgotten to feed the child lunch after the macaroni and cheese fiasco.

"I could use something myself," Gary said, putting away his coping saw. "How about we go have a hamburger?"

"Can we, Mom?"

Danny's hopeful expression seemed to match the one on Gary's face. Gina grinned. "French fries too?"

"And onion rings!" Gary declared as though closing an important business deal.

"And maybe a banana split," Danny added.

"Yeah," Gary agreed.

"Let me get my purse," Gina said, but Gary stopped her before she could move.

"My treat," he said in a voice that was nearly a whisper.

Gina could only nod. It'd been so long since anyone had offered to pay their way or treat them to anything. "Let's go."

Later, with half-eaten burgers on the table and Danny off to climb the restaurant's playground equipment, Gina found herself companionably settled with Gary. It was amazing that a chance encounter with Danny's scoutmaster could leave her feeling as though she'd finally found all the answers to a lifetime of questions.

When Gary reached out to cover her hand with his, she bit her bottom lip and looked deep into serious blue eyes. "This seems unreal," she whispered.

"I was thinking the same thing," Gary replied.

Gina swallowed hard. "You can't possibly understand, but I haven't even been out with anyone since Ray died."

"I can understand. I haven't dated since Vicky and that was high school. I never thought I'd have to do it again, and when she and Jason died, I decided I never would. But there's something about this," he said, looking off to where Danny was happily climbing the wrong way up the slide. "I suppose it sounds cliché, but I don't want it to end. I've been alone for four years and now, all of a sudden, it seems unbearable to go even one more week this way."

"I know," Gina said softly. "I figured I would just handle things on my own. That together, Danny and I could face anything and be just fine. Then Danny started saying things that made me realize how selfish I'd been in hiding away. He misses having a dad around."

"I miss being a dad," Gary said, turning to look at her. His gaze pierced Gina to the heart. "I miss being a husband too. I don't have any interest in the singles' scene or one-night stands."

Gina swallowed hard. "I can't believe I'm saying all this—it really isn't like me to just open myself up like this. But, sometimes, when Danny's asleep and the house is all quiet, I'm almost afraid the silence will eat me alive." She paused for a moment to collect her thoughts. "Other times, like when the car won't start and I haven't a clue what's wrong or when Danny needs a race car carved out of wood, I feel too inadequate to meet the demands of being a single mom."

"It always hits me when I go out to eat, like this," he said, breaking away from the trancelike stare to look where Danny was happily playing.

Gina glanced at her watch and realized it was getting late. She should be making some comment about going home. But she didn't want to. She thought back on the years of emptiness and knew she didn't want to let this opportunity pass her by. It might seem crazy to have such strong feelings on a first date, and not even a real date at that, but something in her heart told her to take a chance. *Please God,* she prayed silently, *don't let me make a fool of myself.*

Gary spoke again, breaking her thoughts. "There are all these couples and their kids and a single man sticks out like a sore thumb. But I come anyway. And that's why I continue as a scoutmaster. Sometimes it's just nice to hear the laughter."

"We laugh a lot at my house," she said softly.

Gary looked at her with registered understanding. "I'm pretty good at fixing cars, and you've already seen what I can do with wood."

Gina smiled. "And I'm sure the house would be anything but silent with you around."

"So where do we go from here?" Gary asked quite seriously.

Gina felt her pulse quicken. He was interested. He felt the same way she did. She gave a light cough to clear her throat.

"I guess we'll have to let God decide the distant future, but for now we have a date for tomorrow. Dinner at my house."

Gary nodded. "Can I bring something?"

She wanted to laugh and tell him he was already bringing the most important missing ingredient in her frustrating life, but she didn't. "Just yourself," she replied with a smile, then remembered the pinewood derby car. "Oh, and some paint."

"Paint?" he questioned, his mind clearly not following her train of thought.

"For the car," she replied.

"Of course," he said nodding. "Danny said he wanted red and I just happen to have a can of cherry-red gloss in my garage."

CHAPTER 2

Sunday dawned overcast and humid. Gina looked from the sky to the half-dressed little boy at her side and sighed. "Looks like another stormy day," she told him, reaching down to button his dress shirt.

"Are we still having s'ketti for lunch?" Danny asked hopefully.

"You bet," Gina replied, helping him tuck the shirt into his pants. "There. Now you look absolutely charming. Every little girl in Sunday school will notice how handsome you are."

"Oh, Mom," the boy replied, his expression very sober, "I can't be worried about that right now. I got lots of time to get a girlfriend and get married. First I want you to get married."

Gina smiled and knelt in front of her son. "I know you want that. And for once in a very long time, I think I want it too. I think we should both pray about it and trust God for the answer."

"I think Mr. Cameron would make a good husband for you. He's strong and he knows how to fix cars and you don't know how to fix cars," Danny said seriously. "Mr. Cameron also told me that you have a smile that's like sunshine."

Gina felt herself blush. "Oh, he did, did he?" Could it be the heart of a poet beat within that Cub leader facade? "Well, we will just have to see what happens. Now, come on or we'll be late for church."

They pulled into the church parking lot just as thunder rumbled low. It continued rumbling off and on throughout Sunday school and church, but always it seemed to hang off in the distance. Gina gave it very little thought, however, as she hurried Danny into the van and headed for home.

She felt as giddy as a schoolgirl going on her first date. A man was actually coming to the house. A handsome man who was interested in her for more than just the pinewood derby.

"Danny, get changed right away and come help me in the kitchen," she called as Danny disappeared into his room. She hurried into her own room and tried to figure out what to wear. She was just reaching for a sleeveless cotton blouse when the weather radio sounded a warning alert. Reaching for the button that would let her hear what the latest weather update revealed, Gina kicked off her shoes and pulled at the zipper in her skirt.

"This is the National Weather Service office in Topeka," the male voice announced. "The Severe Storms Forecast Center in Kansas City, Missouri, has issued Tornado Watch #237 to be in effect from 12:30 p.m. until 6:00 p.m. This watch is for an area along and sixty miles either side of a line from Saint Joseph, Missouri, to Council Grove, Kansas. Some of the counties included in the watch are..."

"Great," Gina muttered. "Just what we needed." The man was continuing the routine speech, giving the names of counties to be on the watch for severe weather and telling what a tornado watch entailed. To Gina, who had lived in Kansas all of her life, the information was something she could quote line for line, including the pattern of counties as they were given for a specific area. But even as she mimicked the weatherman's announcement, Gina took the matter in complete seriousness.

"Danny, we're in a tornado watch," she called out. "Make sure you have your bag ready." Danny's bag consisted of treasures he wanted to protect in case they had to make a mad dash for the basement.

"Did you put new batteries in my flashlight?" Danny questioned at the top of his lungs.

"Check it for yourself," Gina replied, slipping on comfortable khaki slacks.

"Wow!" Danny hollered back. "It shines really bright now. Just like when it was new."

"Well, pack it in your bag and take it downstairs," Gina instructed.

Going to the window, Gina glanced out to check the sky. Nothing appeared overly threatening. There were heavy gray clouds off to the west, but otherwise it actually seemed to be clearing in their area. She knew this could be both good and bad. Cloud coverage usually kept the temperature down, and since higher temperatures seemed to feed the elements necessary for stronger storms, she would have just as well preferred the clouds remain.

Deciding not to worry about it, Gina clicked the radio off and grabbed her own bag of precious possessions. Her bag, more like a small suitcase, contained important household papers and photos that were irreplaceable. Usually when the storm season began, she simply took the case downstairs and left it there; but this year the weather had been fairly mild through March and there hadn't been any real need to worry about it.

Trudging downstairs, Gina found Danny already in the basement. The basement was small and unfinished, but Gina had tried to make it homey for situations just like this. She had put in a small double bed for those times when the storms seemed to rage all night long. It had come in handy last year when the season had been particularly nasty. There were also a table and chairs and several board games she and Danny could play if they wanted to keep their minds off the storms.

There were also more practical things. Under the stairs, Ray had enclosed the area for storage and for protection if a storm was actually bearing down on them. They had heard it was the strongest place for shelter and so it was here that they would take their last line of defense. Gina had placed a supply of batteries, candles, matches, and bottled water on a narrow section of shelving that Ray had built for just such a purpose. There was also a battery-operated television, and Gina stored her extra linens and blankets here as well. The only other thing was an old mattress that had been propped against the wall. Ray had always told her that if a tornado was actually headed for them, they would pull the mattress down on top to help shield their bodies from the possibility of flying debris. They'd never had to use it, but Gina was ready and it made her feel safe just knowing that it was there.

She knew her friends often laughed about the cautious manner in which she dealt with storms, but she still had nightmares about a time when she had been young and a tornado had devastated the farm she'd lived on. After seeing firsthand what a tornado could do, Gina knew she would never take the matter lightly.

"Mom, are we gonna have a tornado this time?" Danny questioned, securing his bag under the game table.

"I sure hope not. Why don't we say a little prayer just in case." Danny nodded and Gina bowed her head. "Dear God, please keep us safely in Your care, no matter the weather, no matter our fears.

Let us remember that You hold us safely in Your hands."

"Amen," Danny said loudly. "Can we eat now?" He looked up at her with a mischievous grin.

"I still have to boil the pasta," she told him. "Let's get upstairs and you can set the table while I see how the sauce is doing."

"Don't forget the bread."

"I won't," she told him, giving his backside a playful swat.

They worked silently, Danny setting the table with the good dishes and Gina trying to imagine what it would be like to have a regular Sunday meal with a man at her table. She tried not to make too much of it. She wasn't one of those women who couldn't cope in life without a man at her side, but she did realize how much nicer it was to have the companionship of another adult. Especially a male adult.

She had just pulled the bread from the oven when the front doorbell sounded. "That's him!" Danny yelled from the living room.

"Well, let him in," Gina replied and hurried to drain the pasta. She arranged spaghetti on each of their plates and had started to ladle the sauce on top of this when Gary came into the kitchen, a two-liter bottle of cola in his arms along with a bouquet of flowers.

"I brought flowers for the lady of the house and drink for all," he announced, giving her the flowers with a sweeping bow.

Gina laughed. "They're beautiful, but you really shouldn't have."

Gary sobered, his blue eyes seeming to darken as he beheld her. "And why not?"

Gina couldn't think of any reason and simply shrugged. "You're just in time. I only need to slice the bread."

"Let me," Gary said, putting the soda on the counter. He immediately glanced around for a knife.

Gina handed him a slender knife and pointed him in the

direction of where she'd placed the bread to cool. Just then the unmistakable sound of the weather radio shattered their companionable silence.

"Danny, please run up to my room, unplug the radio, and bring it down here," Gina ordered. Danny, knowing the seriousness of the matter, took off in a flash and quickly brought her the radio.

Gina punched the button in time to hear that a tornado warning had been issued for Morris County. "A tornado was spotted on the ground five miles west of the town of Wilsey. People living in and around the areas of Wilsey and Council Grove should take immediate cover."

"And so it begins," Gary said, trying to sound lighthearted about the matter.

Gina nodded and continued listening to the information. "It sounds like the storms are moving our way, but not very fast. Maybe we'll have time for lunch before we have to concern ourselves with anything too serious."

"I'm sure we'll be just fine," Gary replied. He held up the bread like a prize. "This is ready."

"Well, let's eat then," Gina declared, bringing the plates of spaghetti to the table.

Gary offered to give the blessing and when he did, Gina felt tears come to her eyes. Ray used to pray over the meals in a similar manner, and hearing Gary's voice only served to bring back the memory in a bittersweet wave.

Caught up in the memory, Gina didn't even realize Gary had concluded the prayer until Danny asked if he could have some bread. She pulled herself together and looked up with a smile.

"Of course you may," she told her son and watched while Gary handed him a slice.

Gary had just begun to tell them tales of his own days as a Cub Scout when the radio went off once again. This time, it seemed, another storm had popped up in Wabaunsee County just to the west of them. It was only a thunderstorm warning, but both Gary and Gina knew how dangerous these things could be.

Danny ate with great enthusiasm, apparently oblivious to the look that flashed between Gina and Gary. The weather was making it impossible for Gina to eat, but she tried to give the pretense in order to keep Danny calm. Gary smiled reassuringly until another tornado warning, this one issued for towns much closer to their own, sounded on the radio.

"You do have a basement, right?"

She nodded, feeling better knowing that if she had to endure a bad storm, she would at least have Gary's company through the worst of it.

"Danny and I are all prepared."

"Why don't we just move our dinner downstairs?" Gary suggested. "Then we can more or less ignore the radio and just have a good time. We can even work on the car down there, although I wouldn't want to paint it there. The fumes would probably make us all goofy by the end of the day. In fact, with the humidity the way it is, I wouldn't suggest painting it today anyway. We can work on the axles and wheels and add the weights. I even brought a scale to make sure it's regulation weight."

Gina nodded as the radio once again sounded the alarm. "I guess we could move everything downstairs. The basement isn't finished or very nice to look at, but I do have a table and chairs down there. And you do have an after-dinner activity. . . ."

"Then lead the way," Gary said, jumping to his feet. "Danny, you grab up the bread and take your silverware. Gina, you bring your plate and Danny's—oh, and don't forget your silver. I'll bring the rest."

Gina liked the way he took charge and only paused long enough to grab the weather radio as she headed downstairs. They might as well have it with them to know what was going on, even if they didn't have to worry about taking cover. Of course, it was always possible a tornado could plop down nearby and then she would want to get under the staircase, but that wasn't something she wanted to think about just now. She wanted things to be calm and for the storms to go away, and she nearly laughed out loud as she made her way down the basement stairs. How dare stormy weather interfere with her date with Gary!

"This is a real adventure," Danny declared as Gina put his plate on the table. "We're having fun, aren't we, Mom?"

Gina forced a smile. "I think you have the right attitude about it. When life gives you a storm, look for the silver lining."

"Or the basement," Gary called out as he made his way down the stairs. His arms were filled and Gina hurried to help him. "I'll be right back," he told her as he put his plate on the table. "I'm going to get our drinks and napkins—and my little red toolkit."

Within a few moments he had returned, and as he took his seat at the ancient plastic-top table, the radio announced additional tornado sightings. Gina felt herself tense. She didn't realize how evident it was, however, until Gary reached over and gave her arm a gentle pat.

"You have a nice cozy place here," he said, glancing around the room.

"We had to spend all night down here last year," Danny told him between bites of food. "We even homeschooled down here."

"Oh, so you're homeschooled," Gary replied. And with that he set the conversation in full swing and soon even Gina was caught up in explanations of how homeschooling worked and what she tried to accomplish. Danny related wonderful field trips they'd taken and how he even joined the soccer team at the local YMCA.

She was so engrossed in the conversation that when the tornado sirens actually went off and the radio weatherman announced that a tornado had been sighted not ten miles from where she lived, Gina was completely surprised.

It was only then that she noticed the rain beating down on the basement window. The window well was already filled with about two inches of water. Lightning flashed and thunder roared right behind it, betraying the fact that the storm was right upon them.

Gina tried to take a deep breath to calm herself. She silently prayed for courage and calm in order to keep Danny from being afraid, but already she could read the fear in his eyes. When he left his place at the table and came to her, Gina wordlessly pushed back from the table and took the boy onto her lap. Eight was a difficult age for a child, especially a boy. They needed independence and rough soccer games and all-night campouts with their friends. But sometimes they still needed their mothers' laps and hugs that reassured them that all would be well.

Gina wrapped her arms around Danny's trembling body and kissed his forehead. "We're in God's hands, Danny," she whispered.

Gary reached over and stroked Danny's back. "Don't worry, sport, it'll be over before you know it." He spoke to Danny, but it was Gina's eyes he looked into.

Gina drew strength from his calm demeanor.

"Why don't we play a game?" Gary suggested.

Danny peaked his head up. "Which one?"

"Hmmm, I don't know, how about—"

Just then a roaring boom of thunder shook the whole house and the lights went out. The room was dark except for the flashes of lightning that seemed to come one right on top of the other and penetrated through the small basement windows.

"How about blindman's bluff?" Gary said with a laugh. "We won't even need blindfolds."

Gina laughed, amazed that Gary's presence could give her so much peace. God had known she would need help, and even though the storm raged overhead and the electricity had been knocked out, she realized she wasn't half as afraid as she might have been had she and Danny been alone. Sometimes it was just easier to bear the storms of life when you had someone to stand beside you.

By evening the storms had calmed and the weather had turned peaceful. The electricity had even been restored, and Gina noted that everything still appeared to be in one piece as they moved back up from the basement. The radio droned softly from the kitchen, announcing the forecast for the evening to be clear.

Gina walked Gary to the front door and laughed. "Well, it wasn't exactly how I figured our first date would go."

Gary stopped in mid step and looked at her seriously. "This wasn't a date."

Gina swallowed hard. Had she misread him? "It wasn't?"

"No," Gary said, shaking his head. "You don't take eight-year-olds on romantic dates. I have something special planned for our first date. You doing anything on Friday night?"

Gina grinned, feeling a sense of elation wash over her. "That depends on what you have in mind. I was going to clean out the refrigerator and wash my hair. Can you top that?"

Gary gave her a look that made her want to melt into a puddle at his feet. "I think I can manage to beat that out. How about I pick you up around seven and we go out for a nice grown-up dinner and then take a walk at the lake?"

Gina tilted her chin up while she considered her options. "Hmmm, that's a tough choice. Dinner with a handsome man and a romantic, moonlit walk or burying myself in condiments and soapsuds." She watched a grin spread across his face. "I guess the fridge can wait."

"Good. Seven o'clock sharp," he said. "Oh, and if you're free on Saturday, we can paint the car. That should give us plenty of time to detail it out for the race."

"Sounds like a winner to me," Gina replied.

She watched him climb into his car and didn't stop watching until he'd backed out of her drive and headed off down Humboldt Street. This was definitely be the start of something exciting, she thought. *Please God, let it be real.*

CHAPTER 3

Gary showed up at seven o'clock sharp. He looked down at his navy suit and red-patterned tie and hoped it would meet with Gina's approval. He hadn't felt this nervous since. . .well. . .since the last time he'd showed up for a first date. Taking a deep breath, he punched the doorbell and waited for Gina to answer.

"God, don't let me push too hard or act out of line," Gary prayed aloud. Just then Gina opened the door and the vision took his breath away. She smiled a smile that went all the way to her blue eyes. . .and to his heart.

"Good evening," Gary said, struggling to control his breathing.

"Good evening," she replied.

He faltered. Should he compliment the way she looked? Should he say that the cream-printed dress looked particularly nice—that he liked the way she'd styled her shoulder-length brown hair? His mouth felt dry.

"Ah. . .um. . .you look really great," he stammered.

She looked down briefly, then returned her gaze to meet his eyes. "Thank you, you do too."

His mind went blank. What was he supposed to do now?

Gina stepped back from the door. "Would you like to come

in for a minute. I just need to check on something upstairs, and I'll be ready to leave."

"Sure," Gary replied, following her into the house. He waited while she went about her business, wishing he felt more at ease. *This shouldn't be such a big deal,* he told himself. But it was a big deal.

It seemed strangely quiet without Danny's rambunctious voice, and Gary figured this would be as good a way to break the ice as any. "Where's your son?" he called out.

"Staying with the Applebee twins," she replied, coming back down the stairs, securing her right earring. "He was very excited to be able to have a sleepover at their house." She lowered her voice to a whisper and added, "They have two horses and some chickens, don't you know."

Gary laughed. "Yes, and a dog who's got a litter of six-week-old puppies as I recall."

Gina nodded. "So are you ready?"

"I thought I was."

This caused Gina to pause and look at him rather sternly. "Is there a problem?"

Gary thought she almost looked alarmed, as if he might back out of their date and ruin the evening. "I'm nervous," he finally admitted.

She grinned. "Me too. I thought I'd pass out when I opened the door."

This finally broke the tension, and Gary smiled. "That makes two of us. Why are we acting like this? We're grown adults and we've been through all this before."

"Yes, but not with each other," Gina replied.

"True, but that shouldn't matter."

Gina gave him a look of disbelief. "But of course it matters.

You haven't learned my hideous secrets yet. You don't know how I look when I wake up in the morning or how I keep house or cook—with the exception of spaghetti."

"Which was fantastic," Gary interjected. "And exactly what secrets could you have that would make the prospects of spending time with you any less attractive?"

"I don't know, but there are bound to be some. You know how it can be. I remember arguing with Ray over stupid little things."

"Like what?"

"Like not leaving dirty clothes all over the floor but rather in the hamper," Gina began.

"A horrible secret, to be sure," Gary teased. "Okay, what else?"

"Well, we used to clash when it came to vacations. I liked to go to quiet places far removed from the tourists. Ray liked to hit all the tourist traps."

"Anything else?"

"I like to read in the evening when Danny goes to bed."

"Hmmm," Gary said, stroking his chin. "Did that habit come about before or after Ray died?"

Gina blushed. "Well, I have to admit, it came about after."

"So...if you had something better to do, you might reconsider?" Gary questioned, a mischievous expression on his face.

"I might."

"Well, I just don't see a problem. I'm a very flexible man. I like most foods, love to travel and try new things, but am just as happy to sit still and do nothing. I have given myself a lot of consideration, and I just don't think I have too many flaws that will interfere or create a conflict with our personalities."

Gina smiled. "In all seriousness, we don't know much about each other."

"That's why we're dating," Gary replied. "And I'm starving, so can we continue this conversation at the restaurant?"

Gina nodded. "I was beginning to think I should just warm up some leftovers."

Gary took hold of her arm and maneuvered her toward the door. "Not that I wouldn't enjoy another sampling of your cooking, but I've got special plans for tonight."

He liked the way she looked up at him, her eyes wide with curiosity, her expression betraying her anticipation. She brought back all the excitement of his youth, and suddenly he believed in love at first sight.

Dinner passed in pleasantries and memories of Danny and days gone by. Gary enjoyed listening to Gina talk about her childhood and tried to imagine the brown-haired beauty as a tagalong child in pigtails.

"I've often thought I'd like to move back to the country and live on a farm again," Gina told him.

"Honestly?" Gary questioned. "I've considered such a thing myself."

"You're just saying that to impress me," Gina teased.

"No. I'm serious. I think a farm could be a lot of fun."

Gina laughed lightly. "It's also a lot of work. Things don't just take care of themselves. I'm always trying to explain that to Danny. Especially when he nags me for a puppy."

"I've no doubt that's true," Gary replied. "I didn't mean I wanted to actually run a big farm. Plow the fields and plant and harvest. I doubt I'd be any good at that, and if that's what you had in mind, then maybe we have reached our first clash of personalities."

Gina shook her head. "No, I don't desire to go back to that headache. But I love the way the air smells in the country. The ground freshly plowed, wheat when it nears harvest, the scent of the trees after a summer rain. . ."

Gary smiled and nodded, then his smile faded as he caught sight of someone across the room. He tried to regain control of his emotions, but Gina was too quick for him.

"What's wrong?"

Gary tried to figure out what to say. He didn't want anything to spoil their evening. But, because the man he'd spied was now walking toward their table, Gary knew his wish wasn't going to come true.

Tensing, he took a long drink of his iced tea and waited.

"Hello, Gary."

Gary looked up at the same time Gina did. "Hello, Jess," Gary said rather stiffly.

"I think this is the first time I've seen you out with a woman since Vicky died," the man replied, his voice clearly hostile.

"Gina, this is Jess Masterson. My father-in-law."

Gina reached out her hand, but Jess clearly ignored her. "I suppose you haven't heard yet, but there's going to be a rather sticky issue brought up before the city council."

"And you're no doubt behind it," Gary replied, not even bothering to hide his hostility.

Masterson smiled. "As a matter of fact, I am."

"So why is this sticky issue something you needed to bring up at my dinner?"

The older man shrugged. "Because it has to do with your pet project of Scouting."

"Scouting?" Gary shook his head. "What in the world are you talking about?"

Masterson glanced around the room, noted his party and

waved, then turned to Gary and Gina. "I'm strongly pushing to drop all funding for Scouting given by the city."

Gary felt unquestionable anger surfacing. "And what did the Scouts do to offend you?"

"They're an elitist group. They force those who join to participate in religious indoctrination. I'm suggesting"—he paused and smiled—"or rather demanding, that the Scouts eliminate any ties to 'God' in their organization or the city will have to discontinue its support. There's that whole separation of church and state thing, you know."

Gary clenched his jaw tightly, and before he could speak, Gina replied, "I'm sorry you feel that way, Mr. Masterson. I'm afraid if they removed the funding from Scouting it would make it more difficult, but I doubt it would do away with the local organization. Even if you could remove a focus on God and country from Scouting, it wouldn't change anything. Scouting is not part of the church or government. We joined voluntarily because we honor the values of Scouting. No one is forcing anyone else to join."

"No, but they are forcing taxpayers to help support the organization. That isn't acceptable when it's such a selective organization."

"And do you speak for the majority, Mr. Masterson, or for a select few?" Gina countered.

Gary wanted to applaud her bold attitude, but he knew that sooner or later Masterson would drag her to the ground over the issue. He started to interject his own thoughts on the matter, but Masterson spoke before he could answer.

"I speak for the law of the land, Miss—"

"Mrs. Bowden," Gina replied.

Masterson scowled as he threw Gary a look of disgust. "Dating married women, Gary?"

Gina slammed down her fork at this. "I am a widow, Mr. Masterson. Not that I think it's any of your concern, but because you are a very rude man I will clear the matter before you continue to prejudge the situation. I am also the mother of a Cub Scout. I fully support the Boy Scouts of America and their desire to put God at the center of their organization. Perhaps if more people put God at the center of their lives, this would never be an issue. However, because you are so intent on bringing up issues of separation of church and state, perhaps you should research the origins of those issues and read for yourself that while our forefathers had no desire to allow government to organize or prohibit religious affairs for the people, Thomas Jefferson wrote quite eloquently of the need for Christian values in government."

"He also wrote of the need to have a revolution every twenty years," Masterson retorted.

"And perhaps we should," Gina replied hotly. "Perhaps if we'd had a revolution the first time someone suggested the elimination of God from the foundations of our society, we wouldn't be in the situation we are today."

"You are naive, Mrs. Bowden."

"And you are out of line, Jess," Gary said, getting to his feet. "I came here for a nice quiet dinner, not for a political-religious debate. I suggest you join your party and allow us our privacy."

Jess Masterson's dark eyes seemed to narrow on Gary as if he were sizing up his opponent. "I simply thought you'd like to know about the situation."

"You could have called me at home. You know the number."

Masterson looked as though he'd like to say more but simply nodded and quickly walked away from the table. Gary watched him rejoin his own group before taking his seat. The evening had been quite successfully ruined as far as he was concerned.

Calling for the check, Gary hoped he might be able to salvage at least part of their date by going on the romantic walk he'd promised. But as they reached the parking lot, a light rain began to fall and his plans were thoroughly thwarted.

But Gina came to the rescue.

"Well, why don't we forget about the walk and go back to my place instead? I have a couple of movies I checked out from the library and I could fix us some popcorn." She slid into the car and smiled. "Or we could just sit and talk politics."

Gary let his anger fade. "I think the first part sounds good."

Coming around to the driver's side, Gary felt as though he should somehow try to explain Jess Masterson and his anger. When he climbed behind the wheel, he sat silently for several seconds, trying to figure out how best to begin.

"I'm sorry for that," he finally said, not even bothering to start the engine. "Jess has been angry at God ever since Vicky and Jason died."

"He blames God rather than the drunk who hit them?"

"Vicky didn't die right away, and Jess, who was always a bit mixed on his feelings about God and Christianity, began to pray as he'd never prayed in his life. He pleaded with God to save Vicky. She was an only child, you see. And with Jason already dead and Vicky so severely injured, Jess wanted to grab at any lifeline being offered."

"But she died anyway," Gina whispered.

Gary turned to look at her. The compassion and understanding in her expression made him want to take her in his arms. She knew that pain and longing. "Yes, she did. After nearly thirty-six hours of fighting for her life, Vicky died. Jess went ballistic, and Cissy,

Vicky's mom, collapsed into my arms in tears. Cissy was a strong believer; so was Vicky. Jason was only four, but he loved to go to Sunday school and church. Cissy and I got through by turning to God, but Jess alienated himself from God and rejected the whole line of comfort. He said if God cared so much He would never have allowed Vicky and Jason to die in the first place."

"I think that's a pretty normal response," Gina replied. "I remember feeling rather hostile myself. I knew God was still there for me, but I wasn't sure I wanted His kind of comforting. After all, He could have kept Ray alive and He didn't."

Gary nodded. "I know. I felt that way too, at least initially. God brought me past that point, however."

"Yes, He did that for me as well, but," Gina said quite seriously, "I wanted to come past that point. I wanted to let go of Ray and the accident and the anger of blaming the man who killed him—blaming anyone. Jess Masterson doesn't appear to be a man who wants to get beyond those things. How does his wife deal with him?"

"She died last year. Cancer," Gary replied flatly.

"Poor man," Gina said, shaking her head. "He must have been devastated."

Gary's heart warmed at Gina's compassion for the man who'd just so angrily berated her. "You're a special lady, Gina Bowden," he said softly, reaching out to touch her cheek.

Gina held his hand in place with her own hand. "I guess this date turned out to be rather revealing, after all. I'm not sorry for what happened. I hope you won't be either."

Gary took a deep breath and let it back out. She had such a calming effect on him. He smiled. "No, I'm not sorry. I'd pay good money to see you take Jess to task again the way you did in the restaurant. I don't think he expected that out of you."

Gina grinned. "Like I said, it's been a very revealing evening."

"Revealing but not very romantic," Gary said almost apologetically.

"Well," Gina said, removing her hand from his, "the night's still young."

CHAPTER 4

Saturday dawned in complete pandemonium. Telaine called early to say that Danny had been begging to come home since six that morning. It seemed to have something to do with the fact he was going to work on his pinewood derby car with Mr. Cameron. Then, after assuring Telaine that it was all right to bring Danny home before the agreed upon nine thirty, Gina had to face the fact that her dryer had given up and was now completely useless.

It had been some time since she'd hung clothes outside, but after wiping down the lines, she went to work and actually found she enjoyed the task. It brought back memories of childhood, when all of their clothes had been line-dried. She remembered how sweet their things had smelled after being outside in the sunshine.

She had just managed to empty her laundry basket when she made out the unmistakable sound of someone pulling into her front driveway. No doubt it was Telaine with Danny. Then a feeling washed over her. *Surely Gary wouldn't be coming at this hour,* she thought, looking down at her watch. It was only just now eight thirty. She felt her pulse quicken.

She hurried through the house, leaving the empty basket in the laundry room, and had just reached the front door when someone knocked loudly from the other side. Opening it, Gina found herself face-to-face with a delivery man and a huge bouquet of flowers.

"How beautiful!" she exclaimed, taking the flowers.

"Mrs. Bowden, will you sign here?" the man requested.

Gina smiled, smelled the flowers, and nodded. "Who are they from?" she questioned as she took the pen he offered.

"There's a card," the man replied. "That should tell you everything you need to know."

She nodded again and handed the man his pen. "Wait a minute and I'll get your tip."

"No need, ma'am. I've already been tipped sufficiently for this delivery."

With that, he was gone. Gina closed the door slowly and savored the aroma of hothouse flowers. She put the glass vase on the kitchen table and opened the card. After sitting up until midnight talking with Gary, she had little doubt that the flowers were from him.

But they weren't.

My sincerest wish is to be forgiven for my rude behavior. If I offended or otherwise caused you pain, I am sorry.

Jess Masterson

"Well, I'll be," Gina whispered, looking at the card again to make certain she'd read it correctly.

The bouquet was clearly an expensive one. Gina didn't even recognize some of the flowers included in the arrangement, but the size alone made her well aware that the cost must have been considerable. Leaving them on the kitchen table, Gina threw another load of clothes into the washing machine and then returned to start some baking. She wanted to bake a batch of Danny's favorite cookies. Chocolate chip with nuts.

"Mom! Mom, I'm home!" came a yell as the front door flew open with a resounding bang.

"I'm in the kitchen," she called to her son.

"Mrs. Applebee says to tell you I was good," Danny declared coming into the kitchen. "I got to ride the horse and play with the puppies. Those puppies are sure cute and one of them liked me a whole lot. Do you suppose we could have one? Where's Mr. Cameron?"

All of this came without Danny drawing a single breath or pausing long enough for a comment or answer from his mother. Gina looked at the rambunctious boy and laughed. "He's not here yet. No, we can't have a puppy right now. I'm sure they were very cute, however, and I'm glad you got to play with them and ride the horse," she replied in reverse order of his delivery. "I'm also glad you were good for Mrs. Applebee, although I can't imagine it was good that you got her up at the crack of dawn to come home."

Danny's enthusiasm remained high. "They have to get up early to feed the animals," he told her simply. "I didn't wake anybody up. The rooster did that." He came up to Gina to see what she was doing. "Are you making something I like?"

"I sure am. Chocolate chip cookies with pecans."

She had thought it impossible for Danny to look any happier. "All right!" he declared and practically started dancing around the room.

Just then the doorbell rang. "Mr. Cameron!" Danny exclaimed, heading at a full run for the door.

Gina knew he was probably right. A part of her wanted to run for the door at the same time, but instead she held back and mixed in the final ingredients for the cookies.

"Hello, Danny" she could hear Gary say from the front room.

She felt flushed just thinking of the way his voice excited her. Last night had been wonderful, in spite of Jess Masterson. They had talked and shared their hearts on so many things. Gary believed in the power of God to move those pesky mountains of life, and he seemed the perfect counterpart to her own beliefs.

"Mom's making cookies," Danny told Gary as they came into the kitchen. "Can we paint the car today?" he questioned eagerly.

"I don't see why not," Gary replied. "Why don't you go get it?" Danny gave a little cheer and hurried off to his room, while Gary turned his full attention to Gina. "Good morning."

She spoke about the same time he spied the flowers. "Good morning. I see you've noticed my morning surprise."

Gary nodded. "Is it your birthday?"

She laughed. "No. They're from Jess Masterson, complete with apology. Here," she said, picking up the card. "Read for yourself."

Gary took the card and shook his head. "You must have made some impression on the old man. I've never known him to apologize to anyone."

"Well, I have to admit, I was stunned. I thought the flowers were from. . ." She paused, realizing how pretentious it might sound to admit the truth.

"From me?" Gary said, fixing his gaze on her.

Gina licked her lips and felt her face grow hot. "Yes," she finally managed to say.

Gary laughed. "I would have, but I ran by the bookstore this morning and then, well, to be honest—I forgot. The place was in chaos. We're having a sale today and there were some last-minute changes."

Gary had told her all about his bookstore, Cameron Christian Books and Gifts. Gina was fascinated to know that after many years of patronage to the store, she'd never once met or seen Gary, the owner. "I really didn't expect you to bring flowers. I just figured they were from you because I didn't know who else would have had any interest in sending them."

Gary sobered. "It sure isn't like him."

"Well, if you have his number, I'd like to call him later and thank him for the flowers. And, to accept his apology."

Gary reached out and touched one of the blossoms. "I just wonder what he's up to."

Gina frowned. "Does he have to be up to anything?"

Gary shrugged. "Unless he's changed; and after seeing him last night, I don't think that's happened."

"I think we should give the man the benefit of a doubt," Gina replied, wiping her hands on a nearby dish towel. "After all, the Bible says we're to forgive if asked."

Gary seemed to consider her words for a moment. "I just don't like it, that's all. I know Jess Masterson too well, and I'm worried that this is just his way of trying to manipulate you."

"Why would he care what I thought?" Gina asked, her temper starting to get the better of her. That Gary would act so callously and be so skeptical about his father-in-law's apology really bothered her.

"Here's my car!" Danny declared, bounding back into the kitchen.

He was totally unaware of the tension and Gina intended to keep it that way. "I'm sure you and Mr. Cameron want to get to work right away. You can either work in here or out on the patio; the choice is yours."

"Outside!" Danny declared.

"Yes, I think that would be best since we'll be spray painting,"

Gary agreed. He looked at Gina for a moment, his expression apologetic, then turned to Danny. "Do you have some newspapers?"

"I've been saving them just like you told me to do," Danny replied with great pride.

"Good, then go spread them on the patio table and we'll get right to work."

Danny nodded and took off through the laundry room and out the back door.

"Look, I'm sorry," Gary said to Gina.

"Are you really, or should I doubt your apology as well?"

"Touché," Gary said, stuffing his hands into his pockets. "I guess I acted out of line."

Gina grinned. "It's all a part of that 'getting to know you' stuff. I just didn't want to think that when my apologies were necessary, you'd believe them less than sincere."

Gary nodded. "Point well taken."

Later that evening with Danny happily preoccupied with a naval battle in the bathtub, Gina picked up the telephone in her bedroom and dialed the number Gary had left for Jess Masterson.

"Hello?" a gravelly voice sounded.

"Mr. Masterson?"

"Yes."

"This is Gina Bowden. I wanted to thank you for the flowers and the apology."

There was silence for several seconds before Jess Masterson replied. "Well, I did feel bad for acting so rudely. I appreciate your willingness to look the other way."

Gina wasn't sure she agreed with his wording, but she didn't want to create yet another scene by challenging his statement, especially when she wanted to ask him more about his stand against the Boy Scouts. "May I ask you a question?"

"Certainly," Masterson replied.

"I wondered why you were so set on fighting this thing out with the Boy Scouts. I mean, I know firsthand there is a lot of local support for Scouting. I suppose I'm just curious as to why you would ruin a good thing for everyone else just because you're angry at God."

"Who said I'm doing it because I'm angry at God?" Masterson retorted, his voice betraying his anger. "I suppose that was Gary's analysis."

"Well, isn't it true? I mean, what does it matter to you if the Boy Scouts make it an issue to honor God and country?"

"It matters that they are treating others unfairly by demanding an allegiance to God."

"I fail to see how it is unfair. No one is forced to join the Boy Scouts. It isn't a requirement in order to be educated in the public school system. It isn't necessary in order to be able to vote or serve in government or other forms of public service. It is an elective club, rather like your country club, Mr. Masterson."

"But my country club doesn't interfere in my religious beliefs. I may still join the country club so long as I adhere to the rules of the club and pay my dues."

"It's no different for the Scouts," Gina countered. "We adhere to the rules. Rules about being honorable to God and country. Promises to do our best, to help other people. Oh, and we pay dues that are a whole lot less exclusive than the dues you pay to your country club."

Masterson was silent for several moments. When he spoke, it so surprised Gina that she could do little more than agree to his idea.

"I'd like to come over and talk about this in more detail. Perhaps you could arrange for Gary to be present as well."

"When?"

"How about tomorrow?"

"We have church in the morning, but the afternoon would be fine. Say around three?"

"Thank you, that would be fine," Jess replied. "I'll see you then."

"Oh, do you have the address?" Gina questioned, forgetting about the flower delivery.

"Yes, it was in the telephone book. That's how I arranged for the flowers."

"Of course," Gina said, feeling rather silly. "Until tomorrow then."

As she hung up the phone, she heard the unmistakable sound of water being drained from the bathtub. Danny had apparently finished with his bath. She stared at the telephone for a moment, wondering why Jess Masterson would make it a point to come all the way over to her house to talk about his fight against funding for the Boy Scouts.

"I'm ready for bed," Danny announced from the doorway. Once again he'd failed to dry off before putting on his pajamas, and Gina wanted to laugh out loud at the way the material clung and bunched.

"Come here," she said with a grin. "Let me get you untwisted." She turned him around and found the entire back of the pajama top was caught up around his shoulders, leaving most of his back bare.

She adjusted his shirt, then prayed with him, and finally kissed him soundly before tucking him into his bed down the hall.

"Mommy," Danny said sleepily, "do you think if you and Mr. Cameron get married, I could call him Dad? I mean, do you think Daddy would mind?"

Gina felt her throat grow tight. "Honey, Mr. Cameron and I are just friends right now. I don't know if God would have me

50

marry him or not, but I'm sure that's a question we don't need to worry about right now."

"I want to call him Dad when you get married," Danny said, not seeming overly concerned with Gina's words. "I'm going to pray and ask God to 'splain it to Daddy in heaven. I don't want to hurt his feelings."

Gina kissed him on the forehead. "I think Daddy will understand perfectly," she told her son. "Now, get some sleep. I love you very much."

"I love you too," Danny said, yawning loudly. "And Mommy?"

"Yes?"

"I had a lot of fun today."

She smiled and tousled his hair. "I'm glad. I did too."

There was a comfort in knowing he was safe and happy and healthy. A comfort that Gina wouldn't trade for anything in the world. Not companionship with Gary or any other man. She wanted to remarry and give Danny a father, but it had to be right. It had to be the right man and the right time. He had to be someone she could love and respect and someone who would love her and Danny as if they had belonged to him from the start. Gary had made a special place in both their hearts, but Gina knew it was important to be careful.

Back in her own room, Gina stretched out on her bed and picked up her book, a wordy intellectual piece on New Age religions. Telaine had suggested it, but Gina found it rather dry and boring. Putting it aside, her mind turned to Gary's comments on whether she read because of a lack of anything else to do. She smiled. Of course, he was partly right. She loved to read, however, and would find time for it whether she was married or single. But this time of night had always belonged to just her and Ray.

She allowed her mind to run back over the memories of her marriage. She was happy as a wife and mother. She couldn't imagine wanting anything more out of life. She didn't mind that other women wanted it all—careers, travel, children, husbands, even politics. But she was happy with things being simple and noninvasive. Even now her modest home was paid for, and she had Ray's life insurance money in the bank, which paid their living expenses. No boss called her to come in when she had something else planned with her family. No political scandal brewed outside her door while the world waited for her to make a wrong step. No one knew or cared who Gina Bowden was. It had become a comfortable anonymity.

Would a relationship with Gary change that? She thought of his involvement with the community. His bookstore. His Scouting leadership. She had learned only that morning that he was heavily active in his church and she couldn't help but wonder how that might change things for her and Danny should their relationship grow more serious.

CHAPTER 5

Gary didn't like the idea of Jess Masterson arranging to speak to Gina. He couldn't imagine what possible good it would do. Did the old man think to persuade her to join his cause? Furthermore, he still found it of concern that after nearly four years of absolutely no communication, Jess Masterson had also requested that Gary be present.

Pulling into Gina's driveway, Gary was just about to switch off the car when the radio announced that the area was once again under a tornado watch. *Good old Kansas weather,* Gary thought as he shut off the engine and made his way to the house.

"You're early," Gina said, greeting him before he could even ring the doorbell.

"I know," Gary said. "I guess I wanted to make sure I got here first."

"Didn't want to leave me at the mercy of the angry councilman?" Gina teased.

"Something like that."

"Well, come on in. I was just cleaning up in the kitchen."

"They've just put us in another tornado watch."

Gina nodded and picked up a dish towel. "Yes, the weather

alert radio just went off. Danny's putting his things downstairs."

"You're acting a bit prematurely, aren't you?" Gary was more than a little aware of Gina's preoccupation with storms.

"As a Scout I would think you'd approve. 'Be prepared!' Isn't that the motto?" She picked up a glass and began drying it. "We don't just sit in the basement the whole time we're in a watch. We just make ready so we can go about our business until the time comes that we need to go to the basement. The last thing I want is to have Danny running around here like some sort of frantic ninny, trying to gather up things important to him and make his way to the basement."

"But the things aren't important," Gary pressed. "Are you sure you aren't teaching him to value possessions more than life?"

Gina continued drying the glass even though Gary could see it was already dry. He'd pushed her too hard, and now she was no doubt angry at him. But to his surprise, Gina put the glass in the cupboard and picked up another.

"I suppose," she finally said, "that it might look that way to you, but it's not. Danny knows the things are unimportant. Property can be replaced and memories will live forever in your heart and mind. Being responsible for his bag of treasures is one way he feels he has some control over the situation. My mother used to do this with me and it helped a lot.

"My parents' farmhouse was built at the turn of the century, so we had to go out into the weather to get to the storm cave and it always scared me. So, my mother decided to do what her mother had done when she was a child and give each of us kids an old pillowcase to put a few of our favorite things in. When the weather looked threatening, she'd have us take our stuff down into the storm cave. That way we had a vested interest in the cave and it was more than just some place to get to when the storms came." Gina put the glass in the cupboard and leaned back against the counter. "I like to believe that I'm helping Danny have some control over his environment. He focuses on what he can do to be ready rather than stewing about the upcoming storm."

Gary nodded. "That makes sense. I'm sorry if I sounded out of line."

Gina smiled and continued drying dishes. "A lot of folks go around doing nothing about the weather. They feel that God will protect them, and of course, He protects us all. But I feel it's important to take precautions. After all, people have been killed in these storms."

The way she looked as she said that final sentence made Gary wonder if she'd lost someone she loved in a storm. "You sound like you know better than some."

Gina nodded. "A good friend of mine died when I was thirteen. She used to laugh at my fear of storms. She and her mother teased me and said it wasn't Christian the way I fretted about things. They lived about a mile north of us, and one spring a bad storm system went through and a tornado hit ground about a quarter mile southwest of our farm. I'd just come from helping Dad turn the cows out into the pasture in case things got bad. We could see it bearing down on us, and Mom and the others were already making a mad dash for the cave. I was so scared I could hardly move. The roar was bad enough, but the sight of that thing. . ." Gina shuddered and grew silent for several moments.

Gary got up and went to her. He felt bad for having made her relive such a nightmare. Gently, he pulled her into his arms and hugged her close. "You don't have to tell me any more."

Gina seemed not to hear him. "It destroyed our farm and it

kept going north, where it destroyed my friend's farm too. Only they hadn't bothered to take shelter. They weren't paying attention to the weather, and we were too far away to hear any warning siren blown in the city. The house collapsed on top of them." She began trembling.

"Shhh," Gary hushed her and stroked her hair. "It's all right."

Gina looked up at him and tried to smile. "I'm sorry. Sometimes it's still so hard to remember."

Gary cupped her chin with his hand. He looked for several seconds into her eyes. Without a doubt he had fallen in love with this woman. And now, seeing her so vulnerable and weak, he loved her even more. He wanted to protect her—to keep her safe from anything that might harm her.

She watched him with an expression that implied concern and curiosity. He hesitated only a moment, then lowered his lips to hers. Just then, the weather radio sounded, startling both of them nearly out of their wits. Gary laughed and Gina pushed away to punch the radio on. As she did, the tornado sirens started up.

"Guess we don't have to ask what the radio has to say," Gary declared, grabbing the radio and pushing Gina toward the basement stairs.

"Where's Danny?" she questioned, seeing that the basement light was off.

"I'll find him," Gary assured her. "You get downstairs." He handed her the radio, then went off in the direction of the living room.

"Danny!" he called, looking around the room. Seeing no sign of the boy, he bounded up the stairs, the constant blaring of tornado sirens in his ears. "Danny!"

The boy came streaking down the hall. "Dad!" He threw himself into Gary's arms. Neither one said anything about Danny's usage of the word *Dad*.

"Come on, sport. Your mom's already in the basement," Gary said, lifting the boy and carrying him downstairs.

As Gary reached the bottom step, he made out the sound of knocking on the front door. Opening it, Gary came face-to-face with a stunned Jess Masterson. "Come on, Jess," Gary commanded. "Basement's this way."

The older man nodded and followed Gary. Gary felt the rapid beating of Danny's heart as the boy clung to him tightly. He longed to comfort the child, but the most important thing was to get them both out of harm's way. Gary hadn't needed to look for long at the greenish-black clouds that he saw overhead when he'd opened the door for Jess. He knew the signs were all there. The color of the clouds. The puffy fullness—indicating wind. They might well be in for it this time.

They made their way down the stairs with Gina grabbing Danny out of Gary's arms before he even reached the bottom step.

"Oh, Danny," she said, holding him tight. "I was so worried about you. Where were you?"

"I went to your room," Danny said, his lower lip quivering. "I thought you were there."

Gina hugged him close. "We're all right now, Danny. We don't have to worry. Did you say a prayer?" she questioned, taking a seat at the table.

"I think we were both saying prayers," Gary interjected, trying to lighten the mood. Outside the rain had picked up and the unmistakable sound of hail pounded down.

Gina nodded and Danny popped his head up. "I prayed." He

paused only a moment and added, "Look, Mom. We found this guy at the door."

Gina looked up and smiled. "Ah, Mr. Masterson. So glad you could join us."

Gary looked over to meet Jess' expression. "You timed that just right."

"I was rather concerned," Masterson replied. "I could see that storm coming up fast and wondered if I'd even get here before the rain started."

The lights flickered and Gary looked at Gina. "Flashlights?"

She nodded. "Danny, go get your bag and get your flashlight ready." The boy seemed to calm at this and nodded. He slipped off her lap and Gina smiled at Gary. He knew what she was thinking. Giving Danny an action, something to occupy his mind, had given the boy a sense of renewed strength.

Gina got up and went to the stairway enclosure. Opening the door, she handed out a battery-operated lantern. "I picked this up the other day. They were having a sale and I figured it would be—"

B–O–O–M!

Thunder shook the house so hard that for the briefest moment before the lights went out, Gary could see Gina's expression of sheer panic. He switched on the lantern, and Danny turned on his flashlight. By the time they could see each other again, Gina had pulled her facade of calm into place. Gary admired that she wanted to appear strong for her child, but he worried about her.

"We may be here for a spell," Gary said, motioning to the table and chairs. "Might as well have a seat, Jess."

The older man nodded and took a seat. Gina did likewise. Gary noted that Danny was already busy rummaging through his bag, apparently oblivious to the drone of the weather updates and the raging storm outside. He was safe and he knew it. He knew it because routine told him it was true and his mother's calm assured him that all was well in spite of the storm. Gary could easily see that even Gina was calming.

"So, Mr. Masterson," Gina said with a smile, "you wanted to talk with Gary and me?"

Jess chuckled. "Yes, well, I wanted to better explain my position regarding the Boy Scouts."

Danny perked up at this. "Are you a Boy Scout?" he questioned, pulling something out of his bag and coming to the table. "I'm a Cub Scout. Do you want to see my pinewood derby car?" His hopeful expression seemed to penetrate Jess Masterson's resolve.

"Sure, son," Masterson said, exchanging a quick glance with Gary before turning to the boy. "Let's see what you've done there."

"We've been working for about two weeks on it," Danny told him. "See how fast the wheels go?" The little boy ran his hand against the wheels and watched them spin.

"They do indeed go fast," Masterson agreed.

Gary listened in silence as the boy explained how they were going to have a race on the following Saturday. Danny's enthusiasm was so contagious, in fact, that when he invited Jess Masterson to be his special guest at the derby, the old man surprised them all by accepting.

Gary shook his head and walked to the window well in order to see if he could make out anything. It was usually on the back side of a thunderstorm that tornadoes made their deadly path. He glanced to where Jess Masterson was nodding to something Danny had said. Compared to his father-in-law, tornadoes were predictable.

CHAPTER 6

"W ell," Gina said as she met Gary at the door to the church community center, "it looks like clear skies for the derby."

"After last Sunday's storm," he replied, "I'm ready for clear skies from here on out."

Gina laughed. "Me too. Thanks for helping me clean up." She could still see the mess of downed tree branches in her mind.

"No problem. Pity you don't have a fireplace."

"I'm just grateful we didn't have any more damage. I heard that the tornado touched down near a housing development on the west side of town. Destroyed about six houses."

"I heard that too. We were fortunate no one was killed," Gary said softly.

"Yes," Gina said nodding. The thought made her shudder, and she turned quickly to watch Danny rush by her, his Cub Scout hat sitting rather cockeyed and his necktie twisted in the back. She compared his haphazard appearance with that of Gary Cameron, who stood before her wearing the adult uniform as if he were born in it. She realized all at once that he was watching her study him. Feeling her face grow hot, Gina looked away to where the boys were playing around the derby's inclined track.

"Is Jess here yet?"

"Nope, not yet. I still can't believe he agreed to come today."

"I know," Gina replied. "He hardly said two words to me after Danny latched on to him during the storm."

"Me either. I tried to call him once during the week, but I only got the answering machine. You do realize the council meets next Thursday night?"

Gina nodded. She knew Gary was worried about Masterson's plans for the Scout funding, but she also knew he was troubled by more than just that. Reaching out, she touched his arm. "What are you afraid of?"

His eyes widened for just a moment before he regained control. Then, as if deciding she deserved his honesty, Gary's expression softened. "I just don't want to see anyone hurt. Especially that little boy." He nodded to where Danny was proudly showing off his car. "I've come to care a great deal about him."

Gina smiled. "I have too."

"Do you know he called me Dad?"

"When?" Gina questioned, remembering Danny's request to call Gary Dad if and when they married.

"During the storm. It was when I found him upstairs. He was terrified and he called me Dad."

Gina nodded. "I don't doubt it for a minute. He cares a lot about you, and. . ." She hesitated to continue.

"And?" Gary questioned, taking hold of her hand as if they were the only people in the room.

Gina licked her lips. "And he asked me if he could call you Dad after we got married."

Gary's expression revealed surprise, almost shock. Gina tried to pull her hand away, fearing that she should never have mentioned the "M" word.

Gary held her hand fast and asked, "What did you tell him?"

"That he needed to give it time and let God show us the direction to take."

"And has He?"

"Has who—what?" she asked, feeling her senses overcome by the way he was looking at her. He seemed to reach into her soul with his eyes. Her mouth felt cottony and her hands began to tremble.

"Mr. Cameron! Mr. Cameron!" one of the Bear Cubs was shouting from across the room.

Gary grinned as if sensing his power over her. "We can discuss it later. But," he said, pausing to lean closer to her, "I think God's already shown me plenty. The path seems very clear, and if I have my way about it, we'll be making derby cars for years to come."

"Danny won't be a Cub Scout forever," Gina teased.

Gary winked. "No, but it'll take a while to get all his brothers through Cubs." With that, he walked away, leaving Gina to stare after him. *His brothers! Gary was implying—*

"Hello, Gina."

Gina turned to find a very casually dressed Jess Masterson. "Hello, Mr. Masterson." She felt both regret and relief that Masterson had chosen that moment to show up.

"Now, I thought we agreed that you were going to call me Jess."

Gina gave him a slight smile and eyed him as one might when considering a rattlesnake. *Caution!* her mind seemed to warn. "I'm glad you could come, Jess," she offered.

He smiled. "I know you are making an effort where I'm concerned, but really I'm not such a bad guy."

"Why don't we take a seat. It will take a while for the leaders to get everything ready. We might as well make ourselves comfortable."

Jess nodded and followed her to a gathering of empty chairs. "I don't want you to hate me, Gina."

Gina realized how very reserved her actions must have seemed to the older man. Asking God for guidance, she took a seat and turned to Jess. "I don't hate you," she began. "I don't understand you, but I don't hate you."

Jess looked at her in a rather puzzled manner. "What don't you understand?"

Gina folded her hands and looked at them as though they were the most interesting things in the world. "Why would a grown man set out to ruin the pleasure of children? Why do grown-up politics have to creep into everything in life?" She forced herself to look at Jess. "I believe in my heart that you are doing this for two reasons."

Jess looked rather surprised. "Do continue."

Gina swallowed the lump in her throat. "I think first of all you're angry at God for not saving Vicky. I can understand that. God knows I was angry at Him after Ray died. See, my husband died in a car accident like your daughter. A drunk driver hit him broadside and killed him instantly."

"I'm sorry," Jess said, stiffening in his chair. "I didn't know."

"I think you want to get back at God, but we both know that won't work," Gina continued. "Secondly, I think you want very much to hurt Gary because he lived and Vicky and Jason died." Jess paled and looked rather shocked. But Gina didn't give him time to answer. "You and Gary could have gained strength from each other, but instead you somehow hold him responsible."

"I don't suppose Gary bothered to tell you, but Vicky and Jason were only in that car because they were on their way to pick him up from a late night of inventory work at the bookstore," Jess said rather haughtily.

"Yes, I know," Gina replied. "And my husband was on his way home to me after a business trip. Should I blame myself? Was it my fault he was killed? Better yet, maybe I should blame Danny; after all, Ray was in a hurry to get back to us because Danny's birthday was the next day." She paused and looked him square in the eye. "Or was it the fault of the drunk behind the wheel? And beyond that, do I blame God because He took away someone I loved, when it was God who gave him to me in the first place?"

"Ah, the old 'The Lord giveth and the Lord taketh away,'" Masterson replied. This time anger was clear in his voice.

"Blessed be the name of the Lord," Gina finished.

"Meaning what?" Jess' eyes flashed in rage.

Gina reacted without thinking and placed her hand on Jess' arm. "Meaning, God is still God whether we blame Him or praise Him. Meaning God is still in charge even when we think He has somehow forgotten our zip code. Meaning God was with our loved ones when those drunks crossed their paths, and He was there when they breathed their last breath on earth and took their first steps into heaven."

Jess' expression remained fixed and rigid. "You can believe that way if it brings you comfort."

Gina smiled and squeezed his arm. "It does, Jess. It honestly does. Just knowing I don't have to bear the weight alone is more comforting than any kind of retaliation I can think of. You can go ahead with your plans against the Boy Scouts, but it won't change the fact that Vicky and Jason loved God." She paused and looked him in the eye, hoping she wasn't about to go too far. "It won't change that your wife loved Him either."

"What do you know of my wife?"

"I know what Gary told me. How she stood fast in her faith in spite of Vicky and Jason's death."

"She turned to God, but not to me," Jess said, and this time his voice sounded tired—resigned.

"She always had God, but maybe when she lost you, God became even more precious."

Jess' eyes widened in surprise. "How dare you say something like that! You didn't know her. You don't know me."

Gina released her hold on him and smiled. "Maybe I know you better than you think. I've been hurt just like you. I've lost people I loved, and I pushed away the love of others because I feared ever feeling that emptiness again. Jess, you go ahead and do what you think you need to do, but it won't change how you feel inside right now. I just want you to remember that."

"Mr. Masterson!" Danny exclaimed. "You came!"

The man eyed Gina for a moment, then turned to greet Danny. "I told you I'd be here and I'm a man of my word."

"Come see my car," Danny said, reaching out to take Masterson by the arm.

Gina forced a smile, Masterson's words echoing in her head. "I'm a man of my word," he'd said, making it both a threat and an affirmation.

~⁓

The afternoon passed in noisy exultation. Gina laughed watching the boys line the pinewood derby track. It was hard to imagine that something so simple could give such pleasure. From time to time, she also caught sight of Danny with Jess Masterson. The man seemed completely caught up in the moment, and Gina actually found herself glad he'd come.

The awards were handed out and Danny enthusiastically received the award for "Best Design." She smiled, knowing that if Gary hadn't bothered to take the time to help the child, Danny would have been racing a block of wood. She smiled, wondering if they had an award for the "Most Boring Design." No doubt she could have helped Danny win that one.

When the celebration was over, they gathered their things, and while Gina helped Gary, Danny was busily talking to Jess Masterson. She headed over to rescue the man, but as she drew close enough to hear their conversation, she halted in surprise.

"I had a very nice time, Danny. Thank you for inviting me. I'd almost forgotten what it was like to be young."

"I'm glad you came," Danny replied, entwining his fingers with Masterson's. "I need a grandpa and you need a boy so you won't forget about being young. Maybe you could ask my mom about coming over all the time. You could even come to church with us."

Jess Masterson looked up to meet Gina's fixed stare. She thought she saw the glistening of tears in the old man's eyes. She knew for certain there were tears in her own eyes. When Masterson appeared to be at a loss for words, Gina rescued him.

"Danny, come give me a hand with the chairs." She smiled at Jess. "You're always welcome at our house," she said as if to answer the unspoken question in regard to Danny's statement. "And at our church."

"Thank you," Jess replied. "I need to go. Will you tell Gary goodbye for me?"

"Of course," Gina replied. She watched the man leave, wondering what the future would hold and whether or not he would accomplish his goal of removing funding from the Boy Scouts.

Either way, she knew he was struggling to find his way out of sorrow and loneliness, and depriving the Scouts of city money wasn't going to change a thing.

CHAPTER 7

Gina and Gary nervously took their seats at the city council meeting. Neither had spoken to Jess after the derby, and neither knew what kind of scene they would have to endure tonight. But, they had prayed about the situation and had agreed to trust God for the outcome. It would be hard on the Scouts to lose the help of the city, but it wouldn't put an end to the organization.

The meeting was brought to order, and after the rhetoric of various reports, the issue of Jess Masterson's proposal was brought to the attention of the council. Jess, who'd arrived late and had barely taken a seat before the meeting started, cleared his voice and shuffled some papers in his hands.

"If it pleases the council," he began, "I'd like to withdraw my proposal. I would also like to propose the council disregard anything I've said over the last few months." He grinned rather sheepishly and added, "I'm not sure exactly what all that might entail, but I'm certain it was probably less than well thought out."

Silence held the room as Jess continued. "I'm afraid my judgment has been altered by the recent events of my life. Some of you know I lost a daughter and grandson in a car accident. Then last year I lost my wife of forty years. Those aren't the kinds of things a man easily deals with. I'm afraid I didn't deal well with them at all."

Gina felt tears come to her eyes and did nothing to try to hide them. She smiled at Jess when he looked her way, hoping—praying—that her expression offered reassurance.

"Instead of my original proposal," Jess said, nodding slightly at Gina, "I'm offering something else." He picked up a stack of papers and handed them down the table to the council. "My resignation."

There were gasps of surprise in the audience, but no one was as surprised as Gary and Gina.

"It's time I retired and did some of the things fellows my age have earned the right to do. There's a little boy out there who told me the other day he needed a grandpa. He also said that I needed a boy to remind me about being young." Jess grinned. "I think he was exactly right."

Gina tightly gripped Gary's hand. "This is unbelievable," she whispered. "I thought it was impossible for us to change his mind."

"I don't think *we* did," Gary countered. "I think Danny did."

Gina nodded. "He sure took to Jess. I guess I just never realized all the missing aspects in Danny's life. It's like he has holes in his life I never even suspected were there."

"Well, we need to get to the business of filling in those empty places, don't we?" Gary said softly.

Gina felt her breath quicken. She knew what Gary was implying. It was time to make a commitment. "Maybe we could leave the meeting?"

The council was already going through the motions of dismissing Jess' earlier proposal and accepting his resignation. As soon as the vote was complete, Gary grabbed Gina's hand and pulled her up with him. They made their way to the back door, and Gary had already opened it when Gina stopped. Turning, she caught sight of Jess watching them. Smiling, she did the only thing she knew would clearly explain her gratitude. She blew him a kiss. Jess Masterson couldn't have looked more shocked had she shaken her fist at him, but then a tiny smile crept across his face.

Gary pulled Gina into the hall, his own expression rather stunned.

"What's the matter?" Gina questioned. "You look as though you've seen a ghost."

"Vicky used to always blow Jess a kiss goodbye whenever we got ready to leave. I guess seeing you do that just now. . .well. . .it just surprised me."

"I'd say it surprised you both," Gina replied, fearful that she'd caused more harm than good. "I hope I didn't upset him."

"From the expression on his face, I think he was touched," Gary said, raising her hand to his lips. "I know I was."

Gina felt overwhelmed by the emotions coursing through her heart and mind and soul. *God always had a way of breaking down doors,* she thought as Gary led her to the car.

They picked up Danny at the Applebees' farm, then made their way to Gina's house. Danny chattered at full speed, telling about the puppies and how much he wanted one. Gina quickly realized that any private discussion she and Gary had hoped for was now out of the question.

Gary must have realized it too because after they arrived home, he told Gina he needed to run some errands and couldn't stay. Disappointed but understanding, Gina bid him goodbye and watched as Danny gave Gary a big hug. Perhaps it was better this way. She needed to talk to Danny about the future and help him through any questions he might have.

As soon as Gary was gone, she turned to her son. "We need to talk," she said quite seriously.

"Did I do something wrong?" Danny asked, his face contorting as he appeared to consider the possibilities.

"No, silly," Gina said, tousling his hair. "Come sit with me on the couch. I want to talk about us. . .and about Gary."

Danny nodded. "Are you going to get married now?"

Gina laughed. "Nothing like jumping right in, eh? Well, we might as well talk it through. Would you like for me to marry Gary?"

"Yes!" Danny replied enthusiastically. "I want him to be my dad."

Gina nodded. "I know you've said that before. But I want you to realize how things might change for us."

Danny sobered. "Okay."

"Having a dad around will be a lot of fun for you. You will be able to do things with him while I do other things, and then there will be times when we have fun all together. But if I marry Gary, you will also have to mind him. Do you understand that?"

"Sure," Danny replied as if what she'd said was a given fact. "I mind him at Scouts already. Mom," he said, reaching out to hug her, "I want a dad. I promise I can mind."

Gina felt her heartstrings plucked in a most evident way. "I know you can. I want you to have a dad, and I think Gary would make a great dad and a good husband. I think God has finally shown me that we would make a good family."

Danny let out a yip of excitement. "I'm gonna have a dad and a grandpa!" He got up from the couch and danced around the room.

Gina laughed at his enthusiasm. "Danny, come back here. Nothing is settled yet. Gary and I haven't even talked about getting married. I mean, not really. We need to talk about it first, and then we need to give ourselves plenty of time to make plans and get to know each other better. I need for you to know him better too."

Danny threw himself into her arms and looked up at her. His baby face was fading more and more each day, and in its place had grown a boy's hopeful expression. "How long will it take?"

Gina laughed again and tickled Danny lightly under his arms. "Not long. Not near as long as it's taken to find the right person for the job."

Gina had fully expected Gary to call her later that night, and when he didn't, she felt an emptiness inside that her newest fiction novel couldn't fill. Then when Gary didn't call on Friday or Saturday, Gina thought perhaps she'd done something to offend him. She thought back to her actions reminding everyone of Vicky and worried that she'd created a major mess of things.

Sunday found her and Danny just going through the paces. How empty it seemed without Gary. It was as if a vital part of their lives had been suddenly taken from them. It reminded her too much of how she'd felt after losing Ray. Finally, on Sunday night she broke down and gave Gary a call.

But he wasn't there. His answering machine clicked on and asked her to leave a message, but that was the only sound of his voice that Gina had. Going to bed that night, she tossed and turned fitfully. What was happening? Had Gary given up on the idea of making a commitment to her and Danny?

Monday morning, Gina awoke more tired than when she'd gone to bed. Going through the familiar routine of homeschool studies and daily chores did nothing to help calm her fears. Gina had just managed to finish cleaning the bathroom, while Danny worked on multiplication facts, when the telephone rang.

"Mrs. Bowden?" a decidedly aged voice questioned from the other end of the line.

"Yes?"

"This is Nora down at Cameron Christian Books and Gifts."

Gina felt her body tense. Why should this woman be calling her? Had something happened to Gary? She could still hear the voice of the police officer who'd come to tell her about Ray's accident.

"Is something wrong?" Gina questioned, praying silently for strength.

"No," the woman assured. "Well. . .that is. . .I hope you'll forgive me, but I've neglected my duties and now I fear I've been the cause of making you worry."

"I don't understand," Gina replied softly.

"Gary asked me to give you a message last Friday and I totally forgot."

Gina felt relief wash over her. "A message?"

"Yes. Gary wanted me to tell you that he needed a few days of prayer for a special situation. He thought you'd understand. He took off for a three-day weekend. I expect him back anytime, but I was supposed to let you know last Friday. I hope you'll forgive me."

Gina was so happy to hear that nothing horrible had happened to Gary that she would have overlooked any mistake the woman might have laid claim to. "That's all right, Nora. I understand how these things go." Gina listened as the woman apologized once again, then thanked her and hung up with renewed enthusiasm for the day.

Danny brought his paper to her. "I'm finished. Can I have a recess break?"

Gina smiled. "Sure thing. Oh, and that was a woman who works at Gary's bookstore. She said she forgot to call us last Friday and tell us that Gary was taking a short trip away from town."

Danny's face brightened. "So he's coming back?"

Gina nodded. "Yes, I'm sure he will. Now, you go play and I'll call you in about fifteen minutes. We still have social studies, but then we'll be done."

Danny hurried out the back door, while Gina followed in order to check on the clothes hanging on the line in the backyard. Silently she thanked God for Nora's call. She looked heavenward, noting the building clouds. It looked like the weather might once again grow threatening. Glancing at her watch, Gina saw that it was nearly three o'clock. Their worst storms took place in late afternoon and early evening. If she was fortunate, the clothes would have time to dry before the rain set in.

By five o'clock, Gina was hurrying to pull the clothes from the line. The area had been put into a severe thunderstorm watch, and from the look of the weather radar on television, storms were popping up all around them. The unmistakable darkness of the clouds to the south gave Gina little doubt the storms would soon be upon them as well.

She fixed them a light supper while Danny played quietly upstairs. The first sound of thunder rumbled in the distance, and Gina silently prayed for safety from the storm. "Danny!" she called, putting two plates on the table. "Supper!"

Danny came bounding downstairs, his storm bag in hand. He put it by the basement door and looked up at his mother. "I brought this down just in case. I don't want to be stuck upstairs again if the sirens go off."

Gina frowned. She didn't want her son so paranoid that he

couldn't go about his business when storms came. Sitting down at the table, she took hold of his hand. "Danny, we don't have to be afraid of the stormy weather. God is watching over us. He will take care of us, no matter what happens. You believe that, don't you?"

Danny's eyes were wide as he nodded. "I think so," he said doubtfully. "But sometimes people die in storms. You told me about your friend."

Gina gently stroked his hand. "I know. Sometimes bad things do happen. Sometimes storms destroy homes and lives. Sometimes people are hurt by other storms in life, as well. But, Danny, I promise you—God has it all under control. He won't leave us to go through it alone. The Bible says He will be with us always."

"But sometimes you get afraid," Danny said quite seriously.

"Yes." Gina nodded. "Yes, I do. But that's when I forget to give it to God. The times I get afraid are those times when I try to take care of everything myself. When I try to be in charge—instead of letting God be in charge. Understand?"

Danny nodded. "But you said that we should be prepared."

"And we should. We should use the knowledge God has given us to help take proper care of each other and of our things. But we don't sit in the basement all day, every day for fear that a little rain cloud might send us a tornado. It's the same way with other things in life. When the threat of bad things comes, we have to do what we know is right in order to get through those times. Sometimes we get hurt—"

"Like when Daddy died?" Danny interjected.

"Yes," Gina whispered, her voice heavy with emotion. "Like when Daddy died. But God brought us through that. He showed us that we were still loved by Him and that we would always be loved by Him. He's taken good care of us, hasn't He?"

"Yup, and God sent us Mr. Cameron."

Gina smiled. "That's right, He did."

The weather alert radio blared out its warning tone, interrupting Gina's conversation. Giving Danny a reassuring smile, she went to the radio and pressed the button. The thunderstorm watch had been changed to a tornado watch after two separate storms had produced small tornadoes in the surrounding area. She was still trying to listen to the details when someone rang the front doorbell.

"Danny, go answer the door, please," she told her son.

She finished listening to the report as Danny ran for the door and came back beaming from ear to ear, Gary Cameron following right behind.

"Looks like we're in for it again," Gary announced. "I don't like the looks of those clouds."

"Mom said God will take care of us," Danny offered.

"I agree totally," Gary replied as lightning flashed.

There was little doubt that a storm of great intensity was nearly upon them. Gina tried to maintain her composure. "Danny, go ahead and take your bag downstairs and then we'll have lunch."

"Can we eat in the basement again?"

Gina laughed and cast a quick glance at Gary. "I don't think we have to go that far. At least not yet. Remember what I said about not being afraid of the storms?"

"But I thought it was fun eating down there," Danny countered, picking up his bag. "It was like an adventure."

"Well, I suppose if you really want to...," Gina said, her voice trailing off.

"Come on, sport," Gary said, picking up his plate. "I'll get you settled downstairs, then come back up and convince your mother that it will be a lot of fun. We'll even play a board game or two."

Danny cheered and headed down the stairs.

"I thought we didn't want him to be paranoid about storms," Gina said in a barely audible voice.

"We don't, but like I said, those clouds didn't look good. Besides, when I come back upstairs, I have some important questions to ask you and I'd like to do it without an audience." He winked at her, then bounded down the steps before she could reply.

Gina felt her heartbeat quicken and her hands go clammy. Did he want to ask her what she hoped he would ask? Had he thought through all the complications in their lives and sorted through his feelings to know that marriage to Gina was the right move to make?

By the time he returned, Gina was leaning casually against the kitchen counter. She tried her best to look disinterested and nonchalant but knew she was doing a miserable job of it. "So what did you want to ask me?"

Gary smiled and leaned against the jamb of the basement door. "How do you feel about having more kids?"

"I've always wanted more children," she said quite seriously. "How many did you have in mind?"

"Three, maybe four?"

Gina bit at her lower lip as if considering the matter. "I think that's workable. What else?"

"Houses and living arrangements," he said flatly. "I prefer to think of us both starting over. A new house in the country is what I have in mind."

Gina tried to keep from smiling, but she couldn't help it. "I know a good real estate lady. Anything else you want to ask me?"

"That just about does it," Gary said. Then without a single word, he crossed the room and swept her into his arms. "I've missed you more than I ever imagined possible." His mouth came down on hers and Gina melted against him in absolute rapture. "I love you, Gina Bowden," he whispered, pulling back only long enough to speak.

Gina tightened her hold on him and let her kiss be her agreeing comment on his declaration. Without warning, he pulled back and grinned. "Marry me?"

She laughed, and as she opened her mouth to speak, the weather alert radio sounded. Both of them broke into laughter as the weatherman announced the need to take cover from the strengthening storm.

"Ah, Kansas stormy weather," Gina mused, allowing Gary to hurry her to the basement door. "Grab the radio, will you?" She turned on the top step to await him.

"Sure thing," he replied, reaching back to the counter.

He quickly retrieved the radio and gave her a gentle push to start her down the steps. "There's never a dull moment around here," he declared.

"I warned you, our house is anything but quiet," Gina replied.

Gary smiled at Danny, who started to babble about the sirens and his good idea to eat lunch in the basement. "We're having another adventure, aren't we, Mom?"

"That we are. Say, how would you like it if I made this an even better adventure?" Gina questioned.

Both Gary and Danny looked at her, but it was Danny who questioned. "How?"

"By letting you in on a great surprise," she replied, enjoying her son's curiosity and Gary's puzzled stare. "Gary just asked me to marry him, and I'm just about to say yes."

Danny cheered and jumped up from the table to hug his arms

around Gary's waist. "I knew you would be my new dad. I just knew it!"

Gary looked down at Danny for a moment before returning his gaze to Gina. "She hasn't said yes yet, sport."

Danny pulled back. "Say it, Mom. Say it so Dad knows you mean it."

Gina laughed in spite of the weather outside. "Yes," she said simply. "Yes, I will marry you, Gary Cameron."

Danny cheered again, but this time Gary joined him and lifted him high in the air to toss him up in joyful celebration. "She said yes, sport! That makes it official." He caught Danny and held him against his shoulder and held open his other arm to Gina.

"Now we can be a real family." The pleasure in Danny's voice was clear.

Gina laughed and came quite happily into Gary's embrace. "A real family," Gina murmured and silently thanked God for the miracle He'd given her. Even stormy weather couldn't spoil the moment.

Epilogue

A year later, on a clear April evening, Gina and Gary were married in the church where Gary had grown up. Gina loved the people and the wonderful way she'd been welcomed into their family, but most of all, she loved Gary and the way he loved her and Danny.

"You look rather pleased with yourself, Mrs. Cameron," Gary whispered in her ear as their guests gathered around to see them cut the wedding cake.

"I am rather pleased, Mr. Cameron," she replied, giving him what she hoped was a rather sultry look.

Gary raised a single brow and Gina thought she saw sweat form on his forehead. Grinning, she leaned against him ever so slightly. "You're looking a bit stressed, my dear." She held up the knife. "But we mustn't disappoint our guests."

"Just remember," he whispered against her ear, "I wanted to elope."

Gina felt a shiver run from her head to her toes. His warm breath against her neck was nearly enough to make her drop her facade of composure. "We're supposed to. . .ah. . .cut the cake together," she stammered.

Gary took hold of her hand and closed it around the knife's handle. "The quicker we get to it, the sooner we can leave on our honeymoon," he teased, and laughed out loud as Gina quickly plunged the knife into the cake.

The reception was a tremendous success, and Gina's heart was warmed by the sight of her son and Jess Masterson sharing company and having a wonderful time. Jess had acted as Gary's best man, while Danny stood up as Gina's only attendant.

"I'm surprised you held the reception in the church basement," Telaine Applebee said, coming to give her best wishes to Gina and Gary. "They have a perfectly wonderful reception hall upstairs. I don't think anyone's used this area in years, at least not for a wedding."

Gina exchanged a quick smile with Gary before answering. "Scout motto."

Telaine looked at her oddly. "Scout motto?"

"Be prepared," Gary countered.

"Yes, I know what the motto is, but what does that have to do with the reception being in the basement?" Telaine asked.

"Gina figured we'd outwit any chances of stormy weather," Gary replied with a grin.

"That's right," Gina replied. "It took me long enough to find this man, I wasn't going to risk losing him in a mad dash for the basement."

Everyone around them laughed at this, while Gina felt Gary's arms close around her from behind. "There wasn't a chance of you losing me," he whispered only loud enough for Gina to hear. "Storms or calm, you're stuck with me for life, Mrs. Cameron."

Gina leaned against him and grinned. "Good thing. See, there's this pinewood derby coming up in two weeks and. . ."

Summer

KING OF HEARTS

Chapter 1

Elise Jost stood waiting impatiently at the receptionist desk. Her college adviser, Dr. Cooper, had summoned her, and with only a week left until graduation, Elise couldn't image what she might need to discuss.

"Elise?" a strong but clearly feminine voice called from the doorway.

"Yes?"

"Come on in."

"I have to say, Dr. Cooper," Elise remarked as she followed the older woman into her office, "this comes as quite a surprise."

The trim professional took her seat and motioned for Elise to do the same. "I'm afraid I have bad news. I am partially to blame for this oversight, and that makes telling you the circumstances even harder." Dr. Cooper shuffled some papers nervously before finally settling into silence. "It seems," she finally began again, "you are one credit short of having the requirements for graduation."

"That can't be!" Elise exclaimed and quickly scanned the pages in her hand. "I've calculated all of this to the last detail. I graduate next week. There must be some mistake."

"There was," Dr. Cooper offered sympathetically. "There was an incorrect entry on your elective credits. One of the classes you were given three credit hours for was only a two-credit class. You'll have to take an additional credit or another two- or three-credit class to meet your requirements for graduation. Of course, they'll still let you graduate with your class next week."

"But I can't!" Elise moaned. "I have the possibility of a job that could very well start in June. I'm in the final cut, and one of the only remaining factors is that I complete my degree by summer."

"I am sorry, Elise. I know how much of a shock this is, but it isn't the end of the world. There are several classes offered during the day that should fit in with your schedule."

"You don't understand," Elise began, weariness mingling with anger. She fell back against the chair as though she'd just been given a death sentence. "I had to rearrange my entire work schedule for this semester. I've turned my life upside down so that I could work from three to ten at night and go to school in the day. Now you're telling me it was all for nothing. I can't even complete my requirements without coming back to several weeks of summer school. That's going to put an end to the government job or at least put it off until fall, and I don't even know if my retail job will keep me on."

"I'm sure there's something we can find." The older woman seemed oblivious to Elise's panic and leaned across her desk to pull out her own copy of the summer schedule. Thumbing through it while Elise collected her thoughts, she mentioned several classes that might be acceptable. "Here's a chorus class. It's only one hour three times a week and it would give you the credit you need."

"I can't carry a tune to save my soul," Elise said despondently.

"Okay," Dr. Cooper continued, "how about an art appreciation class. We have several that are for the nonart major. You would surely enjoy learning a little more about the history of art."

"It might work," Elise said, scanning the hours. "No, all of these are afternoon classes. I have to work then, and I don't dare ask to change my schedule again. Not with the fact that they know I'm just biding time until a real job comes along."

Dr. Cooper nodded and continued to flip through the few remaining pages. "Here, what about this?" She showed Elise the page. "Renaissance Appreciation."

"What does that involve?"

"It's technically an art credit, but it's a combination class that deals with the historical and artistic values of the time. It leans very heavily toward the history aspect and meets both in the Fine Arts Building as well as the Liberal Arts Building. It all depends on the various assigned projects. Dr. Hunter is the professor, and he's excellent. He used to teach here at the college on a regular basis, but he retired to write textbooks and other projects. Now he just teaches this one class in the summer as a pet project."

"I see." Elise noted the time would work, just barely, with her already tight schedule. "I suppose it'll have to do. Can I take it pass/fail so that if I don't have an appreciation for the Renaissance, it won't affect my grade average?"

"Of course." Dr. Cooper smiled, happy to see that this was going to work out for one of the university's brightest nontraditional students. "You've worked hard for your perfect record, and the college has been honored to have you here. Now you go ahead and get scheduled for this. Today's the last day for enrollment in this class, so don't waste any time. I'm glad we could catch this before it ruined your plans."

Elise got to her feet, not at all convinced that it hadn't ruined her plans. "Thank you, Dr. Cooper. You've been a tremendous help over the years."

The woman smiled. "I was in your shoes not long ago. It isn't easy to attend college and work full-time."

Elise smiled. She and Dr. Cooper had had this conversation more than once. "I'll let you know how it goes," she said, leaving the office.

Once outside in the busy hallway, Elise wanted to break down and cry. She went to the restroom and blotted a cool towel against her cheeks for a moment. "This isn't working out the way I'd planned," she muttered to herself. She comforted herself with the fact that graduation was in a few short days. *I can't let this change anything,* she thought while studying her reflection in the mirror. Her cinnamon-colored hair was pulled back into a neat ponytail, making her look younger than her twenty-seven years. Her face, softly rounded and lightly highlighted by makeup, was a bit fuller than she'd have liked, but then so was the rest of her body. For years she'd tried to lose that extra twenty pounds, but it seemed to fall in acceptable places—and since she wasn't trying to look good for someone else, it was easy to ignore.

She continued looking in the mirror for several minutes. It was almost as if she wanted to force some revelation from her reflected image, find the answer to her unspoken questions.

She jumped nervously when the door opened to admit two young, giggling women.

"Daddy said if I did well this semester," one was saying to the other, "he'll get me that new red sports car."

"Not the one you showed me!" the other girl exclaimed.

"Yeees!"

Elise fully expected the girlfriend to break into a high-pitched

"Way cool!" but she didn't.

"Then you can drive us to Kansas City and we can meet some interesting men."

"Forget Kansas City. Let's go all the way to New York or California. That's where the really rich ones are."

"Not only rich, but interesting. New York is where all the really interesting men live," the other fairly panted.

Is that so? Elise wondered. Maybe that was why she'd not run across any of the "really interesting" men. Not that she'd been looking. She knew what could happen when a career-driven woman let a man into her life. She would be expected to put her career on the back burner while establishing his, and then if there was time for her job interest, great. If not, it was diapers and bottles and bye-bye career. Who said old-fashioned notions were dead?

"Daddy says the only reason I came to college was to get my M.R.S.," the first one giggled. "I think that's funny, don't you?"

"Sure," the second one answered, sounding unconvinced. Then she chimed in, "Oh, I get it. Your dad thinks you're here to find a husband. Oh, that is funny!"

Elise rolled her eyes, gathered her things, and went on her way.

Registration passed without much ado. Elise noted with only marginal interest that she had three books to purchase for the class. It was just more money to spend that she'd not planned on having to part with. At this rate, her nest egg wouldn't last until she got a real job.

Passing from the administrative building into the student union, Elise made her way to the bookstore. *Might as well get this out of the way now,* she thought. With a moan, she pushed past a group of girls who seemed to be holding hands and moving collectively through the store. *They should keep us old folks isolated,* she thought and watched the girls with a marginal bit of envy. She'd never had good friends. By her own choice, she realized just as quickly.

Nevertheless, the truth hurt. There just wasn't time for relationships in her life. College had taken what little time she had to give, while work and study took the greater portion of her life. How could she possibly give such a precious commodity as time to another person?

Elise juggled her purse and papers and moved to the fine arts section. Over the last few years, searching for textbooks in the union bookstore had almost become a pastime. She glanced around the section, praying silently that the Renaissance books wouldn't be as big as math textbooks. Why someone hadn't found a way to make a math book smaller eluded Elise. She had yet to take a math class of any kind and have the book weigh less than fifty pounds. Or so it seemed.

"*Life in the Renaissance,*" she said aloud, spotting the book. She glanced down at the list. Yes, this was one of the required books. The other two, *Art in the Renaissance* and *Renaissance England,* were neighboring the slots beside the stack of *Life in the. . .* books. Picking up one of each title, Elise noted they were inexpensively priced paperbacks and that the third book had even been written by the same man who would teach the class. "*Renaissance England,*" she spoke softly, "by Ian Hunter, PhD."

Turning the book over, she read aloud, "The lifestyles and daily routines of *Renaissance England* are explored in this academically crafted work by Dr. Ian Hunter." The descriptive copy continued, but Elise noted the time and realized she had to hurry in order to get home, drop off her things, and dress for work at the mall.

"I wonder if women in Renaissance England had to worry about schedules the way we do in twentieth-century America," she grumbled to herself. The day was rapidly going downhill.

CHAPTER 2

G raduation came and went without much fanfare in Elise's life. Her parents were too far away and too busy to make the trip to see her graduate. There had been a sweet card and surprisingly large check, along with a newsy letter about their neighborhood, but other than that, Elise was alone. The government job was given to another person with the promise that they were still very interested in Elise and would have another position available by fall. Fall was months away, however, and Elise brooded bitterly over how she was supposed to survive in the meantime.

"God, sometimes," she prayed, "I just don't get it. I do the things I think I should. I follow Your Word and feel I understand what You want for my life, and then it all seems to fall apart. I don't want to question You on this one, but I could sure use some clarity."

The Renaissance class offered problems from the very first day when Elise missed her alarm going off. She barely had time to shower and braid her hair before hurrying out the door. Trying to save money, Elise had refused to buy a car. Up until this day, it had worked pretty well, but now she questioned her sanity. The twelve-block walk seemed to stretch for miles, and time refused to stand still.

Finally reaching the college, Elise realized she'd have less than five minutes to make it across campus to the Salinger Liberal Arts Building, affectionately referred to as the SLAB. According to the schedule, the class would have its first meeting in the SLAB, but keeping straight which sessions would be held in the SLAB and which would be held in the Fine Arts Building as the course progressed could prove to be a challenge. Elise figured it was a plot to thoroughly confuse and discourage her. She could well imagine showing up one place, only to learn that she belonged in the other.

Remembering the Renaissance class was on the third floor, Elise made a mad dash for the elevator, only to find a sign taped to the closed doors. OUT OF ORDER! Elise moaned and realized she'd have to climb three flights of stairs.

The next surprise came when she got in class and found a young man at the head of the classroom. Surely this guy who looked five years younger than her wasn't the esteemed, retired Dr. Hunter she'd heard so much about!

"If you'll take your seats," the man called out, "I have some announcements to make. I'm Jeff Moore," he announced. "I'm a senior here and my major is history. Dr. Hunter was scheduled to be back today, but due to a family illness, he's been delayed. In his absence, I am prepared to walk you through the course requirements and give you your first reading assignment. Hopefully, Dr. Hunter will be here next Monday and you won't be forced to endure more of my babbling." There were a few muted chuckles, but Elise's was not among them.

"Dr. Hunter is pretty easy going. As you know, this class is a combination history and art class. It's kind of different from anything else you've probably taken, and as you know, it meets four times a week. However, that's just the beginning. There will be multiple projects that will require extra hours during the week to help with a variety of duties related to the festival. And of course, the festival itself."

Elise nearly dropped her pencil. What projects? What festival? She didn't have extra hours to give. Glancing around her, Elise noticed that no one else seemed in the least bit concerned. The young man to her right, in fact, was drawing designs of motorcycles on his class syllabus, as though he hadn't a care in the world.

"Was everyone able to get copies of the three books Dr. Hunter assigned?" A unified mumbling of affirmation rose from the class of some thirty students and died down just as quickly.

"Great!" Jeff said and held up the book entitled *Life in the Renaissance.* "Your first assignment comes from this book. You're to read the first twenty pages, which is actually chapter one. On Monday, be prepared to discuss the material." Jeff put the book back on the table and looked up. "Any questions?"

"When do we start working on the festival?" a dark-haired young woman asked. Elise perked up, wondering again at the festival reference.

"Immediately," Jeff answered. "Dr. Hunter spends a great deal of energy each year on the festival and prides himself in a job well done. This class will of course be responsible, as it is every year, for the foundational planning, coordination, and execution of the festival."

"Do we get to pick what we want to do?" another voice questioned, this time a young man.

Jeff smiled. "For the most part. You are assigned parts to play, but Dr. Hunter always listens to what a person has an interest in. Of course, because of the multiyear involvement by some people in the pageantry, nobles are selected by committee and titles are retained until a person chooses to retire from involvement. Then again, the nobility have more responsibilities. They raise a great deal of the money prior to ticket sales, and they usually sponsor the various activities. Our college is one of four in the state that sponsors a Renaissance Festival, and because of that, we've divided each college according to suits from a deck of cards. Ours is hearts, therefore our king is the king of hearts."

Elise now realized they were speaking of the Renaissance Festival that took place in July on the college campus. She'd heard about it, but in the six years she'd lived in Jacksonville, she'd never bothered to attend.

"Is it true that everybody gets to participate in the festival?" a girl who barely looked old enough to be out of high school asked.

"It's not a matter of being allowed to," Jeff reminded them. "You must participate in the festival or you will not pass the course."

The words slammed into Elise's brain. "What do you mean?" she said aloud before realizing that she'd spoken.

Jeff shrugged and shook his head. "I'm sorry, I guess I don't understand."

Elise eyed him suspiciously. "Do I understand correctly that I have to participate in the festival in order to receive a passing grade? Even if I take the class pass/fail?"

Jeff nodded. "That's right. The class was created by Dr. Hunter and raises a great deal of money to fund projects for the fine arts department. Class participation sees that everything runs smoothly. It's been a most successful way to coordinate the more tedious tasks."

Elise was beginning to feel ill. The day was now officially ruined. "What about those of us with job obligations?"

"A lot of people take their vacations during the actual festival time," Jeff offered. "Otherwise, Dr. Hunter is very flexible and needs volunteers for both day and evening hours. Now, are there any more questions?"

When nobody else spoke up, he dismissed the class with a reminder of the reading assignment. Elise wasn't about to be put off that easily. There was no way she could take a week out to playact in a Renaissance festival.

"Mr. Moore?"

"Huh?" the man looked up rather surprised by her use of his last name.

"What alternative assignment does Dr. Hunter have for those students who can't participate in the festival?"

"Alternative assignment?" Jeff repeated the words like they were some cryptic code.

"That's right. What can I do to get out of the festival and still pass this course?" Elise knew she sounded a bit on edge, but she was rapidly losing patience.

"As far as I know, and this is only from the four years I've attended this college, Dr. Hunter doesn't let anyone out of the festival requirement. There are no alternatives."

Elise felt her ire rise but kept her temper in check. "No other alternatives. Are you absolutely sure?"

"Positive," Jeff said, gathering his things. "Now if you don't mind, I have to get on over to my regular class. I'm sure Dr. Hunter will be back next Monday. Why don't you just wait and discuss it with him then?"

"I think I'll discuss it with someone over at the administrative office today," Elise said and angrily stormed back to her desk to gather her books.

Of all the idiotic things, she thought while marching down the three flights of stairs. *King of hearts, indeed!*

Making her way to the registrar's office, Elise calmed down a bit. It seemed reasonable that kids would find Dr. Hunter's festival a good way to get an easy credit, but for her it was a complete waste of time.

"May I help you?" an older, gray-haired woman asked.

Elise nodded. "I hope so. I need to talk to someone about a class I'm in. I think I want to change it."

"I see," the woman replied. "I'm afraid you'll have to speak with the department head, but he's out sick with the flu. Why don't you let me pencil you in for an appointment on Monday. If he's still sick, I can give you a call to cancel."

Complete frustration washed over Elise. "Isn't there anybody else I can talk to?"

"Have you spoken to your class instructor?"

"The class is led by Dr. Hunter, and he's not yet made an appearance."

"Oh, yes, Dr. Hunter. Well, we're expecting him back Monday as well. Why don't you talk to him first?"

"I'll start with the department head. Dr. Hunter apparently isn't known for his willingness to work with students on schedule conflicts."

The woman's expression told Elise how incredible she found Elise's words to be.

"Just schedule me early on Monday so that I can still make my class," Elise snapped.

Taking the slip of paper offered her by the receptionist, Elise stormed from the building. "I don't have time to play games!" she said aloud, glad that she was far enough away from anyone so that no one could overhear her. Monday couldn't come soon enough!

CHAPTER 3

To Elise's surprise, however, Monday came quicker than she'd anticipated. She'd put in extra hours at the department store where she worked in designer clothes sales and was left feeling drained and desperately behind schedule. After a quick shower, Elise realized that once again she was running late. Nothing was going right!

Her long, damp hair wouldn't cooperate in forming a bun, so Elise pulled it back and hoped to do something with it later. Halfway to the school, however, the barrette in her hair snapped from the pressure of the bulky mass and left Elise with a tangled cinnamon mess that the wind whipped at mercilessly.

At the college, the registrar's receptionist sympathetically told Elise that the department head was still out sick. "You can make another appointment, dear, but I can't help you other than that."

"I can't believe this. An entire university staff and I can only complain to one man about one class?" Elise's anger was barely in check. "Look, it's not that I can't work with the regulations and procedures around here, but give me a break. Renaissance Appreciation wasn't my idea, and if I didn't need a single credit in an elective to complete my degree, I wouldn't have even taken it."

The woman smiled tolerantly and nodded, which only made Elise madder. She was placating her, and Elise knew it. "Oh forget it!" Elise exploded. "I can't win!"

"Excuse me," a male voice called from behind a stack of books. It was a very tall stack of books, Elise noted. Probably because it was held by a very tall man.

"Yes?" Elise questioned, thoroughly irritated by the interruption.

"I couldn't help but overhear. Perhaps if you came to my office, I could get the details of your circumstances and help."

Elise calmed a bit. "I would really appreciate that."

"Come on then," the voice called. "My office is halfway down the hall."

Elise followed obediently, and only when her escort stopped and tried to fumble with the door did she speak. "Here," she offered, "I'll get it." She took the keys from his hands and unlocked the door.

"Thanks," the man replied, entering the room. "Just have a seat and I'll be right with you."

Elise was too angry to sit, so she walked over to the dusty window and stared outside while the man momentarily disappeared from the room. Running her fingers through her hair to reestablish order, she sighed.

"There, that's taken care of."

Elise turned and met a pair of chocolate-brown eyes and a disarming smile that immediately put her at ease. She guessed him to be about six-two and maybe in his midthirties. The tweed jacket he wore over a black T-shirt only moderately dressed up the jeans that accompanied them, but Elise liked the look.

"Now, what seems to be the problem, Miss. . . ?"

"I'm Elise Jost," she finally replied. Her windblown hair rippled behind her in a ribbon of cinnamon as she crossed the room and extended her hand. The man took it and gave it a squeeze.

"May I call you Elise?"

"Sure, whatever you like."

"Good," he said with an even broader smile. "Now, I understand you have some problem with the Renaissance Appreciation class."

"You might say that." The anger reappeared in her voice. "I didn't even want the class, but I had to take it so I could graduate with my class last semester. Someone in the transcript department miscalculated my credit hours and I came up on the short end of the stick."

"I see," the man said and sat down behind his desk. "Please, have a seat. I find that people in chairs are less likely to throw things."

Elise smiled at this and sat down. "I suppose it wouldn't have been so bad, but I had to give up a good job offer and I feel as though Renaissance Appreciation has rearranged my entire life."

"What exactly seems to be the problem with the class?"

Elise threw her hands up. "What doesn't seem to be the problem would be easier to answer. I don't know the first thing about the Renaissance."

"Isn't that a good reason to take a course on it?" the man interrupted with a grin.

"It could be, under normal circumstances. But nothing in my life is normal. I have to work for a living, and the man who teaches this class, Dr. Hunter, insists on participation in some rinky-dink festival they have every year."

"I know it well. It's a lot of fun and raises a great deal of money for the fine arts department."

"That's great!" Elise said angrily. "I'm very happy for the fine arts department, but it doesn't do a thing for me. I have to work. I can't very well go to my boss and say, 'Oh, by the way, some clown at the college insists that I play dress-up for a week in order to graduate and leave this hole-in-a-wall job for a better one.'" Elise's voice steadily rose in volume. "I'm sure they'd understand that one."

"So have you talked to this 'clown'?" the man questioned.

"No, he's out on some kind of family emergency. I do plan to take it up with him once he comes back," Elise said, nearly losing complete control. She got to her feet, smiled weakly at the man behind the desk, and began to pace. "I promise not to throw anything, but I'm too mad to sit still. Do you have any idea when Dr. Hunter will be back?"

"Oh," he said, sounding guilty, "I should tell you—I'm Ian Hunter, PhD, and clown at your service."

Elise's mouth formed a silent O, and she felt as though she might actually faint from the shock. She grabbed the back of the chair she'd just vacated and tried to remember every insulting thing she'd said. "Please tell me you're joking," she finally managed to say.

Ian laughed. "Sorry, I didn't realize you didn't know who I was until you started in on me."

Elise sat down. She had to. Her knees were suddenly jelly, and she had no reserve strength to fall back on. "I'm sorry. I guess I let my temper once again get the best of me. As a Christian, I must say it's one of my biggest crosses to bear." She knew it was a lame apology, but she was completely mortified and had no idea how to set things right. This man was her professor. He would decide whether she could drop the festival requirement. He would have the power to pass or fail her.

"We all have them, Elise," Ian offered. "I, too, am a child of God and quite often, a most childish child. You're in good company, so relax. I'm not the least bit offended."

Elise perked up a bit. "That's kind of you."

"No, not really," Ian said with a shrug, "but it is realistic and will probably work best in our favor. The requirement to participate in the Renaissance Festival was set the first year the class was created. It gives everyone a chance to get a feel for the times and just have a lot of fun. The money raised helps the fine arts department to put on free performances for the community, especially Children's Hospital."

"So trying to get out of it is like saying I don't care about sick kids? Not fair, Dr. Hunter."

"Ian, please." He said it in such a manner that Elise couldn't resist his charm.

"Ian, I appreciate what you're telling me, but I have to work full-time. I'm a nontraditional student, and I've been working to get this degree for over six years. I've already had to rearrange my work hours, and they aren't very happy about that," Elise added.

"Why did you have to do that?" Ian questioned.

"Before last semester, I was working days and attending school at night. In order to take my final business classes, which were only offered during the day, I had to change my hours at work. I work at the mall in retail sales and believe me, they weren't pleased. But, because I had seniority and had a perfect work record, they felt they had to at least try to work with me on my schedule. Now you want me to take even more time away from work and participate in this festival."

"But most of the festival work will take place during the day, so what's the problem?"

Elise felt herself getting angry again. "I promised the store I would go back to days as soon as I graduated."

"Look, Elise," Ian said in a tone that she recognized meant

he wasn't going to let her off the hook, "I do appreciate your circumstances, but this is a hard, fast rule. If you absolutely can't work with it, then I suggest you drop the class."

"But I can't drop the class! That's the point. I have to have one additional credit hour."

"There are other classes."

"We tried to find something to fit my schedule. There were other art classes, but they were offered in the afternoon. I can't change it now, because I spent all weekend looking over the schedule and there is nothing else. Please, Dr. Hunter," she paused. "Please, Ian, won't you reconsider this?"

Ian got to his feet. "Look, Elise, this is just the way it has to be. I can't make an exception for anyone, although if I were going to, I'd certainly do so for you."

Elise didn't know what to think about that statement, but she did realize with a heavy heart that she was trapped into a course with this man and she wasn't going to get free of the festival.

"So that's it?"

"I'm afraid so," Ian said, coming to stand directly in front of her. "Don't look so defeated. Once you get into the swing of things, it'll be a lot of fun."

"Fun, Dr. Hunter," she said, stressing the formality of the name, "is something I do not have time for." She picked up her things and stormed out of the room.

~⁀�~

Ian watched the vivacious redhead leave his office. She was fire and ice all rolled into one package. With a smile, he crossed to the window and waited for her to come outside. She was an attractive, intelligent woman. When she came into sight, Ian watched as the bulk of cinnamon hair swayed back and forth in the summer sun.

"Beautiful," he said aloud. He watched until Elise was out of sight, then returned to his desk.

Picking up his pen and preparing to write a note to his sister, Ian couldn't get Elise out of his mind. He was just back from his mother's surgery, and even though she'd been quite ill, Ian couldn't help but smile when he thought of their last prayer together.

"And Father," he could hear his mother pray, "please send a good woman to be a mate for my Ian. She'll need to be someone special. Someone with strength and determination and a spirit of love to match my son's."

The words almost seemed to echo on the air. Ian sat back in the chair and thoughtfully chewed on the end of his pen. It looked like his mother's prayers were about to be answered.

"I'm really quite taken with her," he mused aloud. "How about that?" Then posing a more serious question, Ian looked up at the ceiling. "But just what should I do about it?"

CHAPTER 4

W hen it was time for class, Elise took a seat as far to the back of the room as possible. Only marginally more composed than when she'd left Ian's office, she was trying hard to figure out how she could work everything out.

"I want to welcome you to Renaissance Appreciation," Ian said as he came to stand at the podium. "I am Dr. Hunter, although I'd prefer you to call me Ian. My office hours are posted in the department if you need help or guidance. I trust you have a copy of the books we'll be using and the syllabus." He paused long enough to acknowledge Elise with a nod.

"What exactly is the Renaissance? The word means rebirth or revival. How's that for dramatic? To me it conjures up vivid images of a group of downtrodden serfs sitting around one day, late in the Dark Ages. Suddenly one of them stands up and proclaims, 'I know, let's have a Renaissance!' Inspired, everyone begins painting and breaking the bonds of feudalism." He paused while most of the class chuckled at this image.

"Well, it didn't happen that way. Few things come into this world fully developed. This especially applies to the Renaissance. The Renaissance is more the result of gradual change than of a spontaneous and dramatic rebirth. The Renaissance is the end result of changes in society and the way people perceived their world and their place in the world."

Elise tried not to care overmuch about the lecture, but the lecturer had a way of drawing in his crowd. Ian was a gifted speaker and teacher, and not only did she find herself wanting to know more, but she was fairly hanging on his every word. The only thing that made it bad was that he seemed to notice her open interest.

"As few things spring into full existence unaided," Ian continued, "all things must have their roots in the past. Essentially, this is why the study of history is important: to give us a better understanding of the present. To understand what has happened to cause or to bring about an event in history is to grasp a better understanding of that event.

"This is why the first topic on our syllabus is the Middle Ages. Before we can talk about the Renaissance, we must have a basic understanding of the Middle Ages. If the Europe of the Middle Ages can be characterized by one word, then that word is *obligation*. In the Middle Ages, nearly everyone was held in obligation to those above him. The peasants had obligations to the landowners. The nobles had obligations to their lord or king, and all of the people had obligations to the church."

Elise watched Ian sit casually on the table beside the podium. He was definitely in his element, she thought. His teaching style was free-flowing, thought provoking, and easy to follow. What more could a student ask? Before she realized it, the hour was up and Ian was summing up the lecture.

"Therefore, Renaissance is not so much a rebirth as it is a reevaluation of beliefs and attitudes that, when found wanting in terms of what they provided to the enrichment of life, were changed for a better way. Tomorrow's assignment, read chapter two and come to class prepared to discuss your thoughts on the content. I assure you, this will be one of the last classes where I do most of the talking."

The close of his book signaled dismissal, and Elise suddenly realized the time. If she hurried, she could be to work before noon. Maybe if she showed an effort to give the store as much of her daytime hours as possible, they'd lighten up and not be so hard to deal with when the July festival rolled around.

Hurrying from the room, Elise was already to the parking lot when she heard her name being called. Turning, she recognized Ian's lanky form striding toward her with determined purpose. He'd shed the tweed jacket and was juggling it between books and papers.

"Are you rushing off somewhere?"

Elise tried not to be the slightest bit interested in the way the sunlight made his hair turn golden brown. "I, uh, I'm off to work." She struggled into the backpack she'd been carrying.

"How about a lift?"

"No, no thanks." Elise was startled by the invitation but tried to remain reserved. "I walk everywhere, and if I hurry, I can be there to relieve the girls for lunch."

"I can hurry you there faster in the car. I'm parked right here," he said, pointing to a restored classic. The black Chevy gleamed from many coats of hand-waxing.

Elise hesitated. "Surely you don't offer to drive all of your students to work?"

"Nope, just the ones who call me a clown." His lopsided grin told her that he was working hard to get on her good side. "Come on, Elise, I want to talk to you anyway."

Elise agreed to the ride, hoping that with time to reconsider, Ian would tell her of his decision to let her off the hook. She climbed into the car, admiring the restoration work, and then fell silent as the engine roared to life and Ian headed in the direction of the only mall in town.

"Which store do you work at?"

"Gallagher's," she replied, trying hard not to sound too eager for him to continue.

"And what do you do there?"

"Sell women on expensive designer outfits."

"I see," he said, maneuvering through traffic. "And what is the job you had to give up in order to take my class?"

"A supervisory position with the US Customs Department. I was very excited about the position. It's something I've worked for all my life."

"A customs job?" he asked with a teasing smile.

"Well, maybe not exactly that, but a good solid career. You'll need to turn at the next entrance," she said, hoping Ian would drop the small talk and tell her what she wanted to hear.

"Look, Elise," Ian finally began, "I had a motive in offering to give you a ride to work."

"Oh?"

"Yeah, I know this sounds sudden and maybe a bit out of line, but I'd really like to spend some time with you and get to know you better. You know, away from school."

Elise stared at him openmouthed. What was it about this man that gave him the power to reduce her to stammers and stunned silence?

Ian grinned and pulled the car up to the store entrance. "Well, what do you say?"

Elise shook her head. "I don't have time for a relationship."

"Seems to me you don't have time for much. First it was fun; now it's a relationship."

"Well," she said nodding, "that about sums it up. I'm driven to see my career off and running. I can't let anything or anyone get in the middle of that. I work full-time, usually going into overtime, and what with college, I don't have the time to give. I'm sorry."

"I won't take sorry for an answer. What time do you get off, so that we can continue this discussion?"

Elise reached for the door handle. "There's nothing to discuss."

"Look, I'm concerned about you. What time do you get off? I'll give you a ride home and then you can tell me why it's so important to keep everyone at arm's length."

"By the time I finish with receipts and counting the drawer, it's past ten. So forget it. I'm perfectly capable of walking."

She got out of the car, and as she closed the door, Ian called out, "See you at ten."

He drove off before she could protest, leaving Elise once again dumbfounded by his arrogance and self-confident nature.

"Oh, no you won't, Dr. Hunter," she muttered as the Chevy disappeared from view. "Not in a million years!"

From the first moment Elise stepped onto the sales floor, until she was counting out the money drawer at nine forty-five, she faced nothing but a myriad of problems. She argued for twenty minutes with a younger employee who thought the display of new silk suits needed more color.

Then two elderly women who were regular customers demanded to see the latest arrivals from their favorite designer. When Elise showed them what had come in, the women were clearly unsatisfied and wanted to know when the next shipment would arrive. Elise spent half an hour running down the schedule that would let her advise them on the line, only to have them grumble about the delay and suggest that they could take their shopping elsewhere if necessary.

Elise wanted badly to tell them to do just that, but instead she calmed them down by showing them a line of sporty clothes that mimicked their favorite designer. And now, she was trying without much luck to get her register receipts to match the cash and charges in the drawer.

"Elise, we need to talk," said a stern-faced, bleached blond. It was Roselle, the manager of the women's designer department.

"Yes, Roselle?" Elise hoped she sounded more sincere than tired.

The woman took a seat at the table where Elise worked. "You promised to return to your original schedule by now. I want to know what happened and why you're still working evenings."

Elise gave up on the money and receipts. "I explained to the store manager that I was one credit hour short. If I'd only known before last semester, I could have worked it out then, but now I find myself in a summer class that I can't get out of without forfeiting my degree."

"I see," Roselle said, not sounding the least bit sympathetic. "Have you considered that perhaps it's time to quit Gallagher's? I mean, you plan to move ahead with your plans and we have many talented people in this department who should have a chance to move up in ranks. If you're going to resign to take another position anyway, why not go ahead and do it now?"

Elise felt mild panic building. "I can't quit, Roselle. I need the money to live on until I have another job. Look, I've been honest and straightforward with everyone here. I've been good to come in when I wasn't scheduled to work, and I've never missed a day."

"Yes, well, it was just a suggestion." Roselle got to her feet. "We'll just have to see how it all works out."

Elise had a hard time concentrating after Roselle left. She counted her drawer out five times before she finally felt confident that it was all there. After hurrying to turn everything into its assigned place, Elise noted it was nearly ten twenty.

Grabbing her pack and purse, she hurried to where Marty, the security guard, waited to check each employee out for the night.

"Kind of late this evening, aren't you?" he asked in his grand-fatherly way.

"It was a rough one, Marty." She passed through the door stuffing her purse into the backpack. "Hope yours goes better."

Outside, the night was heavy and felt like rain. Elise hurriedly pulled on the pack and started across the dark parking lot toward home. She glanced around nervously as she always did. The can of pepper spray in her pocket did little to reassure her, but this was a small town and the crime rate was very low. Since switching to evenings and walking home in the dark, she'd never once had any problem to concern herself with. Nevertheless, the nightly walk made her nervous and edgy.

Barely halfway across the lot, Elise heard footsteps behind her. The hair on the back of her neck prickled and her hand reflexively grasped the pepper spray. She could hear her heart beating in her ears, almost keeping time with the footsteps. Glancing around her, she tried to figure out a path of flight. There were several cars she could weave around, but should she head back to the store or make a dead run for home?

"Elise."

She barely suppressed a scream, as a hand touched her arm. She whirled around, spray in hand, but stopped short of depressing its button. Panting for breath, she tried to focus her mind on the image before her. Ian Hunter was looking at her with concern.

"I'm sorry. I didn't mean to scare you," he said, watching the pepper spray intently. "You aren't going to skunk me with that, are you?"

Elise drew her gaze away from Ian's amused expression to the canister in her hands and then back again to Ian. "I should," she finally whispered.

"Come on." He took hold of her arm and led her forward. "I told you I'd be here to give you a ride home. What if I'd been a real mugger or worse yet, a murderer?"

"Then I guess I wouldn't have to take Renaissance Appreciation," she snapped sarcastically. Her fear was quickly being replaced by anger. Pocketing the spray, she jerked away from Ian's hold. "I don't need a ride home. I've been doing this for several years."

"Yes, but as I recall, you did most of those years during daylight hours. Now swallow your pride and let me take you home."

They had reached the car, and Ian stood with a look of resolve that Elise had no doubt was stronger than her own. "Okay" was all she trusted herself to say.

It didn't surprise Elise when they pulled into the driveway of her little rental house. Somehow she'd known that Ian would have looked up her address. But instead of being angry, she was rather touched that he was so concerned for her safety. In six years of living on her own, no one had shown her that kind of concern. Oh, there were those people at church who tried hard to keep her in their circle of activities; and there was her mom and dad, of course, but they were a world away in Washington, DC.

When Ian shut off the motor, Elise realized he still intended to discuss their dating. She tried hard to steady her already shattered nerves. Ian was a handsome man with a very dynamic personality. It was hard to imagine that he was honestly interested in her, and for once it was hard to say no to the idea of getting involved.

"So have you given more consideration to my request?"

Elise shook her head. "No. There's no room for consideration." She thought the words sounded rather weak and fervently wished she had the courage to open the car door and walk away. Instead, she remained seated, her gaze fixed on the dashboard.

"Elise, don't say no."

She knew it was a mistake, but she couldn't help looking at him. The streetlight afforded her a good look, and his expression matched his voice. He looked like a little boy who'd been disappointed. Her breath caught in her throat, causing her to cough lightly. Licking her lips nervously, she sighed and tried to find the right words.

"I can't see you outside of school. It wouldn't be right. I don't intend to stick around this town once your class is done, and I don't want to leave any unfinished business behind me. Don't you understand? I've put my life on hold for six years in order to get this degree. I can't mess that up now."

"I'm not asking you to," Ian said softly. "I'm not asking you for anything but a date."

Elise felt her defenses crumbling. She had to do something. No one had ever affected her like this before. "If I date you, will you drop the festival requirement and give me an alternate assignment?"

Ian laughed, and his whole expression turned mischievous. "No, but if you go out with me, I promise you won't be sorry. Come on, Elise. Let some fun into your life."

"Isn't there some rule about professors dating their students?" She knew it was a lame excuse, but she was desperate.

"I'm not a regular professor anymore. I only come in as a guest lecturer for this one class. It's more community service than anything. Besides, you're very nearly graduated. What's six weeks?"

"Then wait six weeks and ask me again." Elise didn't trust herself to remain resolved. "I have to go. I have an early class, you know." She reached for the door handle, but this time Ian quickly jumped out of the car and came around to open the door for her.

"Can't you just think about it?" His voice was almost a whisper.

Elise looked up into his hopeful eyes. She was losing ground, and she knew that she had to get away from this man—immediately.

"Just think about it," Ian said, lightly touching her cheek. "I promise not to take up too much of your time. I know what a bear that professor of yours can be."

Elise smiled nervously. "I wish I had known before signing up for his class."

Ian grew quite serious. "I'm glad you didn't. Now, how about it? Won't you at least consider the matter?"

"All right, Ian," she said, resigning herself to say what he wanted to hear. "I'll think about it."

CHAPTER 5

For two weeks, Elise faithfully attended Ian's class and waited for him to ask her for a decision on his request. And for two weeks, he very nearly ignored her altogether. On Friday, the only day she had off from both regular classes and work, Elise found herself sorting through festival props. There was everything from armor to velvet gowns and knightly swords. Climbing up and down the long ladder to the overhead storage rooms just opposite the stage, Elise felt hot and very dirty.

Two of the young men from her class were inside the storage rooms handing props out through the opening, while Elise alternated with several other students going up and down the ladder to retrieve the things. Ian was nowhere to be seen, having taken another group of students off to another room for their assignment, and for this, Elise was grateful. She was nervous enough about climbing fifteen feet into the air and juggling props back down a wobbly ladder, but if Ian were there watching, she knew she'd never be able to manage.

She had just made her fifth trip up the ladder to receive a large shield when two young women came running past the ladder. They were caught up in a game of chase with another classmate,

Jason Emery. They laughed at the young man's attempts to poke at them with a wooden sword.

"You will be mine!" he called out in deep, dramatic voice, causing giggles to ensue once again.

Elise was barely halfway down the ladder when one of the girls ran underneath, knocking it just enough to cause the entire ladder to move violently to the right. Without warning, Elise found herself plummeting the remaining eight or so feet, landing with a crash on the wooden floor below.

She had tried to catch herself and land on her feet, but this only caused her to twist her ankle badly and crumble beneath the weight. She cried out in pain, but quickly hushed her complaints when Ian came running through the stage door.

"What happened here?" he asked, coming to Elise's side. He reached out to pull her to her feet and Elise refused to grimace, even though the pain was severe.

"It's our fault," one of the girls replied.

"No, it's really my fault," the young man answered.

"Jason, you want to tell me what happened?" Ian asked.

Jason Emery raised the sword as if hoping it would offer an explanation. "I was kind of chasing after Kerry and Leah and we hit the ladder. We didn't mean to cause any harm. Elise, I feel just terrible that you fell. Are you hurt?"

Ian turned to Elise. "Yes, are you hurt?"

Elise felt Ian's gaze bore into her, demanding the truth. "No, I'm fine. I didn't fall that far, and I think the shield broke my fall anyway." She smiled weakly, and all gazes fell to the broken shield on the stage floor.

"You know horseplay is uncalled for in circumstances like this," Ian said sternly. "Elise could have been hurt severely, not to mention what might have happened if you'd fallen with that sword while chasing after Kerry and Leah."

"Yeah, it was real dumb. I'm sorry, and it won't happen again."

"Hey, what's going on down there?" one of the guys working in the prop room called from overhead.

"Just a minor setback," Ian replied. "Jason, since you've nothing better to do, you take Elise's place going up and down the ladder. Kerry, Leah, do you have something you should be doing?" Guiltily both girls nodded. "Then I suggest everyone get back to work."

"Dr. Hunter!" a voice called from the other room.

Ian let his gaze travel the length of Elise. "Are you sure you're all right?"

"I'm perfectly fine."

"Dr. Hunter, we have a problem in here," the voice materialized into the form of yet another classmate.

"Coming," Ian called.

Everyone went their way, and Elise waited until Jason had climbed up the ladder before she tested her weight on the throbbing ankle. With a muffled cry, she fell to the floor and grabbed her right leg.

"So you're perfectly fine, eh?" It was Ian, and he was standing in the doorway, arms folded in a determined stance. He crossed the room with the same determination in his stride.

Elise looked up anxiously. "Really, I'll be just fine."

"Of course you will be," Ian said, surprising her by easily lifting her into his arms. "After the emergency room has a chance to fix you up."

Elise protested. "I'm not going to the emergency room. Ian, put me down."

Jason was apologetically opening the exit door for Ian. "I'm really sorry, Elise."

"Stop this. I can just put some ice on it and—"

"Nothing doing, Elise. I'm taking you to the hospital, and that's that."

"I can't afford it, Ian," she finally said, giving up any hopes of maintaining her pride.

Ian stopped and looked down at her sympathetically. "You don't have to afford anything. The school has insurance, and if they won't pay, I will."

~

"I told you it wasn't broken," Elise said later as the nurse wheeled her out from the examination room.

"Yes, but it is badly sprained," the nurse said before Ian could react. "She'll need to be off it until the swelling goes down, and that might take as long as a week. Here's a prescription for painkillers and the phone number for the doctor's office should you have any questions or concerns. She's been given an injection for pain, but she can take the pills in addition to that." The nurse addressed Ian as though she knew him to be in charge. "Oh, and she'll need these." The woman disappeared into a room and returned with a pair of crutches.

Ian thanked her and helped adjust the crutches to Elise's height. He watched anxiously as Elise tried to coordinate the crutches.

"It isn't as easy as it looks," she commented snidely.

"Do you need any more information for the insurance?" Ian asked the nurse while Elise made her way slowly to the door.

"No, everything is in order."

"Thanks," Ian replied and hurried to where Elise was about to disappear into the night. "Where do you think you're going?" he questioned, scooping her into his arms, crutches and all.

"Ian, put me down!"

"Not on your life. I'm taking you home and seeing to it that you don't get up until that swelling is completely gone."

"I can't do that, Ian. I have a—"

"I know. I know. A job and a class and a life without complications or relationships. Look, I've cut you a wide path these last two weeks. You're going to do this my way, so just get used to it."

Elise opened her mouth, but nothing came out, causing Ian to nod. "Good, I'm glad you're seeing it my way."

Ian wondered silently as he put Elise in the car if there wasn't some way to break through her facade of independent strength. She would never willingly be weak in front of him. It was just too important to her to be strong. Then an idea came to him. Starting the engine, he turned with a smile. "I'll fill the prescription after I get you settled in."

Elise nodded and reached for her purse. "Oh, Ian, I left my purse in your filing cabinet at school."

"I'll get it tomorrow."

"But all my money is in it, along with my credit cards and bank card. I can't just leave it there, and I can't pay for the medicine without it."

"All right, all right. I'll get your purse when I go for the prescription, but I'm paying for your medicine and I won't hear any argument about it."

"Okay."

When Elise said nothing more, Ian laughed. "Okay? Just 'okay'? That shot they gave you for pain must have been pretty potent."

"Well, I'm hardly in any position to fight you right now. But, when I get back out of the car and have my crutches in hand, watch out!" She smiled, and Ian thought his heart would melt into a puddle around his feet.

He pulled the car into his driveway and waited for Elise to comment. She looked past him to the Victorian house and then rested her gaze on Ian's face.

"This isn't my house."

"No, it's mine."

"I see, and why are we here?"

"Because you're going to stay here for a few days."

Elise shook her head and reached for the door. "Oh, no I'm not. I told you the first time we met. I'm a Christian. Not just in name, in deed as well."

Ian reached out to stop her. "I'm glad to hear it, but it doesn't change a thing. You're alone, and you need help."

"So you figure that makes it okay for me to move in with you? I don't think so." She was pushing his hand away. "If you're the Christian you profess to be, you'll understand why I can't stay here. What would people think? What would they say?"

"I don't really care, but I do care about you. Besides, I have a live-in housekeeper, a very respectable older woman named Lillian Greer. She's a wonderful, loving soul who is actually a third or fourth cousin to the tenth power or whatever. Anyway, she needed a home and I needed a keeper. It's a companionable relationship, and she'll not mind one bit helping me keep you in line."

Once again, Elise stared at Ian with an open mouth, and he raised a single eyebrow, waiting for her to refuse. When she didn't, he grinned broadly.

"Now, no arguments about me carrying you upstairs," he said, reaching to take her in his arms.

"But I weigh a ton," Elise protested.

Ian shifted her lightly in his arms. "I'd say closer to 130." Elise blushed and Ian laughed. "I lift weights at the YMCA. I'm getting pretty good at sizing things up."

His face was just inches from hers, and he studied her expression. She seemed so anxious and concerned about her size.

"I think you're perfect," he whispered against her cheek and lightly kissed her. Whether to hide her embarrassment or because she felt the need to get closer to him, Elise snuggled her face against his chest and didn't say another word. Ian liked her like this, vulnerable and yielding, but he liked her with her fiery speeches and her eyes ablaze too. She was perfect, he thought as he carried her into the house. She was just exactly what he'd prayed for.

The next morning, Elise awoke to the aroma of freshly brewed coffee. For a moment, she thought she was back home in DC. It was the sharp jab of pain in her leg that brought her back to reality. With a start, she sat up in bed and tried to focus on the events of the night before. The painkiller they'd given her at the hospital was one powerful drug, she decided, realizing that after the white-haired Lillian had tucked her into bed, she'd instantly fallen asleep.

A quick glance at her watch told her she barely had enough time to get to work. This was Saturday, and a sale day to boot. If she didn't hurry up and get there before nine, Roselle would have a fit. Spying the crutches against the wall, Elise threw back the covers and eased her legs over the side of the bed. Her right ankle throbbed furiously at this change, causing Elise to grimace. Hopping around the room to collect her things didn't make matters any better.

Seeing her purse on the nightstand made her smile for just a moment. Ian had thoughtfully collected it, just as she had insisted. No doubt he was tired and worried, but he'd done the deed, and that somehow endeared him to her just as all his other actions had. Then her mind went back to what he'd said last night and the kiss he'd given her. Maybe she'd just dreamed all of that. Her hand went to her cheek as if to touch the lips he had pressed there.

"You're losing control, Elise," she whispered and pulled the crutches under her. Still trying to master the beasts, Elise made her way out of the room and into the hall. Grateful that the stairs were located directly opposite her door, Elise slowly made her way to the top.

"Just where do you think you're going?" Ian asked, standing in a nearby doorway and wearing a navy-blue velour robe, his face full of shaving cream.

"I have to go to work," Elise protested, trying desperately not to give him her utmost attention.

"Absolutely not. That's why I brought you here. Come on, it's back to bed for you." He reached out for her, but Elise pushed past him.

"I have to go to work. If I don't, I'll lose my job. They're already furious with me for the time I've had off for the festival preparations."

Ian leaned his face down close to hers. "I'm putting you to bed and you're going to stay there. Lillian!" He gave Elise no chance to reply before sweeping her into his arms. The crutches crashed loudly to the polished wood floor.

A woman about sixty years old appeared. She had a brilliant smile that made the wrinkles in her face disappear. "I see our guest is up and about."

"Not for long. Hide those crutches in my room, Lillian."

"You can't," Elise tried to protest, but no one was listening.

"I'll bring her breakfast tray up as soon as you have her settled," Lillian said, retrieving the crutches.

"It may take forever to settle her," Ian said over his shoulder.

Lillian laughed and was out of sight before Elise could say anything about the matter.

"Please, Ian," she said in a pleading tone that stopped him dead in his tracks.

With a grin, he leaned down to touch his lips to her nose, giving her a mouthful of shaving cream.

"Agh!" She spit out the soapy foam. "Stop doing that!"

Ian laughed and deposited her in bed. "Stop being so stubborn, angry, independent, and noble."

Elise wiped the rest of the soap from her face. "I am not stubborn. I'm determined."

"Call it what you will, but stay in this bed," Ian said firmly. "I'm going to shave, and then we'll discuss your job."

After shaving, Ian took the telephone number Elise had given him and went to his study. If this Roselle was the monster Elise made her out to be, he wanted to have a nice quiet corner from which to make his argument.

"Women's Designs," a voice said on the other end of the phone.

"I need to speak with Roselle Goodman, please."

"Speaking."

"Ms. Goodman, I'm calling on behalf of Elise Jost," Ian said professionally. "Elise was injured at the college last night and is under doctor's care. She severely twisted her ankle and is to be off her feet for at least a week."

"I see, and who may I ask is this?"

"I'm Dr. Ian Hunter," he answered, wondering if the woman would think him to be Elise's physician. *Oh well*, he thought, *let her think what she would*.

"Well, Doctor, I'm afraid I can't wait on Elise to return to work. This situation is rather delicate, but Elise was told that should there be any other problems surrounding her work schedule, she'd be terminated immediately."

"But this isn't her fault. She was—"

"It doesn't matter to me whose fault it was," Roselle stated.

Ian barely kept his temper in check. "I would imagine Elise might be able to file a lawsuit of some kind if you are truly threatening her job."

"That, Dr. Hunter, will be up to Elise, although I seriously doubt that she'll have the same notion. She's given her notice to quit by the end of summer, anyway. She hopes for a career in the government, and I don't think she'll want an employment lawsuit hanging over her head for the months, probably years, that it would take to resolve. Please give Elise my heartfelt wishes for her return to health, but also inform her that she is no longer an employee of Gallagher's."

The phone went dead in his ear.

Now he had to deal with Elise, and he worried about how she'd take the news. He had been so confident of being able to smooth things out with Roselle that it never crossed his mind she'd actually fire Elise over the phone. The woman was way, way out of line, but what could he do about it?

The knock on his door gave Ian no choice but to put the matter aside. "Yes?"

Lillian appeared with Elise's breakfast. "I was just taking this up—"

"Let me," he interrupted. "I have to give her some bad news. I might as well see if I can't cushion the blow with your mouth-watering cinnamon rolls."

Lillian frowned, but let Ian take the tray. "Is it her job?"

"Yeah," Ian said with a nod. "They fired her."

"They what?" Elise exclaimed minutes later. "I can't believe this. They fired me? Just like that? After all I've done for them and all the hard work I've given them?"

"I'm so sorry, Elise." Ian sat on a chair beside the bed and reached out to touch her hand. "I tried to reason with Roselle, but she wouldn't hear reason."

"Tell me about it," Elise said, tears threatening to spill. "Oh, this is so awful. Why did this have to happen to me now? I trusted God to work out the details of my life. I trusted Him to keep these kinds of things from happening. I just can't see any purpose in things like this."

Ian leaned closer and smoothed long strands of hair back away from her face. "All things work together for good."

"They can't possibly this time," Elise moaned and put her face in her hands. It had been a long time since she'd cried, but the tears refused to be held back. The last person in the world she wanted to cry in front of was Ian Hunter, but here she was, blubbering like a baby.

Elise didn't stop Ian when he pulled her into his arms to comfort her. Her whole world was spinning out of control, and there was nothing she could do about it.

"It'll all work out, Elise. I'm sure of it. I've had my moments too, and God always comes through."

Elise looked up and met his tender expression. "But all my plans. . ."

Ian put a finger to her lips. "What about God's plans? Don't you think He knows your heart's desires? Do you honestly think He stopped caring about you?"

Elise shook her head. "I know He cares. But Ian, I'm not a wealthy woman. I have a small savings account that was supposed to help me move and see me through to my first 'real' paycheck. It'll never see me through to fall, and even if it did, what would I move on? What would I—"

"Elise," Ian interrupted, suddenly seeming inspired. "I have the perfect solution."

"What?" She eyed him suspiciously, suddenly realizing she was still in his arms.

"Can you operate a computer?" he questioned, not seeming the least bit disturbed by their closeness. Elise tried to push him away, but he held her fast and grinned. "Can you?"

"Yes, but what—"

"You could work for me."

"Doing what?" Elise's financial fears were being replaced by concern for her racing heart and fluttering stomach.

Ian released her reluctantly. "Typing up my textbook notes. I'd pay you well, and you could come here every day after class to use my computer. It would surely get you through the summer."

"You can't be serious. With my savings, I'd have to make at least two hundred dollars a week just to keep the rent and utilities paid and put food on the table. There's no way—"

Again Ian silenced her with a finger on her mouth.

"I can handle it," he assured her. "Two hundred a week seems reasonable for a full-time typist. You can get started right away, and can fix things up so that we can keep you off your foot. How about it?"

Elise shook her head and studied his hopeful expression. "I can't believe this. Are you serious?"

"Quite."

"Then I'll agree to take the job on, but with one condition."

"Name it."

"When I'm back on my feet, I'll take your notes home and work from my house. I don't think it would be wise to spend so much time here." She knew without a doubt that she'd never be able to hold out against Ian's charms if she had to work with him day in and day out.

Ian grinned. "Chicken," he said, seeming to know exactly what she was thinking.

Elise felt her face grow hot. "I am not. I just don't want this thing getting out of control. In less than three months I plan to leave, and I don't want there to be any regrets."

Ian sobered instantly and got to his feet. "Do you honestly think you can walk away from this 'thing,' as you put it, and not have any regrets?"

Elise looked away and swallowed hard. "I can't afford regrets."

$\sim$

"Hey there," Jason Emery said as Ian opened the front door. "I heard Elise is staying here with you, and I brought her these flowers."

"Come on in, Jason. Elise is typing some notes for me in the study." Just then Lillian appeared, and Ian motioned for her. "Lillian, would you take Jason to the study. He wants to make a more formal apology to Elise." Ian smiled at the young man, but something in Jason's tone set him on edge. With Jason's next statement, Ian instantly knew why he felt that way.

"Guess Elise won't have any trouble passing the course now." Jason's laughter caused even Lillian to stop in her tracks.

"And why would that be?" Ian questioned, barely containing his temper.

"Well, I just figured. . .well, I mean, what with you and Elise. . ." Jason fell silent, seeming to realize he'd overstepped the proper bounds.

"Come along, young man," Lillian said in a disapproving tone.

Jason followed after Lillian, while Ian stood trying to regain control of his temper. The world was so filled with suggestive innuendos and foul intentions that even a simple gesture of kindness was rendered a deed of iniquity.

But Ian had to be honest with himself. He had brought Elise here for more than one reason. Of course he wanted to see her cared for, because he was coming to care very deeply for her. She wouldn't go out with him, yet she was always in his thoughts and passing through his day in one way or another.

He was embarrassed to admit that Jason was probably closer to the truth than he knew. Ian's motives weren't just Christian concern. He had hoped to woo Elise with his presence in her life and make her fall in love with him.

"Well, Lord, I guess I made a mess of this. I'm trying to rush Your hand in the matter, and I know that's never going to work." Ian rubbed his chin thoughtfully for a moment. "She just has to be the one, Lord," he whispered. "She's everything I've ever wanted. She is my heart's desire." Just then Psalm 37:4–5 came to mind: *Take delight in the Lord and he will give you the desires of your heart. Commit your way to the Lord; trust in him and he will do this.*

"Okay, Lord," Ian whispered. "I'll try."

Just then Lillian appeared with a tray of refreshments. "I'll take those, Lillian," Ian offered, seeing the perfect excuse to interrupt Jason and Elise.

The older woman smiled. "I thought you might."

Ian shrugged with a grin and took the tray. He stood ready to enter the study when he heard Jason ask Elise, "Are you and Ian a couple?" He held his breath. What would she say?

"A couple?" Elise's voice questioned. "No. He's just been very kind to me, and now I'm working for him." Ian felt his chest constrict. She hadn't even played around by joking or teasing about it.

"So then would you think about going out with me?" Jason asked, causing Ian to tighten his grip on the tray. Jealousy wasn't an emotion he was very familiar with, but Ian recognized it as the feeling that filled his being.

"I'm not seeing anyone, Jason, and I don't plan to," Elise answered. "I'm leaving by the fall, and I don't plan to have a relationship to deal with."

"We could just go out for the fun of it," Jason suggested.

"No, I'm just not going to set myself up for that complication. I want to keep things neat and clean. When I leave, I want to know that I have no reason to look back over my shoulder."

When silence seemed to put an end to the conversation, Ian pushed the door open and entered the small study. "We have iced tea and Lillian's famous butter cookies," he said, trying hard to sound lighthearted.

Elise looked up at him and smiled. For some odd reason, Ian thought it to be a smile of relief, but he passed it off as wishful thinking. Jason, who had been standing very close to Elise, moved away immediately and headed for the door.

"I can't stay. I've still got to get the rest of the concession booth inventory done. I hope you're back on your feet real soon, Elise. See you later, Ian."

When Jason was gone, Ian found Elise studying him with a strange expression on her face. He said nothing, hoping she would explain herself. Her green eyes seemed to bore through his pretense at good-natured ease. Licking her lips and slowly nodding, she finally spoke.

"You win, Ian. I already have regrets."

She turned back to her typing before Ian could answer, but it was just as well. She might not have taken too well to the huge grin that spread across his face. It was something to hope on, Ian thought, putting the tray down on a table by the door, and that was more than he'd had ten minutes earlier.

CHAPTER 6

Elise was trying to get used to being back in her own home when the call came from the US Customs Department. The woman advised her that they had two positions available that were scheduled to begin August 15. The one located on the Canadian border in Montana was the one she offered Elise. Floating on a cloud, Elise accepted the position and immediately called her mother.

"Mom, it's Elise."

"What a surprise. Is everything okay?" Sue Jost asked her daughter.

"Everything is great. I got the job. I'm going to Montana at the end of July."

"That's great, Elise! Will you get a chance to come home first?"

"No, I'm afraid with this summer class I told you about, I'll barely finish with the obligation to the festival before having to turn around and move. But I promise to fly home for Thanksgiving, if I have that time off."

"That would be wonderful. Your dad and I feel like we hardly know you anymore."

"I know and I'm sorry. I try to keep up on the letters, but I know it isn't the same." Glancing at her watch, Elise realized she'd need to hurry or be late for class. "Look, Mom, I need to go. I have class in fifteen minutes. I love you both."

"We love you too, honey."

Elise hurriedly hung up and grabbed her backpack just as the familiar sound of Ian's Chevy roared into her drive. Her knees felt suddenly weak and her breathing quickened. "This has got to stop," she said aloud but knew it was an impossible demand. Securing a gold clasp to hold back her hair, Elise opened the door just as Ian started to knock.

"Taxi service," he announced.

"You shouldn't have," Elise replied, pulling the door closed behind her. "I had fully planned to walk."

"Give the ankle a break," he said with a smile, "and let me be gallant."

Elise rolled her eyes and nodded. "Okay."

As Ian helped her into the car, Elise suddenly remembered her news and declared, "I've got a job!"

Ian frowned. "Don't you like working for me?"

"Silly, I mean I'll have a job when school is finished. I just got called this morning. I'm moving to Montana at the end of July." But even as she said the words they lost some of their appeal. In little over a month she'd be saying goodbye to him—forever.

Ian didn't take the news well at all. He got into the car quietly and was well on the way to school before he spoke again. "The end of July? But that's only a few weeks."

"Yes, I know."

"I suppose congratulations are in order."

"Aren't you happy for me, Ian?"

He looked at her as though she'd lost her mind. The expression of disbelief pierced her heart. "Happy? For your dreams to come true, I'm very happy." He pulled into his regular parking place at the college and shut off the engine. "But for me, I can't say the same. I don't want to lose you, Elise."

Elise felt emotions surge without warning. Slamming her fist into the backpack on her lap, she turned toward Ian. "I told you I didn't want this happening. This was why I avoided relationships. This is why I wouldn't date you, and now it doesn't matter!" She jerked open the door and quickly exited. "I can't let this come between me and my dream!" She slammed the door shut and hurried toward the SLAB.

"Hey, Elise!" Jason Emery called out and ran to catch up with her.

Inwardly, Elise wished Jason would be swallowed up by one of the cracks in the sidewalk, but she bid him a friendly good morning.

"I heard you yelling at the professor. You two having a lover's quarrel?"

Elise knew he was trying to make light of the matter, but she was angry. "No! Ian Hunter is nothing more than a teacher and employer to me."

"I'm glad," Jason said, pulling the door open for her. "I don't think he's all that great at teaching, and I sure wouldn't expect him to know how to treat a woman very well. After all, he's thirty-five and he's never been married. He doesn't date anyone, and he doesn't seem to be interested in anyone. I think he's kind of weird."

"He is not!" Elise declared in defense. She hadn't even had a moment to consider her words before continuing. "Ian is a very good teacher, and he's generous and kind. I don't know how you can say those things about him."

Jason shrugged. "He's got the reputation of being too married to his career to have any time for romance and such."

The words stung Elise. "He's just dedicated."

"He's just dead," Jason said with a laugh. "Some people are too busy with the business of life to ever really live it. Give me a good time and a pretty lady, any day."

Elise said nothing more but hurried to take her seat. Was that how everyone saw her? Was that the way she'd turn out too? Thirty-five and alone?

Ian took charge of the class, but Elise couldn't concentrate. She watched him move mechanically around the room, the joy in his topic clearly ebbing. She'd brought this on him—of that she was certain—and the more she watched him, the more she wished she could apologize for her words.

"Tomorrow read chapter fifteen in *Art in the Renaissance*. Come prepared to discuss three particular pieces of work from the times and why you feel they make important contributions to our society today. Those of you working on the booths tonight, be in my office at five for your instructions. The dry cleaner called and the costumes are ready, so those of you on the costume committee should make preparations to pick them up before Saturday. Thanks."

The classroom emptied out quickly, and Ian headed to his office without another word to Elise. Grabbing her things, she followed him across the campus and without waiting for his invitation, followed him into his office and closed the door behind her.

"Ian, I want to apologize."

Ian turned, pushing back brown hair from his face. "No, you don't have to. You were right to be angry."

"No, I wasn't. I want you to understand where I'm coming from." She tossed her backpack to a nearby chair and went to stand directly in front of him. "There's so much about this that you can't possibly know, but I truly want you to understand it."

"Go on," Ian said, sounding skeptical.

Elise drew a deep breath and sighed. "It isn't easy to explain Elise Jost, but I'll try. I grew up near DC. My father works for the Smithsonian, and my mother. . ."

She paused and looked away. "My mother is one of the real reasons I'm so determined to see this thing through. She was studying to earn a degree in marine biology. It was her dream to work off the coast of Alaska. She met my father in college and they fell in love very quickly. By the time Daddy graduated, he and Mom were talking marriage and family. Mom still had a year to go on her degree, but she quit college and moved to Washington, DC, in order to accommodate my father's new position. They married in the fall, and I was born the following year. There was never a chance for Mom to go back to school, and certainly never a chance for her to work at what she'd always dreamed of doing."

Elise looked up at Ian, praying he could understand where she was going with this conversation. His warm brown eyes seemed to encourage her to continue. "I was determined not to make the same mistake my mother made. I knew I couldn't go to college full-time and work, so I planned out my hours and figured it would take six years for me to complete my degree. I had every single detail thought through and developed alternate plans in case something went wrong. Coming up a credit hour short wasn't something I'd planned on. Meeting you was definitely something I hadn't planned on. Don't you see, Ian? I can't do this. I can't be like my mother and give up my dream career for the man I love."

Ian's mouth curved into a grin, and a certain knowing came into his expression. Elise's eyes widened and her throat tightened. What had she just said? Had she really declared her love for Ian?

Maybe he wouldn't notice. Maybe she could just smooth over the declaration by continuing.

"This job is important to me," she said in a voice that barely croaked out the words. "I think it will be a good adventure, and I like Montana."

Ian just stood there grinning, and she knew she'd lost the battle. Desperate to put the matter behind her, Elise moved to retrieve the backpack, but Ian reached out with lightning quickness and pulled her into his arms. Lowering his mouth to hers, he whispered, "I love you too."

The kiss was tender and sweet, and for Elise, it was the first time a man had kissed her on the lips. She felt her arms travel upward, almost as though they had a mind of their own, to wrap around his neck. When Ian pulled her tighter against him, she thought surely it must be the most wondrous thing in the world.

"Did you hear me?" he asked, pulling away just far enough to speak. "I love you."

Elise opened her eyes to find Ian's searching, penetrating brown eyes watching her closely. "I. . .you. . .oh, dear."

"Say it," he whispered against her lips. "Tell me you love me."

Elise stared at him in silence. How could she admit it? She could barely fathom that she was standing here in his arms. How could she open herself up for the disappointment that was bound to come?

She felt him tighten his grip, and when his lips fell on hers again, she moaned softly in resignation. *But how can I not admit it?* she thought as his kiss consumed her. *I do love him.*

Again he pulled away, searching her face for the answer he needed to hear. Elise felt a rush of dizzy exhilaration. In spite of her fears, she was overwhelmed with the love she felt for this man.

"Tell me," he said, almost pleading.

There was no other way. "I love you, Ian," she whispered. "I love you, but I don't know what I'm going to do about it. I don't know how it can possibly work out."

Ian laughed, kissed her lightly once more, and released her. "The hard part is already worked out. I thought I'd never get you to admit you loved me."

Elise felt her face grow hot. "I've never been in love before."

"I know."

"How could you?" she asked in disbelief.

"Your agenda would have never allowed it before."

"It wasn't supposed to allow it now, either," she said, feeling very vulnerable under his scrutiny.

"I know," he said softly, reaching his hand up to stroke her cheek. "But I'm determined too. And I'm very good at rearranging agendas."

"So now what do we do?" A part of her wanted to laugh and throw her arms around him, while the other half wanted to cry in complete misery.

"First, I suggest we be honest with each other. Then I suggest we pray about the entire situation. On second thought, maybe that praying part should come first."

"I prayed for this not to happen and look where that got me. Oh, this isn't fair," she moaned. "I warned you not to do this."

She looked up at him and could have almost laughed out loud at his expression. He was quite satisfied with himself. "You're not in the least bit sorry, are you?" she questioned.

"Nope." He grinned mischievously. "Not a bit."

After dropping her off at her house, Ian drove away with a smug expression of having accomplished a great task.

Elise wanted to laugh and cry at the same time. "Dear God," she said, closing the door behind her, "how in the world did this happen? I thought I was being so careful. I thought I had guarded my heart so well."

An image of her mother's tender smile came to mind. Suddenly, the only person in the world Elise wanted to be with was her mother. She wanted to be five years old again and crawl up on her mother's lap and be held until the monsters of life had all gone away. Reaching for the telephone, Elise dialed the familiar number and waited for her mother to answer.

"Hello?" The voice warmed Elise from across the miles.

"Mama," she sighed out the word.

"What's wrong? Are you hurt?"

"I'm confused," Elise stated frankly. "I need your advice." With that said, she poured out her heart in a steady stream of words for nearly ten minutes. "I didn't want to fall in love with him. I didn't want to have to give up my career like you did."

"Is that why you've never dated?" her mother asked in disbelief.

"Of course. I didn't want to make all those plans and have to throw them away because my husband's plans took precedence."

"Elise Jost, do you honestly think that your father and I didn't work through all that before we married? Nothing was as important to me as him. I didn't want a life of marine biology if he wasn't at my side."

"I guess, I mean, I just figured that you didn't have a choice."

"Oh, I had a choice. I was even offered a job right here in DC, in spite of the fact that I didn't have a degree. But I was already expecting you, and marine biology didn't sound half as interesting as motherhood. One thing led to another, and I found a whole lot more to life than studying sea creatures."

"But you had a dream," Elise protested.

"I'm living the dream, Elise. I thought I knew what I wanted, but God showed me another path. I had my priorities all wrong, but God straightened me out. Listen to Him, Elise, and you won't be sorry. Your Ian sounds like a smart man when he says to pray about it. That's exactly what you should do, and what I will do."

Elise smiled. "So you don't have any regrets?"

"Not a one."

Her mother's reply would stay with Elise through the weeks that followed. Ian didn't push his attentions on her, but neither did he keep to a silent corner of her life. As though testing a minefield, Elise gingerly stepped into the relationship, feeling a mixture of giddy excitement and nervous anticipation. Whatever God had planned, she reasoned, she would try to face it with a quiet heart, counting on Him to work out the details.

CHAPTER 7

The Renaissance festival began with a spirit of community anticipation that was unrivaled. Elise donned her heavy velvet gown, wondering how in the world women of the times ever managed to maneuver comfortably, especially in light of the fact that they wore an additional thirty pounds of undergarments that Elise had opted to leave off.

Farthingales, petticoats, corsets, and such might have been the attire of the Renaissance woman, but Elise would not be hampered by the likes, especially in the Midwest humidity of summer. She chose instead a single-hooped slip to fill out her gown, and even then, moving while carrying the weight of twelve yards of velvet was no easy matter. But by the time Elise put on the matching burgundy headdress with trailing gossamer veil and ribbons, she was beginning to feel swept back in time.

Ian had coached them on speech and etiquette, all to enhance the pleasure of the visiting crowd. Ladies were to behave submissively at all times, curtsying low when addressed by someone playing their superior in nobility ranking, and always they were to be gracious and ornamental. Of course those portraying peasants and household staff faced different challenges. Elise was glad not to have to roam the festival in tattered rags, with theatrical mud smudged all over her exposed skin.

Moving through the still-quiet festival grounds, Elise knew that she was truly happy. The class and festival preparations had proved to be enjoyable, just as Ian had said they would. She'd learned a great deal in the few short weeks of class, and now that it was nearly over, she could honestly say that she didn't regret the change of plans.

She was nearly to the entrance gate, where she would play hostess and sell tickets to those who had not yet purchased them, when Ian popped out from around the corner. He was still dressed in jeans and a T-shirt, and Elise couldn't resist assuming her role and rebuking him for his attire.

"Sire, you will be mistaken for one of the peasants," she said, curtsying low, then struggling against the heavy velvet to get back up.

Ian laughed and looked her over appreciatively. "I'm going to my office to change, but there were some last-minute problems with the ax-throwing booth. Seems someone forgot to get the axes out of the prop room."

"'Tis the way of this life," Elise said in mock haughtiness. "Good help is hard to secure."

Ian laughed. "Milady, you are so very right. I would like to remain here to drink in of your beauty, but, alas, if you will pardon me," he said with a sweeping bow, "I will retire from your company for but a short while."

"Very well." Elise curtsied again and this time laughed. "They must have had very strong legs in the Renaissance."

Ian chuckled, handed her into the ticket booth, and gave her a brief salute of parting. Elise had very little time to consider him as he departed, for just then, trumpets blared out and summoned the crowds to their appropriate places. Without any difficulty, Elise was immediately transposed from a modern-day play-actress to a gentle-bred woman of the sixteenth century.

By two o'clock, Elise was exhausted and also frustrated by the fact that she'd not seen Ian all day. When Jason appeared to assist her at the gate, she noted the smell of beer on his breath as he leaned down close to her face and told her how beautiful she was.

"Jason, are you drunk?" she asked, trying not to bring anyone else's attention to the matter.

"Only drunk with love for you, Lady Elise." He leaned closer and tried to place a kiss on her lips.

"Jason! What do you think you're doing?"

"Ah, be nice, Elise. Ian said you ladies are to be submissive. Come on and give me a little kiss." He reached out for her, but Elise managed to dart around him. Twenty pounds of velvet didn't seem such a hindrance after all.

"You watch the booth," Elise said, stepping outside. "I'll get someone else to come and help you."

"But I only want you, Elise!" he called after her with exaggerated flair.

Grimacing, Elise motioned to Dave, one of her classmates, and told him what was happening. Dave immediately agreed to cover for her, while Elise went in search of Ian.

"I haven't seen him since this morning," she admitted to Dave. "He wasn't even in costume yet. Where do you suppose I'll find him?"

"Well, he's probably with his council in the center clearing."

"His council?"

"Sure, that's what the king does."

"The king? Ian is the king of hearts?" Elise questioned in disbelief.

"I thought everybody knew that." Dave laughed. "Since he created the festival and works harder than anyone else to see that it's a big money-maker, he's maintained the privilege of being king."

"I see." Elise muttered the words, feeling herself tremble with unexpected anticipation. "I'll go look for King Ian at the council setting."

She made her way through excited crowds of children and their parents. She watched as couples joined hands and found themselves caught up in the revelry. People without costumes were bowing and curtsying as they found themselves faced with costumed actors and actresses, and all around, the atmosphere was one of pure delight and pleasure.

Why have I never come to one of these before? she wondered, making her way past a jousting tournament. Armored knights sat atop equally armored horses and demonstrated to the crowds how an honest-to-goodness joust might have taken place. These knights, of course, weren't classmates of Elise's, but trained professionals who toured the country, working at demonstrations and other festivals.

The festival was set on the edge of a woods that encompassed the college on three sides. The enchanting mood the setting created made it very easy to forget the modern world. Elise heard the minstrels and jongleurs singing songs of love and devotion, all while making grandiose gestures of romantic enticement to the ladies in the crowd. It was amusing to watch grown women actually blushing like schoolgirls when the singers took their hands and kissed them ever so lightly.

Laughing to herself, Elise came upon the crowd watching the

king's council. She worked her way around the gathering, but still had no good view of Ian. Ducking behind a large cottonwood, she managed to squeeze through a place where the temporary fencing didn't quite reach the stage. From there, she moved forward to a place on the stage itself, where props and painted stage settings would keep her from view but allow her to see.

Her first glimpse of Ian made her breath catch in her throat. He was regal and stately in his black doublet trimmed in gold braid. A voluminous and heavily padded short gown of gold and black came over the doublet, but this garment was also trimmed in red hearts befitting the king of hearts. The long black hose on his legs provided evidence of his devotion to weightlifting, and his feet were dressed in traditional square-toed shoes. Elise smiled to herself, noting the simple gold crown on his head. He made a very handsome king.

"The kingdom of Hearts has known peace for many years and prosperity is all around us. There is much to celebrate and—"

"A spy! A spy!" the cry went out from behind her, and before Elise could turn, someone had taken her in hand and thrust her out into the full view of the cheering crowd.

Ian turned a bemused face to her stunned expression. Elise tried to shake loose from the man's hold on her arm, but when Ian came forward, an uncontrollable trembling shook her entire body.

The man was still denouncing her as a spy, and the crowd had picked up the chant. Twisting to break away from the king's guard, Elise was calmed by Ian's touch and reassuring wink. When the crowd saw Ian take hold of Elise, they instantly fell silent and awaited the king's declaration.

Elise stood completely still, and Ian released her to make a full bow. She, in turn, very shakily made a completely floored curtsy, only to find herself too weak to return to her feet. Ian reached out a hand and helped her to her feet, smiling broadly as he did so and seeming to thoroughly enjoy this new turn of events.

Turning to the crowd, Ian led Elise forward. "My good towns-folk, 'tis no spy who breaks in upon us."

The crowd murmured. Everyone was wondering what the king might do next, but no one wondered as much as Elise. She looked out upon the people and felt her legs turn to jelly.

"If she be no spy, Your Majesty, then pray tell, who is this woman?" one of the council members asked boldly.

Ian laughed and tightened his grip on Elise's arm. "This is Lady Elise, my chosen bride." The crowd cheered in unison, so loudly in fact that Elise was deafened by the roar. Ian continued when the noise died down. "For many years now, my mother has encouraged me to take a bride, but until now there has been no one worthy of that place. If Lady Elise consents, we will hold the wedding here on the final day of the festival." Again the crowd cheered, and Elise thought she would faint.

Looking into Ian's teasing eyes, Elise couldn't help but wonder if there was something of truth to his statement about searching for a bride. She felt her heart pound faster at the expression of love she read on his face, and suddenly it seemed as though they were completely alone. What might it be like, she wondered, if Ian were asking for her hand in truth? Swallowing hard, she shook the thought away.

"What say ye, Lady Elise?" another councilman questioned when the crowd again fell silent.

"Yea, milady," Ian whispered. "What say ye?"

"My liege does me honor," she replied. "I will quite happily take the vows with him."

A chorus of cheers rose up from the crowd, and no one but Elise saw the look on Ian's face, a look that strongly suggested he wasn't playing at this—that he was quite serious.

Finally he turned from her and raised his hands. "My good people, if you will be so kind as to return at two o'clock on Friday afternoon, we will hold the wedding here for the pleasure of all."

"Seal it with a kiss!" someone yelled from the crowd. This brought another affirming cheer.

"Yes, kiss the bride!"

"Kiss Lady Elise!"

Ian looked at Elise with a mischievous smirk. "We mustn't disappoint our subjects, milady."

"But Ian," she tried to say, before he swept her into his arms and kissed her soundly. Amid the yells and comradery, Elise lost her will to argue.

Ian pulled away, but not before saying against her ear, "I love you."

By Friday, there was no explaining the exhilaration and happiness Elise felt. She'd seen very little of Ian except in postfestival meetings where progress reports were the focus. Someone had suggested that Elise be fitted with a special gown for the wedding day, and Ian quickly agreed, noting a crate of unused costumes in his office. This extra attention caused Elise to blush scarlet, but when Friday finally dawned, she was fully delighted by her transformation.

Resplendent in heavy, pale blue silk, complete with many of the Renaissance undertrappings she'd avoided with the velvet gown, Elise moved amid the crowd feeling very much like a bride. With braided hair secured beneath a beautiful headpiece of silver and blue, Elise became a queenly vision.

Her only duty for the day, besides the wedding, came at noon when she was to cover the entrance gate. Taking her place there, Elise daydreamed about what it might be like to become Mrs. Ian Hunter for real. He was everything she wanted in a man. Educated, strong, handsome, and most importantly, a Christian who could share her faith in God. But he didn't live in Montana.

"Oh, Ian," she murmured, grateful that no one else was around. "Why does life have to be so complicated?" She felt a bit of melancholia engulf her. In a few days, she'd be leaving and would probably never see Dr. Ian Hunter again. Putting the thought from her mind, Elise resolved to deal with it later. *I will be happy today,* she declared to herself.

It was growing closer and closer to two o'clock, and still Jason Emery hadn't shown up to relieve Elise from the ticket booth. Glancing again and again at the clock, Elise finally decided there was no other recourse but to close the booth, take the day's earnings, and secure them in the fine arts department safe before taking her place in the wedding procession. The festival had grossed over $600,000 during the week, with Friday already taking in $30,000 in gate receipts alone. Most of that had been shifted to the safe early on, but several thousand dollars were still in Elise's hands, and she couldn't just leave the money unprotected in the booth.

Putting the money in a bank bag, Elise locked the booth and made her way toward the entrance gate. Without warning, a black-cloaked figure appeared before her, and before she could protest, he'd hoisted her over his shoulder in barbaric fashion.

"Help!" she yelled out over and over.

The man seemed momentarily to consider his route of escape, while the crowd clapped heartily. Elise relaxed a bit, realizing she was caught up yet again in the role-playing of the festival.

"Are you come to steal the king's bride?" she questioned the man from over his shoulder.

"Yea!" was the grunted reply.

Elise looked out to the crowd. "Someone fetch the king and tell him that his bride has been taken!" Again clapping and cheering rose up while several people moved away to seek out the king of hearts.

Her captor wasted no more time and quickly moved through the remaining crowd, heading deeper into the woods. Elise felt nauseous from being slammed against the man's shoulder and demanded he let her walk.

"We're away from the people now," she cried out. "Put me down or I'm going to lose my lunch!"

The man stopped and did as she asked. His heavy cloak fell away to reveal Jason Emery.

"Jason?"

He smiled nervously. "Hi, Elise. Isn't this great!"

"I agree it's good for the crowd, but you could have hurt yourself hoisting me up like that. I'm a good fifty pounds heavier with this costume." Before Jason could reply, however, Elise noticed the money bag in her hands. "Jason, I need to get this money into the safe. Let's go around the long way and—"

Jason reached out and grabbed the bag away from her. "You don't get it, Elise. I'm taking the money, and I'm taking you too."

CHAPTER 8

Your Majesty! Your Majesty!" Ian looked up to find a collective crowd of festivalgoers approaching him. "Your bride has been stolen!"

Ian stared at them in disbelief for a moment. What in the world were they talking about? As if sensing his questions, one of his students approached to explain.

"A hooded man has taken Lady Elise from the ticket booth. He hoisted her over his shoulder and ran in the direction of the woods."

Ian heard other comments of how wonderful this additional playacting was and how it brought real intrigue and crowd participation to the festival, but inside he felt sick at the knowledge that no such demonstration had been planned by his department. Elise was missing, someone had her, and that someone wasn't part of the festival.

"We will go in search of her," Ian announced. But in the back of his mind he wondered at the best recourse. He made his way with the people to the ticket booth, where the first thing he realized was that the festival proceeds were missing. It was clear now, Elise had been taken in the midst of a robbery. Security would have to be notified and the people kept at a safe distance.

"Good folk of the village, we request that thee leave this area free for our men to observe. There are tracks which lead into the forest and other signs that will be obliterated if thou shouldst traipse about. We beseech thee, therefore, to await our appearance at the inner circle." He made a broad bow, and the crowd clapped.

Motioning to several of the Renaissance students, Ian confided in them that this was no game. He sent one for security and instructed the others on how to maneuver the crowd back to his council stage. With this done, Ian could no longer ignore the sinking feeling in the pit of his stomach. Elise had been taken and could very well be hurt or even dead.

~○

Jason pulled Elise deeper into the cover of trees. Protesting loudly at his treatment, Elise was stunned when Jason produced a gun and threatened her into silence.

"I didn't come this far just to let you blow it for me," he said, shoving the gun into her stomach. "Now be quiet and move that way. The woods end at the river, and I've got a boat there for our getaway."

"But Jason, I don't want to come with you." Elise struggled to steady her nerves. She wanted to sound reasonable and logical. "Robbery is one thing, but kidnapping could get you a life sentence."

Jason laughed. "Only if they catch me. Now move." He pushed her forward, and fighting against the extra weight of her Renaissance costume, Elise stumbled and nearly lost her balance.

"I'm hardly dressed for a hike in the woods, Jason." She hoped he'd see reason in one way or another. "This dress doesn't allow me to move very quickly."

"Then take it off," he said, glancing around them as they came into a clearing. "Hurry up. Just get rid of it. I know you're wearing a T-shirt and shorts underneath—remember, I was in the dressing room when Kerry was strapping you into some of those contraptions."

"I need help to unfasten the hooks in back," Elise said, hoping it would buy her some time.

Jason glanced around nervously. "No, there isn't time. Just keep moving to the river. We'll cut it off then if we have to, but we're losing time."

Elise had only taken a couple of steps when Ian's voice sounded from behind her. Turning, she saw him step into the clearing. "Let her go, Jason! Take the money, but leave Elise here."

"No way, Ian. She's my insurance policy. If I let her go, there'll be no reason to keep security from coming after me. Elise stays with me."

"No," Ian said, taking slow, determined steps forward.

"Ian, don't!" Elise called out. "He has a gun."

"Yes," Jason said, leveling it at Ian. "I have a gun, and I have no qualms about using it."

The sound of Jason cocking back the hammer of the revolver caused Elise to forget herself. All she could see was Ian in danger. Rushing forward, she tripped against the weight of her gown and fell against Jason. The gun fired, but Elise had no way of knowing whether it had hit Ian or not. Jason thrust her back violently, and before she could so much as put out a hand to break her fall, Elise hit her head hard against a fallen log and knew nothing more.

Elise struggled to focus her eyes. A blur of images seemed to circle her head, and dizziness made it nearly impossible to think clearly. Where was she?

"Miss Jost?" a woman's voice called out to her through the haze.

"Where am I?"

"County Hospital," the voice answered. "I'm Nancy, your nurse. Can you tell me how many fingers I'm holding up?"

Elise closed her eyes and opened them again. The blurred double image focused into one. "Three."

"Good," the nurse replied. "You have a slight concussion and five stitches in the back of your head, but you're going to be just fine."

"What happened?" Elise questioned, even as bits and pieces of memory came to her.

"You were in an attempted robbery. The assailant pushed you down and you hit your head."

Elise nodded. Yes, that image seemed to be somewhere in her mind. "Your fiancé has been waiting to see you. Should I send him in now?"

"My fiancé?" Elise questioned. Putting her hand to her head, she knew her expression was one of confusion.

"Don't worry," Nancy said reassuringly. "It'll all come back to you in a little while. Your injury isn't very bad, and you'll only have to stay overnight for observation. I'll go get your boyfriend."

Elise nodded and tried to piece everything together, but when Ian appeared at the door still dressed as the king of hearts, all the confusion cleared away. "You're okay!" she exclaimed and grinned. "Forgive me if I don't curtsy, Your Majesty."

Ian's expression changed from gravely serious to one of amusement. "I suppose we'll let it pass this time." He came to her side and lifted her hand to his lips. "I was so worried."

"Me too," she said. "At least I think I was. The whole thing is still a little fuzzy around the edges, but I do remember Jason and the gun. What happened?"

"When you very stupidly jumped Jason, the gun went off and you hit your head on a log. Jason got caught up for a minute with what had happened to you and it gave me enough time to cross the clearing. By that time, security was there, and they took him into custody."

"So the money's safe?"

"Who cares about that!" Ian exclaimed. "I thought I was going to lose you, Elise. I couldn't stand it."

Elise smiled in spite of the pain in her head. "I felt the same way. I thought at first it was just more of your playacting. By the time I realized what was really going on, Jason had me too far away to do any good."

"I wish I'd never forced you to participate in the festival," Ian said, releasing her hand. He put his hand to his head and realized he still wore the king's crown. Taking it off, he stared at it for a moment. "Maybe the festival isn't such a good idea."

"Oh, stop it," Elise said with more strength than she felt. "The festival isn't to blame, and you know it." The throbbing in her head caused her to grimace. "I've spent most of my life in relative good health, but since meeting you I've been to the hospital twice. You're a dangerous man to be around."

Ian shrugged and offered her a lopsided grin. "You'd better get used to it if you're going to spend the rest of your life with me. I love a good adventure and can't see giving it up just because we're going to get married."

"Ian Hunter, are you proposing to me?"

He sobered and nodded. "I very much want you to become my wife. I knew it long ago, but when I declared you my bride at the festival and you agreed to the mock ceremony, I so wished we were doing more than acting out parts. Please say yes."

"Yes," Elise said with a giggle.

Ian's eyes opened wide in surprise. "Do you mean it?"

Elise nodded, and before she could speak again, he covered her mouth with a very serious kiss that made her tingle down to her toes.

In this glorious moment of ecstasy, a black cloud of despair draped itself over Elise's joy. Pushing Ian away, she asked, "Ian, what about my job in Montana?"

"What about it?"

Elise felt her chest tighten and knew there was no other recourse but to deal with the issue. "I'm supposed to leave next week. You know how important this job is to me—"

He put a finger to her lips. "You worry too much. Yes, I know how important your new career is to you. It made you put up with me and the Renaissance class, didn't it?" He was smiling as though they were discussing nothing more important than the weather.

His expression grew serious, but the soft tenderness in his eyes was not to be missed. "I would follow you to the ends of the earth, Elise. My work can be done anywhere I have a computer and access to the Internet. We can be married as soon as things can be arranged with our families, and then we can move to Montana together."

"Oh, Ian," she said, reaching her arms up to beckon him

forward. She let her fingers entwine themselves behind Ian's head. "Just how long have you had this solution planned out?"

"I started packing the day you told me you'd accepted the position."

"But you said nothing."

"I was afraid you'd think me too forward."

She laughed. "You are too forward."

"It got me what I wanted though, didn't it?" Ian's look of satisfaction was firmly back in place.

"Amazing," she murmured. "God had it worked out all along. Your class, which at one time didn't seem to make a bit of sense to me, put us together; and in a few short weeks of knowing each other, we feel confident enough to agree to marriage."

"All things work together for good," Ian whispered against her cheek.

Elise released her hold and gently touched his cheek. "I love you, Ian. You'll always be king of my heart. With God, of course, being King of kings," she added with a grin.

Ian kissed her nose. "I'm the happiest man alive and all because you were a credit hour short and had to take my class. God used a simple Renaissance class to create a miracle of love and a lifetime of dreams."

"Speaking of classes, Dr. Hunter," Elise said in a very formal tone. "Have I completed all my requirements?"

"Indeed you have. Summer school is out."

"Do I pass?" she asked, narrowing her eyes ever so slightly.

Ian laughed out loud and pulled her into his arms. "Ah, Elise," he said and kissed her lips very briefly, "you got an A-plus long ago."

Fall

FALLING FOR LOVE

CHAPTER 1

Autumn in Kansas was Karen Jacobs' most beloved time of the year. Something about the trees changing colors and the humid air turning a little crisper gave her a sense of anticipation. She couldn't quite put her finger on it, but it always gave her a good feeling. Maybe it was because she could look back on the year and see that she'd accomplished quite a bit.

Like this year, she and Mom had managed to have a very successful garden and now the apple trees were loaded, as well as the black walnut trees. There was still plenty of work to be done, but they'd canned a lot of vegetables and would soon do the same with the apples. It gave her a sense of pride to know she would have plenty throughout the winter and into next spring. Prices at the store seemed to rise by the week, but she wouldn't have to worry about that. She had half a steer in the freezer and had prepaid to receive half a hog in November. They were set. At least as far as food was concerned.

She walked along the small pond that had long been her place of comfort. Since she was born, she'd lived on this land, although there was a lot more of it back in the day. At one point there had been a thousand acres planted in wheat. Her great-grandfather had bought the Kansas land with an inheritance he'd received and farmed it faithfully, then passed it down to his two sons, splitting the land in half. A thousand acres of wheat didn't exactly provide for millions, but it gave the men of the family a sense of duty and accomplishment.

Karen's grandfather and great-uncle had continued to farm until he and his brother signed up to do their part in the war. Granddad had been wounded shortly after reaching Europe in '42 and was sent home, but Great-Uncle Clinton had been killed during the D-day invasion. His wife was so broken up over it that she sold their portion of the farm and took her two children back to Pennsylvania where her family lived. Granddad never forgave her. He had wanted to buy the family land back, but he couldn't raise the money. Eventually her great-uncle's five hundred acres were sold to others, and later the land was subdivided to put in new homes for the rapidly growing community. . .after the war. It made Granddad all the more unhappy.

"I thought I'd find you out here," Mom said, coming to join her. She was using a walking stick rather than a cane. She said it made her feel less old. Frankly, Karen was impressed with how well her mother got around for a woman of her age.

"The day was too pleasant not to enjoy this walk."

Mom glanced around. "I heard geese flying over last night. Barking like dogs, as your father used to say. Can't believe he's been gone for nearly seven years."

"Or five years for Stan," Karen said, gazing out over the still water. Her husband, Stanley Jacobs, had fallen over dead of a heart attack at the bank where he was vice president. The doctor said it happened so fast he probably never knew what hit him. Karen liked to think of it that way—that there was no pain, no fear. Of course, Stanley had a strong faith in God, so she knew he had little fear of death.

"Seems like they were both here just yesterday." Mom came to where Karen stood. "I keep expecting your father to come in from the barn, hollering for me to find something he's lost."

"Yes, or to tell you some new idea he has for something to build." Karen turned and looked back toward the ranch-style house. That design with the walk-out basement had been her father's idea. After having lived through numerous bad windstorms and tornadoes, he said he wouldn't live in a house that didn't have a basement. The old homestead house, as they called the original home, only had a storm cellar. That required them to go outside in the storm in order to take cover. Dad liked the idea of a two-story house that opened up in the back with a deck off the upstairs and a nice patio out the basement doors. There was a nice safe shelter in the basement that was buried underground, while the part that opened to the outdoors made the main living space light and airy. Not at all like a traditional basement.

Dad had put four bedrooms in the basement as well. He and Mom had always figured on having four children. Two boys had come along without any trouble, but Mom had difficulty with Karen and after that there were no more pregnancies. Three would have to suffice.

Mom insisted when the house was built that each room have its own bathroom, which Dad said was a waste of money, but Mom stood firm. She said it was going to be best in the long run, and somehow she had convinced Dad. Karen remembered her and her brothers living down there and feeling almost like they had their own apartment. When the boys became teenagers, Dad had even put in a little kitchen so it really was self-sufficient.

They had popped thousands of cups of popcorn, baked hundreds—if not thousands—of snacks, and enjoyed a good life. Even the boys knew they were luckier than most. Now that it was just Karen and Mom, it seemed like much too much house, and they lived upstairs. But Karen loved what was left of her great-great-grandfather's dream.

Only ten acres remained of the original thousand to remember the Armstrong family, and Karen was the keeper. Two houses, a barn, and three outbuildings, as well as pens, a pond, and a good-sized stand of trees including twenty apple trees and five giant black walnut trees was all that remained. Frankly, it was all that Karen and Mom could manage. But she liked to think of when the land all around them had belonged to her family.

"Penny for your thoughts?"

Karen smiled at her mother. "I was just thinking about how this had once been a thousand-acre farm."

Mom smiled and gave a nod. "My grandfather had been so proud to pass it to his boys."

"It's such a pity Great-Aunt Cloris couldn't have sold it back to Granddad."

"Yes. My father was so angry that she wouldn't even try to work a deal with him. She was always out of place here, however. She never liked Kansas or country living. It just about broke my mother's heart to see my father so upset and to lose their only connection to Uncle Clinton—his two girls. Their mother must have soured them something fierce on this family, because although Mother wrote to them and always remembered them on their birthdays and Christmas, she rarely got so much as a thank-you card from them."

"That is sad. To know you have family out there somewhere,

but they want nothing to do with you is a terrible feeling."

"It is," Mom agreed. "Speaking of family out there somewhere, have you talked to the boys lately?"

Karen had two sons, one living on the West Coast in Seattle and the other on the East Coast in the Washington, DC, area. "I talked to Stan Jr. last Sunday. He had some fundraiser to attend in the city that evening, so he couldn't talk for long. He sounded good."

"And what about Rodney?"

"It's been a couple of weeks since I talked to him. He said this final semester of law school is keeping him far too busy to talk on the phone to his mother. He's applying to various law firms around the country, as well as there in Seattle. He said he hasn't a clue where he'll end up."

"Such busy boys."

"Men. It's hard to believe, but they're both grown and I'm nearly fifty." Karen shook her head. She didn't feel that old. Where had all the time gone?

They walked to a nearby bench and took a seat. Karen could remember her dad making the bench as a gift to her mother one birthday long ago. As a child she had loved to come here and sit by the pond and watch the fish skim the surface for dragonflies and mosquitoes.

Her phone vibrated and Karen glanced to see who it was. "Well I'll be. Marlene is calling." She hadn't heard from her cousin in some time.

"Put it on speaker so we can both talk to her," Mom suggested.

Karen nodded and answered the phone. "Hi, Marlene. I'm putting you on speaker because Mom and I are sitting here at the pond and that way we can both talk to you."

"I think that will be a great idea, because the reason I've called includes you both," Marlene replied.

Karen frowned wondering if Marlene's mother was sick. Aunt Leticia was Mom's oldest sister. Karen whispered a prayer that the older woman was doing all right.

"So what's up?" Karen glanced at Mom, who was also looking a bit worried.

"Well, you probably didn't know this, but Leo retired early and wants to move to California. His folks are there, as you probably remember."

"I do. California is quite the change." Karen looked at her mother and shrugged. It was still unclear what Marlene wanted.

"Yes. And we won't even have to buy a house. His folk's house is huge and very nicely kept. They remodeled it like every ten years or so. It's really quite up-to-date and even has one of those chairs that goes up and down the stairs."

"Well, that ought to be good for Aunt Leticia. I know she doesn't do stairs anymore."

"What does Lettie think of the move?" Mom asked.

"Well, that's the reason I'm calling."

Marlene gave a long pause and for a moment Karen thought they'd lost the call. "Are you still there, Marlene?"

"I'm here. I was just trying to think of what to say. I guess I'll just spill it. Mom refuses to move to California. She said she was born and raised in Kansas and that's where she's going to stay and die."

"Oh, dear. That does sound like Lettie. She's never wanted to travel far," Mom confirmed.

"Yes, and it's making things very difficult for us. Frankly, I had no idea what to do about it, but then Mom said something that got me thinking."

Karen figured she was about to get to the point of the call. "And what did you come up with?"

"That's why I'm calling. Mom said her happiest years were living there on the farm. I wondered—well, I hoped and prayed—that you might. . .might let her come live with you."

The shock of the moment caused Karen's mouth to drop open. She looked to Mom, who was just as surprised.

"Look, Karen, I know it's a lot to ask, but Mom is still able to get around really well. She has trouble with stairs, but otherwise she goes for walks, and you know she has a clear mind. There's no sign of dementia or any health issues except for being borderline diabetic. But she's watching what she eats and doesn't even have to take medication. . .yet."

Karen couldn't think of what to say. Such a big change would require discussion with her mother—and prayer.

Marlene continued, "I wouldn't come to you, but I don't know what else to do. Leo is set to move, and the only other thing we can do is put her in a nursing home or assisted living."

"It is a lot to take in at one time," Karen finally found the right words. "Let me talk to Mom about it, and of course we should all pray about it."

"I haven't said a word to Mom," Marlene admitted. "I didn't want to get her hopes up. We leave in two weeks. The house sold in just one day after we put it on the market. Sure never expected that. I hate to just dump this on you, but remember, Mom has money and can pay whatever rent you need. She can provide for her own groceries and anything else she needs."

"I wasn't concerned about that," Karen replied, looking at her mother.

"Marlene, give us tonight to talk about it and Karen can get back with you in the morning," Mom said, looking to Karen.

Karen nodded. "That would give us time to discuss how this might work, and then I'll call you tomorrow, Marlene."

"Thanks so much, Karen. I know Mom would be so happy out there. I'll talk to you tomorrow. Love you."

"Love you too. Goodbye." Karen pushed the button to end the call and looked to her mother. "Well, I certainly wasn't expecting that."

"No, but I don't see why we can't work it out. You took me in." Mom smiled and shifted on the bench to look back at the pond. "Lettie is opinionated and strong willed. Typical firstborn. It doesn't surprise me she refuses to move to California. Frankly, I'd do the same."

Karen could understand her aunt's misgivings about moving so far away. She had always loved the farm, and when she'd been younger, before Dad had arranged the sale of the property, Aunt Lettie always came out with Uncle George just to spend time on the farm. She'd disappear for hours just to walk around the property with her husband and tell him stories of the old days. Many had been the time Mom and Dad had invited all of Mom's sisters and their families out to the farm for a big picnic or cookout. It had always been so much fun to have all the cousins there. Even if most of them were older than Karen.

"You know, when I married, I knew it would come to me to take care of your granddad and grandmother eventually," Mom began. "Your dad and I talked about it before we said 'I do,' because I wanted him to understand that this was my choice and desire. When I told your grandparents that Curtis and I would like to stick around and help with the farm and take care of them in their old age, Mama actually cried. She had been worried about the future.

I don't know why in particular, but she had started praying that God would make it clear what they were to do. She knew there would be the need to sell off most of the land eventually because there was no one left in the family who wanted to farm. I think it surprised everyone when Curtis stepped forward and told Dad he'd like to learn how to farm and keep it all going."

"Most farmers are born into it," Karen admitted. "Dad had been born into a city family, and his father had an office job."

Mom laughed. "He surprised even me. I told him it would be the hardest work he'd ever done. I reminded him there would be times when storms came up and took it all, and other times when the rains wouldn't come or we'd have a plague of grasshoppers. He didn't care. He told me God had called him to be a farmer, and he intended to answer the call. How could I tell him no?"

Karen met her mother's joy-filled expression. "He was certainly good at it."

"He was, and my dad said he'd never met a man more inclined to farm than Curtis. Curtis became the son Dad never had and we all lived here so happily. First in the little homestead house, but then when we found out the twins were coming, your granddad suggested we build ourselves a house. This place has always been about family, so if you want my thoughts, I'd say let Lettie come. She's as much a part of this place as I am. If you don't want her in the main house, she and I could move into the homestead house."

"No way. That place needs so many repairs. No, she could have one of the lower-level bedrooms."

"I'd move down there too. We could set it all up like our own little apartment—just like you and the boys did when you were younger. We'd each have our bedroom and bathroom. Then when we wanted to be together we'd have the commons area. The tornado shelter room would still be available for all of us, and Lettie and I wouldn't have to worry about hurrying downstairs. With the walk-out aspect of the house we could even park my car down there, and if she needed or wanted to come upstairs, I could drive her up."

It seemed to Karen that every obstacle was already accounted for. "There are things we'd have to do to improve it for you two. Grab rails and other provisions. Maybe one of those electric chairs on the stairs. I'd need to get some remodeling done."

"We'd pitch in to pay for it since it would be on our behalf."

Karen shook her head. "Mom, it's not like Stanley didn't leave me well set. Then there's the fact that you gave me this place and the ten acres after Dad retired, and you sold the rest to split among your sisters."

"Well, you were the one who agreed to take care of me and your dad. You took on the responsibility, and the boys certainly didn't want this place. They made that clear when they took off for Texas and Georgia."

"I don't think there's really any question of it." Karen got up, and her mother did likewise. "I will pray about it, but as far as I'm concerned, Aunt Lettie is welcome to join us here."

Mom put her arm around Karen. "You have such a tender heart. You have always been such a caring person. I remember when you were little and the cat had kittens. You were out there at the crack of dawn to make sure that the mama cat had plenty of food and water so that she could feed her babies. Then later when the dog got hit by a pickup truck, you were the one that pulled him through."

Karen remembered both situations. She couldn't help but care for things. Her pets, her folks. Now Aunt Lettie. It just seemed right.

She put her arm around Mom and hugged her. "I can't imagine Aunt Lettie having to go to a strange place, much less an institution. Especially when we have all this space." They headed for the house. "The pot roast should be ready for us. It's been in the slow cooker all day."

"And I'm starved." Mom stopped and her eyes lit up. "You know, Lettie makes some really amazing dishes."

"I remember." Karen laughed. "Another good reason to let her come stay."

CHAPTER 2

It wasn't much past eight when the phone rang. Marlene was on the other end, apologizing for calling so early—before Karen had even had a chance to call her cousin. "Of course she can come stay with us, Marlene."

"You don't know what this means to us. To me. I just couldn't bear the thought of her having to go into another place— especially some sort of old folks' home."

"I understand. Mom thinks it will be a lot of fun. We're going to remodel and fix up the bedrooms downstairs and the commons area and that way it will be like they have their own apartment. They'll each have a bed and bath all their own and then the little kitchenette. I think we'll all be quite happy. And I can use the help with the apples and black walnuts."

Marlene laughed. "Mom knows full well how to help with both."

"Exactly. So when does she need to come?"

"Well, I was hoping by the end of the week. We're getting everything sorted. I called the kids and found out what they wanted. I figure to ship it to them. Then we're going to be ruthless and get rid of most everything. Leo promised we could buy what we need when we get to California. Besides, his folk already have a houseful of furniture and knickknacks."

"True, but you'll want your own things around you." Karen glanced around her kitchen. She couldn't imagine not having her things with her. When Marlene said nothing, Karen figured she was waiting for an answer regarding the time. "Well, Aunt Lettie is welcome to come whenever. I'll still have to make some repairs and add some grab bars and make sure the floors don't have any places to get hung up on."

"Karen, I can't thank you enough. I think, if it's all right with you, I'll come out later today with Mom and let her look things over. That way she can feel like it's at least partially her decision."

"That's fine. I'll be here all day. I have apples to can."

They ended the call and Karen looked to her mother. "Marlene and Aunt Lettie will be out here later today to look things over."

"Good. We might as well let Lettie choose which room she wants and then we can focus on getting it ready for her."

Mom was already sorting apples. "You know, I'm glad we have that kitchen machine that lets us just put the whole cooked apple in and gives you back applesauce without seeds or skins. I don't think I want to have to core and peel all of these." She motioned to the twelve boxes of apples sitting along the kitchen wall and on the counter.

"For sure," Karen replied, her mind still on Aunt Lettie. "Do you suppose Aunt Lettie will really be happy here? I mean, she's been with Marlene for over ten years. I'm sure she'll miss her daughter."

Mom put down the paring knife. "I think she'll be so happy she won't know what to do with herself. She once told me the hardest part about getting married was having to leave the farm. This was such a happy place for all of us. I know people look at me like I must be crazy when I say we were always happy here. Sure we had moments of conflict, but we worked through it as a family. . .or individually if that was needed. But we were happy here."

"I know. I love the stories you all used to tell when we'd get the family together. While a lot of the others were running around outside or riding horses, I was listening to the old people talk."

"Old people, eh? We were no older than you back then."

Karen chuckled. "I know. I thought of that as well."

A little after three that afternoon, Marlene and Aunt Leticia arrived. Karen hadn't seen her aunt in over a month—maybe two. She and Mom had been so busy with the garden that they hadn't been much for visiting anyone. They barely managed to get to church.

They went together to meet Marlene and Leticia in the yard and walked down the sloping drive that led to the back of the house. Karen figured it would be easier to do this and later Marlene could drive down and get her mother.

"Meredith, I always loved what you and Curtis did with building the new house," Aunt Lettie began. "The farm needed a big family place like this. Remember all of us trying to live in the homestead house?"

Mom smiled. "I do. All of us girls sharing space upstairs." She turned to Karen. "We were almost like two sets of twins, me and my sisters. We were so close in age, just a year or at most two years apart from the next one."

Lettie nodded. "I loved the times everyone would get together out here, didn't you, Marlene?"

"I did. The food was always incredible, and it was fun coming back to the farm. Especially when you guys still had horses and other animals to play with." Marlene gazed off across the yard. "I used to love to swim in the pond."

"Mercy, but we all did," Aunt Lettie replied. "When we girls were young, Mother couldn't keep us out of it during the summer. She used to have to threaten to send Dad to fetch us. We knew we'd be in big trouble if our disobedience forced Dad to leave important work in order to handle us, so we always came running at that warning."

They reached the back of the house and stopped a moment. Karen looked up at the deck that stood over the downstairs patio. It needed some attention, and she'd been meaning to get to that ever since Stan died. In fact, he was the one who pointed out the problem areas.

"Shall we go inside?" Mom asked.

Karen pulled her attention back to the others. "Of course. That's why we're all here."

She opened the french door on one side and flipped on a light. The illumination revealed a large open room with a couch and several stuffed chairs. Against the far wall were the kitchenette and a door. Karen started the tour.

"As you can see there's a little kitchen area. Refrigerator, stove, sink, microwave. Just about everything you'd want except a dishwasher."

"Oh bother," Aunt Lettie declared. "I never liked them. Always washed dishes by hand. Gets them cleaner."

"Mom always thought that way too, until I showed her what a really good dishwasher could do."

Karen continued the tour. "This door leads to storage." She

opened it to reveal a very neatly organized storage room. Shelves lined the walls, and on those shelves were a variety of things including most of the vegetables and fruit she and Mom had canned that summer.

"Looks like you two have been busy," Marlene said, nodding toward the canned goods.

"Yes. We had a really good garden this year, and all the berry bushes produced in record numbers. We made jellies and jams and pie filling until we didn't care if we ever saw another berry. Now we're working on apples, and next it will be black walnuts."

"I remember those days," Aunt Lettie said, nodding in approval. "This looks good, Meredith."

Karen backed them out of the first storage room and showed them another before moving on to the room they used for tornadoes. "This is the room where we take shelter when the storms are bad." She opened the reinforced door and revealed a small room with a bunch of folding chairs leaning against the wall. Another door was on the other side of the room.

"That door goes into one of the bedrooms. Dad insisted there be two doors in case one of them got blocked if, say, a tornado hit the house full on."

"Your father was always worried about storms," Mom admitted.

Aunt Lettie gave a tsking sound. "We had to go outside in the storm just to get to the storm shelter. Used to terrify poor Rachel."

Aunt Rachel was just a little older than Karen's mother and the only one of the sisters who never married. She was one of those people who seemed afraid of her shadow when she was little, but then turned out to be a schoolteacher of younger grades and didn't seem to fear anything—not even the occasional snake that was brought to show-and-tell.

"Well, if you'll recall, Lettie, Curtis did endure a time of dealing with the storm shelter while we built this place."

"Oh, I do recall that," Aunt Lettie replied. "Seems like a thousand years ago. I was so impressed with how fast this house went up."

Mom chuckled. "Well, he had friends in the construction business who had extended family also in the construction business, so it made it very nice and cut down on the months and months needed to build a house."

Karen motioned them from the storm shelter and moved on to the bedrooms. "The boys had these rooms on the west side, so you'll still see a few of their things. I'll get those packed up this week and the rooms thoroughly cleaned just in case you want one of them. I even plan to paint."

They inspected the rooms, which were in much better shape than Karen remembered. Even the bathrooms were clean and orderly. They moved back across the living area.

"The fireplace is gas and really warms up the room if you put down all the thermal shades on the windows." The windows she spoke of included the french doors and the two large windows on either side.

She crossed to the two east bedrooms. Opening the first door, she showed them what was once her old room. Then they moved to the other room, which had always been used for guests.

"And that's just about everything. There's more storage under the stairs over there by the dining-room table and chairs."

"I'll be bringing my rocking chair," Aunt Lettie announced. "I need it for my back."

"Of course," Karen replied with a smile. "You can bring most anything you need. Just keep in mind that space is limited down here. If you have a lot, we might have to put it in the homestead house until we can figure it all out."

"Nonsense. I won't be bringing that much. I've gotten rid of stuff over the years." She frowned. "I just want my chair. I don't even need to bring my clothes. I'll live in my nightgown if I have to."

Karen hadn't meant to offend her aunt. "The chair and whatever else will be just fine, Aunt Lettie. I just wanted to make sure there'd be enough space in your room."

"Mom, it will be just fine. Don't be sarcastic. No one is denying you your clothes."

Karen's phone began to ring. She looked at the caller ID. "It's Aunt Helen." Her aunt had become a widow three months earlier, and Karen hadn't heard or seen her since the funeral.

"Hello, Aunt Helen?"

"Karen?"

"Yes, it's me. How are you doing?"

"I'm fine, but I heard that Lettie is coming to live with you."

Karen glanced around at her mom and the others. "Yes. She is. In fact, she and Marlene are here right now looking at the space."

"Put her on speaker," Mom said.

Karen's mom loved putting folks on speaker so that everyone in the room could participate. She did as Mom suggested. "Aunt Helen, I'm going to put you on speaker so everyone can hear you and you can talk to them." She punched the button. "Can you hear us?"

"I hear you," Helen replied.

"Hello, Helen. It's Meredith."

"Meredith. I presume Lettie can hear me too."

"I hear you," Lettie answered. "Why are you calling?" Lettie always got right to the point.

"I heard you were going to live there on the farm."

"I am. I'm going to move into the house with Karen and Meredith."

There was a long pause, then a rather teary-sounding voice asked, "Can I come too?"

"What's that?" Lettie questioned. "You want to move in here too?"

"Yes." She sniffed. "I'm sorry for the tears. It's just after losing Gary. . .well. . .I've been so lonely. The kids went home to their various places, and I'm here by myself all the time."

Karen looked to her mom, who nodded. "Of course you can move in with us, Aunt Helen. But as I was just telling Aunt Lettie, we'll have to be mindful of how much stuff each person brings. My house was already full, and while I plan to get rid of a lot, we. . .ah. . .need to be cautious."

"Just get rid of everything like I did, Helen. Have the kids come and take what they want after you box up your personals. Then call an estate sale agency. They'll come out and sell off everything else." Aunt Lettie was not in the least shy about dictating to her younger sibling.

"I'll call the kids immediately and let them know. It might take me a week or two, but I'll get one of them to bring me."

"Well, keep us posted when that might be." Karen could hardly believe she was taking on yet another one of her aunts, but somehow it felt right.

She ended the call and looked at the others. "I guess we'll soon have a full house."

"In keeping with that idea," Mom interjected, "why don't we invite Rachel to join us. There are four bedrooms and we can all live quite easily with each other so long as Lettie doesn't get bossy."

"Me?" Lettie replied, rolling her gaze heavenward. "I'm not the one to worry about. If Rachel goes into her schoolteacher mode, we're all in for it." They all laughed.

That night as Karen got ready for bed, she thought of how empty her life had seemed—how lonely she'd been despite Mom's presence in the house. Soon, however, the house would be filled to capacity. Aunt Rachel had been delighted at the idea of leaving her tiny house nearly fifty miles away and moving back to the farm. She had her little community of friends, but it wasn't the same as being with family.

Karen opened her Bible to read and pray for a little bit before sleeping. She and Stan had followed this routine each night, and she'd kept it up after he'd died. How she missed him. Something about having a man around balanced everything out.

She read from the Psalms for a few minutes, then prayed for guidance and direction. This was going to be a big change in her life, and who could say how it would all fall together? The sisters hadn't lived under one roof in a long, long time. They might all be so set in their ways that they'd find each other's company impossible.

"I guess the only way we'll know for sure is to try it." The only problem with trying was it might all go terribly wrong, and then where would they go? Her aunts would have sold their houses—or in Lettie's case, said goodbye to her daughter—and they'd be on their own. Karen knew they all had enough money to take care of themselves, but if they didn't get along, it would probably fall to her to somehow make it right.

She sighed. "Please God, make this work."

~⁓

Dan Polk finished making a couple of sandwiches then headed for the living room. A college football game was on TV, and he intended to enjoy it. He'd even silenced his phone, not that he was expecting any calls. His boys, Mark and David, had gone dove hunting on a friend's farm in the Flint Hills. They'd be gone all weekend—no doubt much too busy to worry about calling.

He turned up the volume and sat back in his favorite recliner. That was when it dawned on him he'd forgotten something to drink. He put the sandwiches on the table beside his chair and got back up and headed to the kitchen.

The fridge was full of their favorite sodas. Ginger ale for Mark, cola for David, and orange soda for Dan. He'd always been fond of fruity flavors, but orange was his favorite. Having grown up in a strong Christian family, Dan had never been one to drink beer as did many of his contractor friends. It just never appealed. He'd gotten his fair share of ribbing over it, even a fight or two, but after years of seeing him unwilling to consume alcohol, most just took it in stride and accepted him as he was.

Dan had raised the boys to be the same way. When he'd married all those years ago, he and his wife, Geena, agreed there would be no liquor in the house. They didn't make it a spiritual matter, so much as a health one, but nevertheless it covered all bases. Only once had the boys broken the rule about drinking. They'd done it together, as they did most everything. Mark had just graduated, and he and David were in a celebratory mood. David of course was only sixteen, but Mark didn't see that as a problem and got them a bottle of something to share. Neither much cared for the taste, and both got sick and threw up. When Dan found them, he didn't have to chastise them—they were already suffering and swearing they'd never touch the stuff again. And they never did.

Grabbing a couple of orange sodas, Dan made his way back to the living room and the game. It was a good way to spend the afternoon. He'd spent many a weekend this way. After the accident, Dan had never had much interest in getting out to go anywhere.

Thoughts of the accident always brought to mind the loss. A drunk driver had hit his wife Geena's car head-on. She and their three-year-old daughter, Kaitlyn, had been killed instantly. The boys had been injured. Dan had been working at a subdivision on the north side of town when a stranger called him to say he needed to come to the hospital as his wife and children had been in an accident. They'd offered no other information, and Dan drove ninety miles an hour on the interstate, praying all the way.

It was as if it had happened yesterday instead of fifteen years ago. When he'd arrived at the emergency room, a nurse had taken him to a small room to wait for the doctor. Dan knew the news wasn't going to be good if they were isolating him. He waited nearly ten minutes before someone showed up.

The look on the doctor's face caused the bottom of Dan's stomach to drop out. He tensed and readied himself for whatever the doctor would say. He hadn't been ready enough.

"I'm afraid I have very bad news," the doctor began. "There was a head-on collision. A drunk driver ran into your wife near Tenth and Jackson. I'm afraid your wife and daughter didn't make it."

Dan felt as if time stopped in that moment. "And the boys?"

"They were injured. We need to get the oldest one to surgery. There are forms for you to sign."

The rest of the day was a blur of doctors and nurses, forms, and that antiseptic smell of hospital rooms. Once the boys were stable, they were put into the same room in the pediatric ward, and Dan was able to be with them. He could still see how tiny and helpless they looked. They were only seven and five. Way too young to have to face something like this.

He put the memory aside and blew out a long breath. Fifteen years. He'd been a widower raising two sons for the last fifteen years, but sometimes it seemed like only yesterday he'd gotten the call—seen his sons fight for life—buried his wife and daughter.

CHAPTER 3

K aren had driven her mom and aunts up to the small Kansas town where Aunt Rachel lived in order to have, as Aunt Lettie called it, a conflab about the future and to plan out Aunt Rachel's move. The drive was only fifty miles from the farm, but already Karen was second-guessing her decision to take on all this responsibility.

Lettie bossed everyone around the entire trip, while Aunt Helen complained and Mom played referee. Karen imagined these were the roles they'd had all their lives. She couldn't help wondering how Rachel would fit in. Despite all the years of them coming to visit at the farm, Karen had never really paid much attention to their interactions.

Rachel was waiting with refreshments when they reached her house. Karen noted it was a very small house, probably no more than five hundred square feet, but once they were inside, she was even more concerned about the amount of stuff that Aunt Rachel had crammed into the place. Every nook and cranny had boxes stacked with numbers written on them.

"What in the world are all these boxes, Rachel?" Aunt Lettie posed the question before Karen could.

"My memories." Aunt Rachel poured Karen a cup of coffee and offered her cream. "I taught school for nearly fifty years. Those boxes are packed with memories from each of my years as a teacher. Each one represents a year. You can see I wrote that on the outside of the box.

Well, that answered the question as to how many boxes there were. Karen had been doing her best to count them without appearing too obvious.

"Rachel, there isn't a lot of room at Karen's place. You can't bring all of this."

"But they're my memories—my life," Rachel said, stopping everything she was doing. "I can't just get rid of them. They aren't the kind of things you can take to Goodwill or sell off to someone. Most are pictures my students drew for me, or letters from them or their parents. Some of the papers are my journals from my school year. And there are photographs."

Lettie shook her head. "There isn't room at Karen's for fifty boxes. We have to be mindful that Karen is giving up the entire basement of her house for us to live. It's a wonderful setup with four bedrooms and baths, but there simply isn't room, even in your bedroom, to house all of this."

Aunt Rachel's eyes filled with tears, but Lettie wouldn't back down. "Now, crying won't make more room. It's simply the way it is." Lettie reached for one of the little cakes Rachel had laid out.

Mom patted Rachel's hand. "Now, deary, don't let it overwhelm you. We will figure something out."

Again, Mom acted as referee to calm the situation. Karen had never really thought about it, but her mother often played this role. Even in the women's group at church, Karen had seen Mom take on this part.

"You know, they have small sheds you can buy," Helen offered. "I'm sure you have enough money that you could buy one of those, and Karen would probably let you put it at the farm."

Karen nodded. "There's plenty of room for something like that, Aunt Rachel."

"There's also the homestead house. We could store things there until we got a shed put in for you," Mom said, continuing to pat Rachel's hand.

Rachel looked at Karen's mom as if to judge whether she was telling the truth. After a moment she nodded, apparently satisfied, and Mom looked to the others.

"The same goes for everyone. If we find it impossible to contain the things you want to bring, we'll work it out. We'll build storage or buy it."

"That does bring up an important question," Lettie said, taking the position of leader once again. "What about money?"

"What do you mean?" Karen asked.

"Rent and utilities, food and gasoline. . .you know, for transportation to our appointments and such."

Karen hadn't really thought about how she was taking on every aspect of care for these women. Only Mom still drove, and she was doing that less and less. Karen would have to drive them to wherever they needed or wanted to go. Her life would no longer be her own.

"Ah. . .well. . .I don't want rent. I don't need it. Stan took good care of me. He had 401(k)s and other investments, as well as large life insurance policies from his work. I don't need your money."

"Well, we're certainly going to take care of our own needs. Food and medicine, clothes and such," Aunt Helen joined in. "You'll soon be broke taking care of an additional four people if you don't allow us to help."

"She's right, Karen. Just as I help." Mom looked to her sisters. "I guess we'll need to get an idea of what monthly groceries will cost. We'll watch the utilities and see how much they go up and act accordingly."

"I can figure out all of this," Rachel said, overcoming her tears. "I had to make budgets for the school. We need to make lists of everything we'll need to buy—special foods, body needs, medicines, supplements, et cetera."

"There, you see?" Aunt Lettie nodded and looked to Karen. "We can manage this for you. We'll get it all figured out and take care of our costs. You are doing us all a huge favor by taking us in. There are few options left to us, and this is like. . .well. . .it's an answer to our prayers."

Aunt Rachel and Aunt Helen nodded, and Mom just smiled. "'Religion that God our Father accepts as pure and faultless is this: to look after orphans and widows in their distress and to keep oneself from being polluted by the world.' That's James 1:27. I think we all fit that verse in one way or another. We'll look after each other."

Karen thought of how perfectly that verse fit them. Rachel might not be a widow, but she was now an orphan. An eighty-some-year-old orphan, but her parents were dead nevertheless.

"I hope we didn't make you feel obligated to do this, Karen." This came from Aunt Helen, but the others watched Karen carefully as if looking for some sign that their sister's comment might hold truth.

"I don't feel obligated at all. The truth is, since I lost Stan, I've been lonely. Even with Mom around. She had her own sorrow to deal with, and I know each of you do as well. We can bear one another's burdens, and then perhaps none of us will be overwrought with the sadness life has dumped on us."

"I may not have lost a husband, but I do feel as though I lost my children," Aunt Rachel said, tearing up again. "For all those years I had those little ones to teach and train. They still stop by on occasion, or I'll see them all grown up at church. They're special to me, but since I can no longer work my job—I feel as if they're so far away." A tear slipped down her cheek. "It's all I've ever had."

Aunt Lettie didn't chide or reprimand; instead she put her arm around Rachel and nodded. "I think we need each other. We always had each other when we were little. No one came between us, but then we found husbands or jobs, and those things took precedence. Now we're back to a place where no one else wants us, but we still have each other. I think we should be thankful for that. Few families remain as close as we have."

"It's true," Aunt Helen agreed. "I'm very close to my children, but what I have with my sisters goes well beyond that. It's a bond that I can't begin to explain. It's completely different from anything I had with friends or other family members."

"And now we'll draw Karen into our little group," Rachel said, sniffing back her tears.

Mom reached out, took hold of Karen's hand, and smiled.

"Thank you." Karen felt such love from these women. It was something she hadn't even realized was missing. Even her mother had been rather distant since losing Dad. It was funny how they had both been living separate lives in the same house. Even the times they came together to work or share meals, there had been a kind of wall between them—a wall of sorrow. Karen felt a huge piece of that wall give way.

"I'm so glad you have allowed me to share in your love," Karen said, fighting back her own tears.

Karen made her way to Sunday school class. Her mind wasn't at all on the study they'd been doing on the book of John, but rather on all the work she needed to get done on the house. Aunt Lettie was set to move in on Tuesday, and the grab bars still weren't up.

"You look pretty preoccupied," the class leader, Jean Stumbo, said as Karen took a seat.

"I guess I am. I've suddenly taken on a big responsibility, and I need to get some remodeling and repairs done on the house, and I don't even know where to start."

"Talk to the Over-Fifties class leader, John Thompson. You know that helping people in the fellowship is the mission of that class. They have contractors and designers, plumbers and electricians. Talk to him and he's bound to be able to connect you with the people you need."

"I'd totally forgotten that's what they do. I'll talk to him after class. Thanks for the suggestion."

Karen felt a little more relaxed as the class began and they spoke of Jesus talking to the woman at the well. She loved that story—loved that Jesus overlooked all of the social taboos and spoke to not only a Samaritan, but a woman to boot.

After class she went to where the Over Fifties met. Next door was the Sunday school class she and Stan had attended—the couples' class. When news came of her husband's death, no one even asked what she wanted before moving her over to the Widow and Widowers class. She didn't even have a chance to say goodbye to the many couples that she and Stan had called dear friends.

Of course, they had called or come by to see her after the funeral, but that didn't last more than a few months. She supposed her widowhood made them uncomfortable—a very obvious reminder that it could happen to them as it had to her.

Karen had tried not to take it personally, but it had been hard. She would never have stopped being friends with them had it happened the other way around.

John Thompson was still gathering his things when Karen knocked on the classroom door. The place where the class met was huge, and her knock seemed to echo in the now empty room.

"Hello, how can I help you?" John asked, stopping everything he was doing.

"I'm Karen Jacobs. I need to find someone who can help me remodel my house. . .well, maybe *remodel* is too strong a word. I have several older aunts and my mother who are going to be living with me. The house needs to be better set up for the elderly. You know, grab bars and such, but also just painted and some repairs to the floors here and there."

"Dan Polk. He and his boys would be perfect for the job. I'll give you his number, and I'll also give him a call to let him know you'll be in touch." He went to where his things were and wrote down the phone number and name. "Dan's a good friend, and I know he'd be fully capable of doing anything you needed."

He came back with the slip of paper. "Dan owns his own construction company and I know he just finished up a big job. He and his sons work together, and I'm thinking they'd have time to knock this right out for you."

"Thank you," Karen said, taking the piece of paper. "I appreciate that you offer this kind of help. I'll turn fifty next year, but I don't have any real skills to share that I can think of."

"We're all good at something. Sometimes we just don't think about it," John said smiling. "We've even had some of the ladies teach the younger girls how to clean house and cook, so don't sell yourself short."

Karen laughed. "I could teach them canning. I've been canning all summer and into the fall. Now I'm taking care of apples and black walnuts."

"See there, you have talents you weren't even thinking about. By the way, if you're of a mind to sell any of those black walnuts, I know my wife would like to stock up. She makes the most amazing banana nut bread and fudge using black walnuts."

"I'd be happy to sell you some." She put away the piece of paper John had given her and pulled out her own pen and tore off the top of her church bulletin. She jotted down her name and phone number and handed it to John. "Just give me a call. I can bring them with me to church next week. They'll be from a previous crop, however. This year's haven't dried out."

"That's not a problem. Thanks." John looked at the paper. "Karen. Thanks a lot."

Dan had just finished up supper and with the help of the boys loaded the dishwasher. They had been discussing their next project when his cell phone rang.

"This is Dan."

"Dan Polk?"

"Yes. How can I help you?"

"My name is Karen Jacobs. I got your name from John Thompson at church. I need some repair and remodel work done on my house. I've agreed to take in my three elderly aunts, and I need to arrange things for them—you know, freshen the place up and add grab bars. That kind of thing."

"Sure, I understand. My boys and I could come out there tomorrow and check things out. Would that work for you?"

"Yes. I'll be here all day."

"Good. Let's say about ten tomorrow morning."

"Sounds good," the feminine voice replied. She rattled off her address, and Dan barely had time to reach for a pen and paper.

"Will your husband be there also?"

"No, I'm a widow, Mr. Polk."

"Well, that's quite all right. I'm a widower. I'll see you in the morning." He shut down the call and looked to his sons. "Looks like we have a job. A lady from church needs help remodeling for her elderly aunts. Can you two come along with me in the morning?"

"Sure," Mark replied, putting away the butter.

"I was going to swing by the college to ask about midyear admission," David answered with a shrug, "but it can wait."

"Awesome. It's out of town a bit. North of the city. Doesn't sound like a bad job." He looked at the piece of paper where he'd written her address. What was it she said her name was? Johnson? No, Jacobs. Karen Jacobs. He added that to the paper.

CHAPTER 4

Karen wished her aunts could wait to move in until after the remodeling was complete, but it just wasn't to be. She managed to get a fresh coat of paint on the walls at least, but that was as much as she could manage. As it was, she'd been down there painting every night until the wee hours of the morning, and frankly, she was exhausted. It was funny. She could remember doing tasks like these twenty, even ten, years ago and not feeling so completely done in. Where had the time gone and why had it robbed her of so much?

Dan and his sons had shown up right on time, just as promised. She liked the look of the trio immediately. The boys favored their father, who was tall and lean with muscular arms. His brown hair was cut short in a no-nonsense fashion, and his boys had followed suit.

"Mrs. Jacobs," Dan said, extending his hand in greeting. "I'm Dan Polk. Just call me Dan. These are my boys, Mark and David."

"Please call me Karen," she replied, shaking his hand. "I'm very glad to meet you all."

"You've met us before," one of the boys declared.

"I have?" Karen shook her head. "When was that?"

"Sunday school," the other answered. "You were our favorite teacher."

She laughed. "Well, that was certainly a long, long time ago."

"It was. It wasn't long after we lost our mom. You were so kind and always helped us when we needed it."

Karen had vague recollections of two little boys who had been injured in a car accident that had taken their mother and sister. "I do remember you. Mark was the oldest and David didn't want to be separated from him, so the Sunday school superintendent asked if I minded having both boys in my class for second graders."

"That was us. I'm Mark, by the way." The young man smiled. "You really helped us get through a bad time."

David nodded. "I was so afraid to let Mark out of my sight. I constantly worried for over a year that I would lose him too."

"It was a hard time for everyone, that's to be sure," Dan interjected. "However, I'm sure Mrs. Jacobs—Karen—would appreciate if we focused in on her needs for the time being."

Karen looked at Dan. The sadness in his eyes she recognized all too well. It wasn't so much a sense of ongoing mourning as it was recognition of the loss. The subtle reminder of something precious that had been ripped away before its proper time.

"It's really all right. I remember your boys quite well. They were so quiet and sad. I remember wanting to ease their minds and help them to mend. I couldn't imagine the pain they had to be going through. But in all that time, I don't believe I ever met you, Dan. It seemed their grandmother came for them after class."

"Yes, she did. I went through a time of anger at God. I wouldn't step foot in church. I thought He'd been quite unfair toward me and mine. I'm ashamed to say I put up a wall between us. Thankfully, some Christians in my life wouldn't let me leave it that way." He smiled, and it went straight to Karen's heart. Here was someone who understood. Someone who knew the sense of loss that she felt.

"I'm glad you were able to work through it," Karen said, uncertain what else to say.

Dan nodded but was clearly uncomfortable. "So tell me about this remodel."

Karen showed him the lower level of her house. She told him what she had in mind. Dan's son Mark took notes, but all three were very attentive to her comments.

"I need to make sure that the rooms are easy for an elderly woman to manage. The windows need to be easy to open; there needs to be grab bars in the bathrooms." She opened the bathroom door in one of the bedrooms.

Dan stepped inside and seemed to consider the situation. "I don't know what you had in mind to spend, but if all the bathrooms are set up like this, I would suggest a remodel of the tub and shower."

"How so?"

"I'd remake it to an easy walk-in shower with a bench seat. There would be a bar along the side for easy reach, a handheld shower at a handicap level, as well as an overhead shower that could be switched off on the handheld device. We can make sure the floors are safe against slipping. They have some great kits nowadays."

"I hadn't even considered how hard it would be to climb over the edge of the tub to take a shower," Karen admitted. "That's a really good idea."

They came out into the commons area, and Dan nodded toward the stairs. "What about those? Are you getting a chair to go up and down the stairs?"

"I hadn't really thought about it too much. I wanted to do something for sure. What do you suggest?"

Dan walked around and looked at every nook and cranny before opening the french doors to step outside. He walked out under the deck and onto the gravel drive and looked up at the back of the house.

Karen followed him not knowing what else to do. She couldn't imagine what he was pondering, but soon enough he revealed his thoughts. "What about an elevator? They are more expensive, but it looks like we could put one in here on the back side of the house. I'd have to see what your situation is upstairs, of course."

"Do you put in elevators?"

He shook his head. "No, but I've got a good friend who does. Nowadays a lot of the well-to-do houses have them, and he started specializing in them. If you want, I can get him out here to look it over."

"Yes, that would be great. I'd like to at least know my options."

After another hour of discussion and exploration, Karen offered refreshments. "Why don't we go upstairs and have something to drink, and you can tell me what you think."

They followed her up the stairs, which came out in her large kitchen. She already had lemonade and cookies waiting and ushered them into the living room, where her mother was crocheting.

"Mom, this is Dan Polk and his sons, Mark and David. I used to teach them in Sunday school."

"I remember them well," her mother replied. "Your wife was part of our women's leadership team. I was so very sorry to lose her."

"Her work at the church was always important to her," Dan replied.

Once everyone was seated and the refreshments meted out,

Karen turned to her mother. "Dan had an idea about us putting in an elevator. We know that Aunt Leticia can't do stairs, and they're very difficult for Aunt Helen too. It won't be long before they could become a problem for all four of you."

"I hate elevators," Mom said, giving a shudder. "I always worry about getting stuck inside. However, I think it's probably a very good idea. If we needed to get up- or downstairs quickly, the elevator would seem the logical solution."

"It can be built so that it can hold all four of you," Dan said. "Of course, that's based on weight."

"None of the aunts are big women," Karen said. "I imagine if you put all of them together with Mom, the weight wouldn't be over six hundred pounds. Probably a lot less. I don't think Aunt Rachel weighs more than 110 dripping wet."

Her mother nodded. "It would be nice if everyone could ride together, especially if we needed it because a bad storm was on the way. Of course, that could be worrisome because of the electricity going out."

"It would have battery backup," Dan said. "In fact, we could set the whole house up with a generator system that would give you power all the time."

"What a great idea," Karen said. "We always lose power at least once every spring and sometimes more. I remember when we lost power for three days several years ago due to that late-spring ice storm we had."

"That was a bad one," Dan admitted. "A generator would be run on propane and could be set up so that the transfer was automatic, and you wouldn't have to do anything. If a storm knocked out the electricity, the generator would just automatically take over."

"Oh, that does sound nice," Karen's mother admitted.

Mark jotted something in his notebook, while David helped

himself to another cookie. Karen felt a sense of calm settle over her. She hadn't realized how concerned she had been about the house being safe. It seemed Dan had lots of great ideas.

After agreeing to all the changes, Karen wrote Dan out a deposit check and saw him and the boys to the door.

"Thank you so much for all the wonderful ideas. I think this is going to make the house so much nicer for everyone."

"My pleasure." He smiled, and Karen thought it charming the way the lines around his eyes crinkled. It had been a long time since Karen had even bothered to notice such things.

"I think that went very well," Mother said, coming to stand beside Karen.

"I do too. I feel so much better just knowing Dan knows what to do. I certainly wouldn't know where to start."

Her mother laughed. "Of course you knew where to start. You got help from someone who knew what they were doing."

Karen smiled. "I suppose you're right."

Two days later, family members moved Aunt Leticia into the house. Marlene, her husband, and their kids showed up with Leticia at eight in the morning. By noon everything was moved in and partially arranged.

"We're going to be having a bunch of work done, so I wouldn't unpack everything," Karen told Marlene. "No sense in having to just pack it up again so that the workmen can do what's needed."

"You didn't need to make a lot of changes for me," Aunt Leticia declared. "I'm perfectly capable of stepping over the edge of the tub. Seems a waste to put in a whole new shower."

"I did it more for myself than you," Karen replied. "I want

to know that you'll be safe. I would feel terrible if something happened to you and I could have prevented it."

"Bah! I've been taking care of myself for a long time. You needn't fret."

"I'm glad she's arranging for all these changes," Mother interjected. "I want life to be easy for all of us. I even insisted we hire someone to clean once a week. I know we could do it ourselves, but honestly, I'm getting lazy in my old age."

Leticia nodded. "I suppose a cleaning girl would be nice. I can't get down on the ground to scrub around the toilet anymore."

"We have a nice group of people at church who share their talents with the congregation. I know for a fact there are several who have cleaning services, Aunt Leticia. So not only will it help us, but it will give them extra business as well. It will be good for all of us."

"When is Helen coming?" Aunt Leticia asked.

"Next week. She's still arranging for all of her extra stuff to be sold. Rachel said she wanted to order a shed for her things, but I told her I could get Dan to just build one while he's here. I guess we'll see which way is better suited to our time schedule."

Mother smiled and looped her arm through Aunt Leticia's. "It's going to be so good to have all of you here. Just like old times."

"We're going to leave now, unless you need something else," Marlene declared. "I'll be back to see you before we leave for California, Mother. So if there's anything else you need, just let me know." She turned to Karen and smiled. "You don't know what this means to me. I know she'll be safe and have loved ones around her. It gives me great peace of mind."

"I'm glad to do it." Karen gave Marlene's shoulder a pat. "Don't worry about a thing."

"Glad you could meet me. This won't take long," Dan said as he sat down to lunch with Robbie Mercer.

"It's good timing for me. I'm not on any jobs at the moment." He picked up a menu and gave it a momentary glance before casting it aside. "I don't know why I bother to look. I get the same turkey club every time I come here."

Dan chuckled. "I know what you mean. For me it's the cheeseburger and fries."

The waitress came and took their orders, then returned quickly with the coffeepot. She filled each man's cup and smiled. "Cream?"

"No, this is fine," Dan said, knowing Robbie drank his coffee black.

Once she was gone, Dan asked about Robbie's wife and kids and then got right down to business. "There's a group of women from my church. Well, at least two of them are. I imagine the others will soon follow suit. Anyway, these women live north of town. The owner, Karen Jacobs, is a widow who lives with her mother and is soon to have her mother's three sisters move in with them as well. I'm remodeling to make it more accessible and safer for the older women."

"Where do I come in?"

"We've discussed the possibility of an elevator. Given the setup, I think it would be better than getting a chair lift for the stairs."

Robbie asked questions about the house and Dan filled him in on the details. "I don't think it will be complicated. I can construct anything you need."

"Can I come out this afternoon?" Robbie asked.

"I have to admit, I was hoping you might have the time. We

need to get on this as soon as possible. I'm already working on the remodels and hope to have those all taken care of before November."

"I'm not sure I could get the elevator in that quickly."

"No, probably not, but we're not overly worried. It's mostly a precaution for storm season and situations where the women can't manage the stairs. I know Karen has already made arrangements to see to their needs in the meantime, but the sooner the better as far as I'm concerned."

The waitress returned with their orders. She waited only long enough to see if there was anything else they needed, then left the two to their discussion.

Robbie pulled out a small pocket notebook. "Give me the address, and let me know what time works for you, and I'll be there."

Dan took the notebook and jotted down the address along with a couple of directions. "It can be confusing as to where to turn, but this will see you through."

"Thanks. I'm not familiar with that end of town. Grew up on the south side." He looked over the address and instructions. "This seems clear enough."

Dan picked up his burger. "Good."

An hour later, Dan showed Karen the shower kits he'd picked out. "As you can see, there's a seat, as well as built-in grab bars. The entry step is low, and I'll attach grab rails on the outside to make it easier for them."

"These are lovely. I like the built-in shelves for their shampoo and bath wash. I can't imagine that they won't be pleased."

"I'll get them ordered. My supplier told me he has four in stock, so I can pick them up today and get started tomorrow."

"That's wonderful."

He met her smiling gaze and felt something he hadn't felt in over fifteen years. He couldn't exactly explain it. It was like a tug—a pull on his heart to take notice. But notice of what he wasn't exactly certain.

Karen was like no one else he'd known. She was very casual and laid-back. Not at all anxious about what was going on with her home. Dan had already been impressed by her willingness to take in her family, but the fact that she was willing to do so much to consider their every need had really touched him.

And it didn't hurt that she was pretty. He'd heard her mention that she was almost fifty, but she didn't look it. He would have guessed early forties. She had brown hair that didn't show even a hint of gray. Of course, she might color it.

"Did you hear what I said?"

He shook his head and forced his thoughts to focus on what Karen was saying. "I'm sorry. Daydreaming, I guess."

"I said someone just pulled up. I'm thinking it will be your elevator man."

Dan nodded. "Good. Now we can really get down to business."

Karen laughed. "I thought we were already doing a pretty good job of that."

Dan wondered if she felt the strange energy that seemed to flow between them. He was clearly attracted to this widow. He could even imagine himself spending time with her. . .a lot of time. These were thoughts he'd never had before, and for a moment he enjoyed the feeling. But soon enough he remembered the only other time he'd tried to date after Geena's death. That hadn't gone well at all. Maybe this wouldn't either. Maybe he should just forget about it and resign himself to staying single.

CHAPTER 5

Two weeks later with all of her aunts finally settled in the house, Karen sat in church marveling at the way her life had changed in such a very short time. She had been bored and lonely, but now there was very little time for that. Every evening the family gathered downstairs at the house and shared thoughts about the remodel and plans for the days to come. Karen had to admit it was actually going much smoother than she'd figured.

"Ephesians 2:8–9 is where I'd like to start," the pastor began. There was the routine shuffling of pages as nearly four thousand people in the congregation turned to the passage in their Bibles.

"'For it is by grace you have been saved, through faith—and this is not from yourselves, it is the gift of God—not by works, so that no one can boast.'" He stopped and looked out over the congregation. "This is a critical passage about who we are in Christ, and I hope today that if you have any doubts about your salvation or the way to come to salvation, this passage will make it clear to you."

Karen glanced over to see Aunt Leticia was already growing sleepy. Old age and a life of hard work had taken its toll on her.

"I have to say that today's message was laid on my heart through a series of circumstances. One conversation in particular that I had with a young man at the prison in Lansing comes to mind. This young man explained to me about good behavior and how being good could merit him an early release. It was all a matter of him doing the right thing. As we talked about salvation, I could see that he had the same thought for getting right with God. He told me that he had been taught that if he was good and did good things, he would go to heaven.

"I countered, however, that nothing we do can give us salvation, and I shared these verses with him, reminding him that it is only by God's grace that we are saved. That was hard for him to hear. After all, he was in a system where it very much mattered what he did and didn't do. He had the power to bring further chastisement onto his head if he did wrong. Or he could do right and bring reward. But that's the way this world works.

"We know if we do wrong there will be consequences. Very seldom do we get away with doing wrong. There are also consequences for doing the right thing, and sometimes those aren't all that pleasant. As a Christian we strive to do good—to do God's will to His glory. As Ephesians 2:10 states, 'For we are God's handiwork, created in Christ Jesus to do good works, which God prepared in advance for us to do.' But don't get confused. Those good works will not save us. Only the blood of Jesus Christ spilled out at the cross will cover our sins. Only Jesus can show us the way, because He is the way."

Karen nodded, as did many of the others around her. She had grown up in this church, remembered a time when there were no more than one hundred people who attended. Many of those folks were still attending and sat nearby. They were like one big family, and it truly blessed her in a way she couldn't explain.

When her husband died, Karen had been deeply touched at the way the church stepped up to offer consolation and care. This was a body of believers who put their lives into action to be the hands and feet of Jesus. Of course, they had moved her out of her beloved Sunday school class, but even that was done with the belief they were helping her.

"Of course we often hear folks complaining because bad things happen to good people. It's hard for us to accept that, when we belong to God, everything doesn't just fall into perfect order. Give me a show of hands: How many of you have questioned why bad things happen when you faithfully belong to God?" Hands went up from nearly every person in the sanctuary, including Karen.

The pastor smiled and nodded. "I thought as much. See, one of the things that folks have gotten wrong is that a man or woman of God will never face adversity or difficult times. I'm telling you though, Satan is going to do his utmost to cause you trouble. You might as well have put a 'kick me' sign on your back."

There was a lot of chuckling at that, but Karen knew the truth of it. She had struggled with a lot of grief in her life. Frustrations and problems that God could have made go away He allowed to remain in her life. She remembered as a girl asking her mother and father why God let these things happen. Her mother said it was to grow her faith. Her dad just pointed to the fact that the world was fallen.

When Stan died, Karen had felt as if God had abandoned her altogether. For those first few days she had alternated between sobbing out her heart to Him and railing at Him. The loss had been greater than any she had ever known, and it seemed so unfair. She was a Christian. She served at church faithfully. She gave to charities and supported missionaries. She tried to always have a good attitude and live an example of God's love. And still Stan died without warning.

"Many a person believes that if you become a Christian, everything in your life will fall into order and be perfect. I'm telling you that nothing could be farther from the truth. God never promised us an easy time of it. Even Simon Peter faced the fact that Satan had asked to sift him as wheat." He paused for a moment and stepped to one side of the podium. "Jesus told him this and that He was praying for him. I have to admit, had I been Simon Peter, I would have said, 'Well, instead of praying, can't You just make Satan leave me alone?'" There were nods of agreement and a few chuckles from the congregation.

Karen had to admit she had thought that herself. She glanced over at her mother, who was smiling. Their gazes met and they nodded at each other.

"But Jesus knew in Peter's case, just as He knows in each of ours, that the bad times can help us to develop our faith, and when that faith is fully developed, we can be of use in helping others.

"Life is hard, folks. That's the way it is. But as Christians we need to get it right and understand that we aren't alone in any of this. Our salvation comes as a gift of grace. We don't earn it, and we cannot buy it. Jesus already bought it with His blood. There's nothing we need to do but accept or reject. That is one choice God has left up to us.

"It's the same when bad times come. We have the choice to turn to God or turn away. We can bear misery on our own or give ourselves to God's care and protection."

He closed his Bible. "Ultimately, no matter how things go, remember that as children of the living God, you are put here to bring Him glory. Glory in the bad times and good. Glory. . .even when you don't understand why things are the way they are."

He added a few more thoughts, then prayed. Karen tucked her Bible inside her large tote purse and prepared to stand for the final song. It was a routine she knew only too well. One which actually gave her a sense of order and well-being.

The pastor stepped aside for the worship band to take over, and soon music filled the church. Karen's mind was already on the rest of the day. She had a casserole warming in the oven at home with fresh apple butter and homemade bread to go along with it. After that she'd work with the black walnuts.

"Ready to head home?" her mother asked.

"I am. What about the rest of you?" Karen looked at her aunts.

"More than ready. I didn't sleep well last night. I think it's being in a new place," Aunt Rachel declared. "I'm going to need a nap."

"We're all going to need a nap," Aunt Leticia countered. "That's what Sunday afternoons are for. Resting in the Lord."

Karen smiled. "Well, as for me, after lunch I'm going to be doing the walnut stomp."

"I'll help you with that," her mother said. "I don't need a nap."

They walked out to Karen's Sequoia. She put her things on the driver's seat and went to help her aunts climb aboard. It dawned on her that here was something else she needed to change. The SUV was much too high for her aunts, and without help, they were hard-pressed to get into the vehicle.

She had just gotten Aunt Leticia settled when she heard someone calling her name. Karen turned and found Dan approaching.

"What can I do for you?" she asked, closing the car door.

"I wondered if you'd mind if I came over to take a few measurements. I thought I had everything but can't seem to locate a couple of important notes." He smiled, and Karen had to admit it did something to her.

"Of course. You can join us for lunch if you want. It's nothing special, just a chicken casserole and other odds and ends."

"No, I'll have lunch with the boys and then be over. Probably no later than two."

She nodded. "We'll see you then."

Dan was surprised when the boys decided to follow him out to Karen's. They drove separately because they were talking about catching a movie later.

The boys had changed into old clothes, while Dan still wore his Sunday slacks and button-down shirt. He knew the measurements weren't going to require he get dirty, so he figured he'd just save time and go as he was.

"It's nice to see you again," Karen's mother said in greeting. He liked Mrs. Langley. She was just down-to-earth and full of joy. He'd seldom seen any other woman her age be as happy as she was.

"Sorry we didn't get a chance to talk after service. I hope you're feeling better than on Friday. Karen told me you were having trouble with neuropathy pain. I've heard that can be a terrible thing to deal with."

"It can be, but I'm much better now. Thanks." She looked beyond him to the boys. "Good to see you two, as well. Karen's out in the little grove of walnut trees. She's picking up walnuts and then stripping off the green husks. You can't miss her."

"You boys go ahead; I'm just going to get those measurements up here and then clear out and leave you to your afternoon."

"I'm just going to be helping Karen. My sisters are taking naps.

Do you need to go downstairs?" Mrs. Langley asked.

"No. I just needed to make sure of the elevator compartment. I'm meeting with Robbie to go over the final blueprints. I'm sure we have everything, but I always like to double-check and take multiple measurements."

"The old 'measure twice, cut once,' eh?" She smiled and it reminded him of Karen's smile.

"Exactly." He turned to his sons. "I guess I'll see you later." He headed off to the far end of the kitchen where they had determined to put the elevator. A part of him felt strangely jealous that they were going to be spending time with Karen, while he might not even see her.

How had that happened? How had Karen Jacobs managed to capture his attention so quickly? Especially since Dan was determined to never give his heart to anyone again.

~~♬~~

"Well, hello," Karen said as she hoisted a box full of walnuts into the back of the utility cart hooked up to her riding mower.

"We came to help," Mark declared.

"Oh, no. I can't have you doing that. You'll stain your clothes and hands."

"We don't mind at all. It's been a long time since we helped with black walnuts," David said. "Besides, we've got work gloves in the truck. I'll go get 'em."

He walked off at a good clip, while Mark began nudging walnuts into a pile with the toe of his boot. "Turned out to be a nice day, didn't it? I thought from the look of the sky this morning that maybe it was going to rain."

Karen wiped her forehead with the back of her sleeve. "I still think it'll rain. Probably later this evening.

David was already headed back, so they focused on the work at hand. Karen was grateful that the boys were such hard workers. Her aunts had tried to help the day before, but they weren't steady enough to roll the walnuts underfoot to tear off the husks, and it was hard for them to bend and pick up walnuts off the ground. Karen had suggested they wait and help with arranging them to dry, and they agreed.

The boys were young and strong, and they made the work seem easy. Time passed quickly, and before Karen knew it, they had cleaned up the area under three trees.

"This will hold me awhile, boys. Thanks so much for the help." She straightened and stretched her back. It was so much harder to be bent over for hours than it used to be. It was just another reminder that she too was getting older.

Mark pulled off his stained gloves. "I guess we'll wash up and head to town. David and I plan to catch a movie."

"Well, once these nuts have cured, I'll see to it that you get some. As it is, I can send you home with apple butter, jelly, and sauce."

"That sounds good," David replied. "I'm a fan of all three."

They walked back to the house while Karen drove the mower over to the barn. Inside they had an entire setup for processing the walnuts. She didn't bother to unload the boxes but parked them close to the area where some of the other walnuts had been spread out to dry. She was just closing up the barn door when Dan appeared.

"I didn't know you were still here."

"I got to talking with your mother," he answered. "Time just slipped away."

"Mom can be that way. What did you talk about?"

"Mostly you." He smiled and Karen felt her stomach clench. She smiled in return.

"That doesn't sound like a very interesting topic."

"On the contrary. I was most impressed to learn about your life here on the farm."

Karen wasn't at all sure what her mother had been telling him, but she wasn't about to make this conversation about her. "So what did you think of the sermon this morning?"

"Which part? That we can't earn our salvation, or that bad things will happen to good people, but it's to God's glory."

"The latter. That's a tough pill to swallow. How can bad things bring God glory? I mean truly evil, bad things. They are as far removed from God as anything could be."

"True. Like when a drunk driver killed my wife and daughter and injured the boys."

They had started walking back toward the house, and Karen paused. "Exactly. That's not glorifying in any way that I can see."

"I asked myself that too. The first few months I was a mess. Had it not been for good Christian friends who came after me, I would have walked away from God. I didn't see anything of Him in what happened. I felt He had betrayed me—that He was cruel."

"Do you still feel that way?"

He gave a sigh. "No, but I didn't come to that conclusion easily. I don't think God wanted my wife and daughter to be killed by that drunk. I don't think He was pleased that a seven- and five-year-old had to struggle to survive the accident. I don't even think God particularly wanted me feeling so hopeless and desperate that I was ready to take my own life."

"No!" Karen hadn't meant to speak out loud. "I'm sorry, I guess it just stunned me. I wouldn't expect that of you, but then I really don't have a right to say one way or another. We don't know each other all that well."

Dan looked at her and nodded. "But I'd like to know you better."

Karen knew in that moment that she wanted nothing more. "I'd like that too."

For a minute, neither one said anything more, but then Dan started to speak again. "I don't often talk about the accident, but a real miracle came out of it, and that was to God's glory. I still experienced loss and pain. My wife and child still died, and my boys had a long road to recovery, but my faith was forever changed. My relationship with God was deepened in a way I can't begin to explain. Not only that, but the man who caused the accident. . .found God."

"He did? I guess I wouldn't have stopped to think about how he came out in all of that."

"I didn't want to," Dan admitted. "But once I was on the road to healing, I came to realize I had to go see the guy and forgive him."

Karen frowned. "That couldn't have been easy."

"It wasn't. My boys were still struggling with the loss of their mother, but I was convicted by my Bible studies that I needed to extend forgiveness to that man. He was young, and as my friends pointed out, what I did or didn't do might have a profound effect on him for the rest of his life."

"Still, that couldn't have been easy."

Dan shrugged. "That's an understatement. It wasn't, but it was the right thing to do. I went to see him at his parents' house. He was just twenty. I had learned that he had at one time had a full scholarship to the University of Kansas. He was a brilliant student with top grades, but when he went off to college, he got caught up with the wrong crowd and started drinking. He was coming home for the weekend when he hit Geena's car head-on. He wasn't even hurt." Dan paused for a moment. "Well, that's not exactly true."

Karen waited for him to continue. She heard the sadness in Dan's voice and couldn't help but feel for him. It had been such a terrible loss. She knew that loss—at least from the aspect of losing a spouse. A dearly beloved spouse.

"That boy was a mess. The accident had left him devastated, and when I showed up, he told me later, he'd hoped I'd come to kill him. He just couldn't live with what he'd done. He couldn't bear the truth that he'd killed two people and wounded two others. Children, at that.

"We sat there in his living room, and I explained that God had helped to get me through the pain and that I wanted to come and tell him that I forgave him. I knew he would have to live with what happened the rest of his life, but I didn't want him to bear it without knowing that I wasn't going to hold it against him."

"That had to be difficult for him to understand." Karen tried to imagine herself in the same place.

"It was. His family wasn't involved in church or a faith of any kind. As I sat there and explained my relationship with God, they seemed to drink in every word. Before I left, they were asking me how they could know more. I told them about our church, promised to send someone out to see them, and invited them to one of my Bible studies. It was the start of changing that entire family."

"How wonderful. That must have been so amazing to see."

"It was, and it didn't stop there. That boy went on to give his life to God in a big way. He ended up going to seminary and eventually served on the mission field."

"So the bad thing that happened to good people brought

God glory," Karen murmured.

"Three people came to the Lord because I forgave, and who knows how many others through that young man's ministry. I made sure the boys knew about it and why it was so important to forgive. It was hard for them, but in time they came to understand. It's made all the difference for us. It would have been so easy for me to turn to drink, and who knows where that would have ended up. I could have ended up taking someone else's life."

"Thank you for sharing that with me. I guess I was just not seeing the possibilities of what God could and would do."

"Sometimes it's hard to see, but we need to keep trying. If we ask, God will show us."

Karen smiled. "I do believe that."

CHAPTER 6

After that, Karen and Dan's relationship changed. They spent a lot of time talking after Dan finished his work for the day. Karen even started helping him with little projects that didn't require her being very knowledgeable about construction.

Karen wasn't at all sure where the relationship was headed, but she found herself hoping it would continue—that maybe they had a future together. She was still rather awestruck to even be thinking that way. Stan had only been gone five years.

"But he is gone, and he's not coming back," she whispered to herself in front of the mirror that morning. She thought of Stan and knew that he'd like Dan. They would have been friends in another place and time.

Leaning forward, she checked for gray. She was glad to find it was still absent. She didn't like the idea of it changing. As it was, she'd cut her hair much shorter than she ever thought she would. When Stan had been alive, she'd worn it long because he liked it that way. After he died, she'd cut it off at the shoulder for ease of living. Now it was even shorter. She wondered if Dan liked short brown hair with a bit of natural curl.

She made her way out to the kitchen and gathered the things

she'd need to make pancakes. Her mom and aunts had mentioned the night before that they were hungry for blueberry pancakes, and Karen had volunteered to fix them for everyone.

It wasn't long before Mom showed up with her sisters in tow. "I'll be glad when we have that elevator," Mom declared. "Driving back and forth isn't a chore I would cherish come winter."

"No, I'm sure not. I was just thinking that I need to rethink my car situation. The Sequoia is too tall for easy access."

"You don't need to change it for us," Leticia said, joining them in the kitchen. "You've already had so much to change."

"It's not safe. Besides, the Sequoia's getting long in the tooth. I was thinking of trading it in anyway. Maybe a nice car with a backseat to sit three. You all are small enough so that it wouldn't be too crowded, and even if it is, it would just be for a short trip."

She whipped up the pancakes and had just started pouring them on the griddle when Aunt Leticia spoke up again.

"So you and Daniel make a nice couple. I think the two of you should consider courting."

"Nobody courts anymore, Sister," Aunt Helen countered. "They date."

"Or as the kids say, they hang out," Aunt Rachel added with a nod.

"They've already been hanging out," Aunt Leticia continued. "I think they're good together. It's easy to see that he needs a wife. His shirts are always wrinkled."

"Aunt Leticia, I'm sure they're wrinkled because of the hard work he does." Karen flipped the first of the pancakes. They were nice and golden brown.

Mother grabbed the dishes. "It would be nice for you to go out with someone. You're too young to stay a widow."

"I'm nearly fifty, and I don't see that as too young to remain a widow. It's not like I have children who need a father. And I certainly don't need a husband to help share expenses. After all, I have all of you now." She beamed them a smile and began depositing pancakes onto a platter.

"There's more to life than kids and money," Aunt Rachel said thoughtfully. "I had both of those things, but I still wished sometimes that I had a husband."

"You should have married," Aunt Leticia replied. "We all thought so." The sisters nodded in agreement.

"Maybe it's not too late," Karen said, her tone teasing. "There are a few older widowers at the church."

"Goodness, no." Rachel's face flushed. "I'm well past all of that. And now I have all of you. I have no need for a husband."

"Well, I still say Karen needs to find someone, and Dan seems perfect. As a widower, he knows the pain of losing a spouse, so he'll understand Karen's heart.

Karen focused on the pancakes so that her aunts and mother wouldn't know just how deeply their comments were disturbing her. Ever since Dan had come into her life, she'd been considering the idea of remarriage for the first time. There really was something about him—about them when they were together. It both frightened and exhilarated Karen.

Dan picked up the newspaper and was hit with the past. There on the front page was a photograph of Nora Edwards Fisher. The woman he'd dated a few years after Geena's death.

He hadn't wanted to date, but everyone insisted that he needed to find a mother for the boys. He reminded them that the boys had a mother, but they insisted that they needed a woman's influence in their lives.

Nora Edwards worked in the building permits office, and she and Dan found they were often thrown together on one project or another. He had enjoyed talking with her, discussing the future and things they both wanted to do and accomplish.

She was a beautiful woman, even now. He glanced again at the photograph. She was dressed impeccably—probably some expensive designer that he'd never heard of. Her blond hair was perfectly coiffed, and her smile still seemed to light up the room around her.

He had asked her to join him for one of the church's picnics. That had been their first date. She had actually flown kites with the boys—something that gained her extra points with the two. He remembered how they had talked and talked while the boys played. She was an intelligent woman—and so beautiful. She was the very epitome of grace and elegance.

Dan turned the paper over. She was also the epitome of betrayal. Dan had come to the conclusion after a few months of dating that she was the perfect woman to step into Geena's shoes. She understood his feelings toward his first wife. She agreed that they should keep pictures of her around the house to remind the boys of who she was. Dan had thought her very nearly perfect in her detailed attention to his needs as well as those of the boys. But all of that changed.

Without much of any warning, she broke off their relationship. The pain it caused Dan was nothing compared to that of his sons. They had become quite accepting that she was going to be their new mother. They were delighted at the prospect, but then she had crushed them by leaving Dan to take up with James Fisher, a politician with big ambitions.

Dan had asked her why…what had he done wrong? She had laughed it off, telling him he was just much too serious for her. She wasn't looking to get married and start a family. Dan remembered telling her that it would have been nice to know that before his boys had gotten attached.

Anger resurfaced as if it had been yesterday. How could she have been so cruel? Within a few months she had married the very wealthy James Fisher and helped with his campaign for governor. He had won, making her the First Lady of the state, a role she played with great enthusiasm.

He shook off the memory and forced back his anger. That was the past, and there was nothing positive that could be done by allowing it to have a role in the present. He thought of Karen. She was much more down-to-earth, and she loved God. Nora hadn't had time for a deep relationship with God. Church was merely a place to be seen. Dan had convinced himself that it didn't matter, that once they were married, Nora would see the importance of God. Thankfully, things fell apart.

As he drove north on Highway 75 to Karen's, he remembered his conversation with Karen about making everything bring glory to God. Nora certainly hadn't been one of those things. Dan hadn't been gracious or kind when she broke up with him. He'd railed at her for her betrayal and the hurt she was going to cause his boys. His anger had managed the entire scene.

"My boys have come to care a lot about you. They were thinking you might become their mother."

"I don't want the responsibility of children. I've never wanted children," she had snapped. "I thought I made that clear."

"I thought by the way you were continuing to be with me that you had changed your mind." Dan could barely keep his tongue civil. He wanted nothing more than to say all the hurtful, mean things he was feeling. Anything in order to hurt her as much as she had hurt him.

He turned off the highway and made his way down the long country road. Why did Nora have to come to mind now? He had no interest in her anymore. She was a wealthy widow who, as the paper noted, was quite busy with charity fundraising. They had nothing in common and no need to ever cross paths again.

Karen's place came into view, and Dan forced Nora from his thoughts. He prayed for peace of mind and forgiveness for his anger before heading up to the front door.

To his surprise, Karen's mother opened the door before he could even knock. "Welcome. Come in. We were just finishing breakfast. Would you like some pancakes and coffee?"

Dan smiled. "No thanks. I had breakfast already."

"Well at least come in and say hello to everyone."

He followed her into the kitchen. Karen sat at the table sipping her coffee. A single, half-eaten blueberry pancake remained on her plate.

"Hello everyone," he said, nodding toward each of the ladies. "How are you all this fine day?"

"It is quite fine, isn't it?" Rachel declared. "I've been contemplating a walk around the pond."

"That sounds like fun," her sister Helen replied. "I'll join you if you don't mind."

"Dan, would you like something to eat? Or maybe some coffee before you get started?" Karen asked.

"Your mother already asked, but no thank you. I ate breakfast."

No doubt those blueberry pancakes were much tastier than the whole grain toast he'd had.

"We were just finishing up. Is Robbie still coming this morning?"

"Yes. We're going to really get going on the elevator."

"Glad to hear it," Leticia told him. "We definitely need to have it in place before first snow."

"Well, hopefully that will be a while yet." Dan smiled, but the older woman didn't so much as nod.

Karen got up and moved her dishes to the counter beside the sink. She opened the lower cupboard door and cleaned her plate off into the trash can. "I'm excited to see how all of this works. It's been fun watching the shaft go up. You've made it all look so simple."

"I've been impressed with how the new addition for the elevator looks as though it had always been there," Karen's mother declared. "It's quite impressive that you could do that."

Dan smiled. "I'm glad you approve."

"You go ahead with Dan," Leticia said, coming to take Karen's dish from her. "It's Rachel's and my turn to clear the dishes."

Karen allowed her to take charge and looked to Dan. "I guess that's that."

"Someone's pulled into the drive," her mother said. "I suppose that will be your man."

Dan nodded. "I suppose it will be."

He and Karen made their way downstairs and out the back french doors, just as Robbie brought his truck to a stop at the back of the house. Behind him was an even larger truck that no doubt had the elevator equipment.

"Good to see you made it," Dan called as Robbie exited his truck.

Dan pulled the tarp off the bottom of the elevator compartment. Robbie had asked him to leave it unfinished to make installation easier.

"My guys and I will get to work. You two should probably stay close by, but out of the way." He smiled. "Like maybe have a seat at that table over there and wait for further instructions."

Dan laughed. "I guess I'm game if you are, Karen."

"Sure. Why not."

They took a seat at the table and watched as Robbie and his men began unloading things. Dan had never seen his friend actually put in an elevator and was torn between getting up close and personal and remaining seated with Karen.

"I am still amazed to think we're going to have an elevator in the house," Karen said, zipping up her jacket.

"It's a little chilly out here. Would you rather go inside?" Dan asked.

"No, this is fine. Feels good and I know it's going to warm up quick. Just look at that clear sky. The sun will have nothing to hide behind." She shifted to look at him more directly. "I've been thinking about what you said about how God was glorified in the death of your wife. I honestly can't say that I did anything to bring Him glory when Stan died. I was in such a state of shock that I barely functioned. At church they moved me quickly from the couples' class to the widow and widower's class. I realized yesterday that I never really had a chance to say goodbye. Not to Stan, nor to the friends who were such an important part of our lives. Everything just sort of stopped."

He nodded and drew a deep breath. "I had no chance to say goodbye either. I think that might have been one of the hardest parts."

"I just keep wondering if there is still a way to bring God glory."

"There's always a way to do that, but you know, I think you have brought God glory in Stan's passing."

"How so?" Confusion was clearly written on her face.

"Well, just look at what you've done here. You've taken care of your mother and now your aunts. You've given of yourself in a way that you might not have been able to if Stan were still here. I'm sure if folks in heaven know what we're up to here on earth—that he's very proud. You've lived the very example of God's love."

"I don't suppose I would have thought of it that way. It just seems right to take care of family. Especially if you have the means."

"But some folks don't see it that way. They hang on tight to their money and talents for fear they might need them someday for personal use. Not that saving for the future is wrong, but they give little thought to the folks who so desperately need them in the present. You aren't that way. I'm betting you've always given freely of yourself. Helping out where you could. Loving folks and making them feel cared about. You even make me feel cared about."

"You are cared about." She glanced away as if she'd said too much.

"So are you." His words were barely audible, but they made her look back.

"When I lost Stan," she began, "I wasn't sure I would ever be able to enjoy life again. Little by little I've found ways to appreciate things around me. Things that Stan and I enjoyed together. Things that I've learned to love since losing him." She frowned and shook her head. "I never thought I'd consider finding joy in another person—like I did in him. But. . .well. . .I'm starting to think that things are changing. I think God is healing my heart, and maybe that's where I can glorify Him."

Dan nodded. "Like I said, I think you've glorified Him all along, Karen."

She met his gaze. "Thank you. . .for saying so. . .for being here to talk to. I've never been able to talk much about Stan before, but you make it easy."

"Maybe because I know what it's like to suffer that loss." He smiled. "But on the other hand, I find it easy to share my thoughts with you. Maybe God has brought us together for more than a remodel and an elevator."

She laughed. "I think you may be right. No, I'm sure you're right."

CHAPTER 7

The next few days saw the installation of the elevator go off without a hitch. Dan was impressed with the work Robbie did and told him so.

"I knew you were good at this, but you make it seem easy, and I know it's not," Dan told him as Robbie packed up for the day.

"Well, when it's all you do, you can get pretty good at it. Look, I'll be back in the morning, and I think I'll be able to finish off by noon or so. You can feel free then to move forward with your final touches. It'll be easiest for future inspections and such to arrange things at the bottom like we discussed."

"Not a problem. The boys are working on another project of ours, but they'll be here tomorrow to help me. We'll do it up just as you instructed."

Robbie nodded and gathered his things. "See you then."

Dan replaced the tarp and secured the still-open area of the elevator shaft. He was meticulous in seeing it done exactly right. No sense at this late date doing anything to risk the project.

"You always that focused on details?" Leticia asked him.

He turned and gave her a smile. "I've learned over the years that attention to detail will often save your entire project."

"I'm one for details myself," the old woman replied. "I've enjoyed watching you on the various projects you've done for us. I have to say that the arrangements have made my life much easier. I'm sure my sisters would agree with me when I say that you've done good by Karen."

He finished with the tarp and checked for any forgotten tools before walking over to the patio, where Leticia sat. Overhead was the upstairs deck, which reminded him that he still had some work to do on it.

"I'm glad I could help. Glad I had the time. We've just taken on a new house build, so my time will be more limited in the weeks to come. We're going to strive to get the frame up before winter so we can spend our time inside when things get really cold and messy."

"You like my niece, don't you?" she asked without warning.

Dan could feel his eyes widen, but he did his best not to act shocked. "I do. She's a very nice person, and we share a lot of common interests."

Leticia nodded. "I think there could be more for the two of you."

Her bold thoughts on the matter left Dan momentarily speechless, but that didn't stop Leticia from continuing. "Karen has been too long alone, and it seems the same for you. God said it wasn't good for man to be alone."

"Indeed He did," Dan replied.

"Well, it's not good for a woman either."

Dan wasn't sure what to say. It was obvious the old woman was doing her best at matchmaking.

"You're both old enough to know that life is too precious to waste. Time passes much too quickly. You've already wasted fifteen years being alone. Don't you want a companion?"

He cleared his throat nervously. "I have to admit, until taking this job, I really didn't. But I'm starting to think like you, that there could be something more for Karen and me."

"Good." The old woman gave him a nod. "As long as you're working in that direction. My sisters and I think we could tolerate you well as a member of the family."

This made Dan smile. "I'm honored you think that way."

"We don't have that opinion of many folks, so don't make a mess of it."

"So what are the two of you talking about?" Karen asked as she came to join them.

"This and that," the old woman replied. "Dan was just finishing up his day."

Karen nodded. "I figured as much. That's why I thought I'd come ask you if you wanted to stay for supper. We eat early around here, as you know. So supper will be ready in about half an hour."

"Have to eat early in order to get it properly digested before we go to bed," Leticia interjected. She got to her feet and grabbed her cane. "I'll leave and let the two of you decide what you want to do." She headed past Karen into the house and closed the french door behind her.

Karen smiled. "So what do you think? I made a roast with potatoes and carrots."

"Sounds wonderful, but I can't tonight. I promised the boys I'd come over to the job site and take them out to dinner afterward."

"I understand and that's quite all right. I think my mom and aunts have enjoyed having a man around. They were actually the ones who told me I should invite you. Not that I didn't want your company." She chuckled nervously. "I guess we all enjoy having a man around."

"I'll try to accommodate another time. I have to say the food has been excellent when I've had the opportunity to share a meal. You're a great cook, Karen."

"I've had a lot of practice. Mom saw that I learned what I needed to know. She said cooking a good meal was the way to win a man over."

"And were you trying to win me over?" He couldn't help but ask the question after dealing with Karen's aunt.

"Do I need to?" she countered with a smile.

He laughed. "No. I think I'm convinced of the benefits."

That night, Karen sat in front of her master-bedroom gas fireplace. The night had grown quite chilly, and it was nice to have a fire. When the phone rang, she checked the number to see if she wanted to be bothered. It was Stan Jr.

"Well hello. I haven't heard from you in a while," she said, putting him on speaker.

"Hi, Mom. I was just telling Dee Dee that I needed to call you, or you'd be calling us to find out what was wrong."

"Is something wrong?" She tried not to sound anxious.

"No. Everything is really good. I got a promotion, and Dee Dee and I are thinking of moving. This apartment has always been too small."

"I think that would be wonderful. Don't forget that I have that money set aside from your father's insurance to help with your down payment."

"I haven't forgotten. So how's it going now that you have a houseful of old ladies?"

Karen laughed. "Quite well actually. They are very helpful and insist on rotating chores, and I'm hearing some wonderful stories about their childhood."

"And were you able to get the construction done?"

"It's almost complete. Dan and his sons have been the perfect choice for the work. I've enjoyed having them around. Maybe more than I anticipated."

"Meaning what?" Stan asked.

"Meaning that I might want to spend more time with Dan."

For a moment the line was silent, and Karen worried that she'd upset her oldest son. "Are you still there?"

"I am. I'm just. . .well. . .I've been praying for you, Mom. I worry about you being alone. I mean, I know you have Grandma and now the aunts, but Rod and I have long thought you needed to remarry."

"Oh really?" She was surprised by this and wasn't at all sure what to say.

"I know it may seem like none of our business, but we worry about you. You've been so quiet and not at all the active person you used to be. You've hidden yourself away from the world, and frankly, I was going to suggest you might want to talk to someone."

"Therapy?" She smiled. "I didn't realize I'd gotten all that bad."

"Not bad, just withdrawn. I'm glad to hear about your interest in Dan."

Karen curled her legs up under her. "So you would be happy for me. . .if I found someone. . .to be with?"

"You've been alone for five years. You have been amazing in that time, always looking out for me and Rod. You've been taking care of Grandma and now the aunts. I can just imagine God saying, 'Well done.' You've brought God glory, Mom."

His choice of words didn't escape her notice. Glory. She had worried about the opportunity to glorify God when Stan died, and now her oldest was telling her she'd accomplished that.

"Thank you for saying so. Sometimes I can't see the forest for the trees."

"You've done good, Mom. Now it's time to do something nice for yourself. Give it a try—go out with Dan and see what you think."

"I just might do that."

Later as she prepared for bed, Karen reconsidered her phone call with Stan Jr. He was twenty-seven and full of opinions and thoughts for his own future, but he'd never been one to try to direct hers. The fact that he'd spoken up about the very issue that weighed on her heart seemed like a God thing.

"Lord, I definitely need Your guidance in this. I don't want to get hurt." She found herself standing before the mirror again. "I'm afraid to love again. Afraid to set myself up for the possible loss. Help me, Lord. Please show me what to do."

~⁀

Dan went to bed early, but he couldn't sleep. He kept thinking about Karen and all that her aunt had said. He knew his feelings for Karen were growing, but he wasn't sure he wanted to act on them. What if she turned out to be like Nora?

No, there was no possibility of that. Karen and Nora were as different as night and day. Nora was always caught up in her appearance and the price of her clothes and car. She wanted to be wealthy more than anything else. She'd once flat out told him that. She saw herself as a woman who needed a grand home and a glorious lifestyle. Nora was all about impressing. That's why it had seemed so appropriate for her to be the state's First Lady.

Karen on the other hand wasn't at all pretentious, and although she had plenty of money, she lived simply and didn't put on airs. She wasn't trying to impress anyone.

He smiled. Geena was that way. She lived for him and the children and worked hard to make them a good home. Her kindness was noted by all sorts of people, from those at church to those at his job sites. She had a reputation for her gentle spirit and devotion to God and family. Dan figured if he dug deep into those who knew Karen, he'd find the same spirit present. Of course, it was God's Spirit pouring out of obedient hearts. He'd been around long enough to know that.

"It's time to ask her out," he said aloud. Speaking the words seemed to make them more real.

"I'll ask her tomorrow. Maybe suggest dinner and a drive. Or would a movie be more appropriate?" He had no idea. He hadn't been to a movie theater in years. What was even showing these days? Good grief, what did people their age do on dates?

He laughed to himself and turned off the light. It was going to be an early morning. He and the boys were headed to Karen's to finish up the elevator's exterior. After that, his work for Karen would be done, and he'd have no more excuses to be there. It was definitely the right time to move their relationship forward.

CHAPTER 8

But the best of plans were often interrupted by other problems and issues, and that's exactly what Dan found on his plate the next day. The weekend was soon upon him, and then before he had even had a chance to talk to Karen on the phone, it was Monday and he needed to get over to her house and finish up on the elevator.

He grabbed up plans from his office desk and started for the door, when he spied someone coming up the walkway. He'd always had his office in a side room off the house, and anyone who had worked with him knew this was where he'd be if he was home during working hours.

There was a light knock and the door opened. When a woman peered inside, Dan thought for a moment she was lost. But then he recognized her. Nora.

"What in the world are you doing here?" he asked none too friendly.

She gave a weak smile. "I hoped we could talk."

He shook his head. "I have nothing to say to you."

"Please, Dan. I know I don't deserve consideration, but I want to try and apologize for the past."

He gave a huff and put his papers back on the desk. "There's nothing you can say or do regarding what happened. You devastated my boys and really hurt me. I don't see that we need to dredge up the past and hash it all out again."

She closed the door behind her. "Dan, I know that I don't deserve your time, but I'm begging you to hear me out. I've come to God and know that what I did was wrong. I'm trying my best to make amends with everyone I hurt."

Dan leaned back on the desk. He could hardly turn her away when she made it clear God was a part of her approach. Still, he was skeptical.

"Well, what is it you want to say?" He crossed his arms against his chest as if it might protect him from any attack.

"May I sit?" She nodded toward the chair in front of his desk.

"Suit yourself." He moved to the back side of his desk and took a chair. He liked having the piece of furniture between them.

Nora settled herself and smiled. "Thank you. . .for letting me talk to you. I had hoped to talk to the boys too. Are they around?"

"No. They're already at the job site. Why don't you tell me what you've come to say and I'll pass it along?"

Nora nodded. "I'm sorry. I'm sorry for what I did to you and the boys. It was wrong. I was so wrong. I was such a mess back then. As you know I certainly wasn't serving God. I made a pretense at going to church, but all that mattered to me was money and social position."

"Yes, you made that abundantly clear."

She met his gaze. "Yes. That's all I thought was important. But not now."

Dan said nothing. He just wanted her to finish with her apologies and go. He wasn't going to be taken in by whatever game this was that she was playing.

"Dan, I really wish you could understand all that's happened to me. I've changed. I truly have. I'm not here to force you to see it, but I just want to make amends before. . ." She let the words fade off. "I hope you'll see that I'm sincere."

He let out the breath he'd been holding. There was something off in the way she looked. Pale, drawn. She'd lost weight and didn't have it to lose.

"Why is it so important to come to me now?"

"Because I don't have a lot of time left." She shifted on the chair. "Dan. . .I'm dying. I have stage four breast cancer. It's spread throughout my body. Losing James and finding myself with cancer, well, needless to say my entire world has been turned upside down."

"I am sorry." He meant it.

"Facing this alone was almost more than I could manage, but I'd broken ties with my family and so many of my friends. I learned soon enough that money would only take me so far." There was genuine sorrow in her voice. "I sought out spiritual advice, and it changed my life. I came to see God in a completely different light. He cares about me and has offered me comfort and strength. But He's also given me direction, and making amends is one of the things that He laid firmly on my heart."

Dan didn't know what to say, so he let her continue talking. Clearly, she was dealing with devastating news, and he had no desire to treat her with contempt.

"I don't think there was anyone I wronged more than you and the boys. In the beginning of our relationship, I honestly thought I wanted the family life. I thought you were a wonderful man—you are, you know?" She smiled. "I wished I'd understood it sooner."

"Understood what?"

"Your deep relationship with God. I didn't realize it at the time, but in looking back, I think I rejected it because of my jealousy. You had something with God that I didn't, something that consumed you and guided you every day. I listened to people talk about accepting Jesus as Savior—that He died for my sins and that I had only to accept Him. It all seemed nonsensical to me. You were so confident in your faith, even though there are hundreds, maybe thousands of faiths out there. I thought it was silly. How could you know that this faith was the one true way?"

This made Dan smile. "Funny, I remember asking questions like that when I came to God."

She smiled and nodded. "I see it now. I wouldn't have made it through these last months without my faith firmly rooted in the truth. Oh Dan, I made such a mess of things. It was never my intention to hurt you or the boys. I was just running scared."

"Scared of what?" He couldn't stop himself from asking.

"You. God. Life. When James came along, all I could see was dollar signs. I knew that no matter what problem came into my life, James would have enough money to fix it." She shook her head. "I was so blind."

"We can all be that way."

"I was convinced that if I had enough money, nothing bad could happen. Yet look at me now. I have a fortune, and I can't buy myself a few more years of life."

"I am sorry about that, Nora. Seems a terrible thing for you to have to go through. I know that you've taken good care of yourself over the years and that appearances are important to you."

"They were. Appearance used to be everything, but not now. It can't do a thing for me." She gave a hollow laugh. "I'll be the best-looking corpse in town." She glanced up. "Sorry."

Dan could hear the pain in her voice. He wasn't about to chide her for her comment.

"Do you think you can find it in your heart to forgive me, Dan?"

He hadn't ever considered forgiving her until that moment. The pain she'd inflicted on him and the boys had been deep. He had figured they would marry and be a family. Nora had assured him that she wanted to be a mother to the boys. She had pledged her undying love to him. Then without warning she was breaking off their relationship, telling Dan she'd never been all that serious. Explaining that there was someone else.

"There was a time when I would have said no. Even though I know what the Bible says about us forgiving so we'll be forgiven. But lately I've found someone, and she's very important to me. I can't carry hatred and bitterness from another relationship into this new one." He paused for a moment and then nodded. "I forgive you, Nora."

Her shoulders dropped a bit as if some heavy burden had been lifted. She looked to the floor. "Thank you, Dan. Do you suppose we could meet up with the boys so I can apologize to them as well? I have a dinner reservation that I was going to have to cancel. Why don't we meet for dinner? It's at Chez Yasu for five thirty. I know that's really early, but it was a last-minute favor to me and the only time they could fit me in. My other party had something come up, and I haven't yet canceled the reservations. Let it be my treat."

"You don't need to do that, but sure. I think the boys and I can make it. We've never gone there, although we've heard plenty about it. It's French food, right?"

"Yes. They do a wonderful job. I've eaten there so many times. James and I were regulars." She got to her feet. "I'll go now and expect to see you at five thirty tonight. Thank you, Dan. You can't imagine how heavy this has weighed on me since getting my life on track with God. I have never wanted anything more in my life than your forgiveness. . .and that of the boys."

Dan stood and watched her as she headed for the door. He couldn't help but pose a question. "Nora. . .uh. . .how long do you have?"

She turned and smiled. "They don't know for sure, but they don't think it will be more than a month or two. But don't be sad. I know where I'm going. For the first time in my life, I really know."

~~~~

"And then she walked out of the office and left me reeling from the visit," Dan told his sons.

"Wow, that's heavy-duty," Mark said, shaking his head. "Dying. I don't think I've ever known someone who was terminal."

"Me either," David replied. "How old is she?"

"Forty-eight." Dan had already thought of that himself. She was much too young.

"And she has all that money and can't save herself." Mark's words were matter-of-fact.

"Well, I told her we'd meet her. I hope that's all right."

The boys exchanged a glance. "Sure. Where?"

"She has a reservation for Chez Yasu."

"That expensive French place?" David asked. "Man, I sure didn't figure on eating there anytime soon."

"We'll need to finish up on the job site early and give ourselves plenty of time to clean up."

"Sounds good," Mark said, still shaking his head. "Never expected something like this."

"I didn't figure it would ever happen," Dan replied. "Just goes to show you what God can do."

~⌒⌒⌒⌒~

"Thank you so much for doing this," Nora said as the boys joined her at the dark wood table. "I can hardly believe how handsome you two have grown up to be. Just look at you." She turned to Dan. "You've done right by them."

"They're great fellas. We all work together, although David is thinking of starting college soon."

They took their seats at the table and gave their drink orders before settling in. Dan wondered if Nora would just approach the boys as she had him with her bold request for forgiveness. He didn't have long to wait.

"I suppose your dad told you why I asked you here tonight."

"He told us you'd come to see him about forgiveness," Mark replied. Then he added, "Because you're. . .uh. . .sick."

"I'm dying. You can say it. I've learned to face it, and while it's not what I would choose, it is the situation at hand."

Dan watched Nora as she dealt with his sons. She had taken great care with her clothes and hair, but the look of sickness was still evident.

They ordered appetizers to share, choosing the shrimp cocktail to be followed by the yellow squash soup. Dan had to admit the food was delicious, but not something he'd want to eat all that often.

"I appreciate so much that you boys have come here tonight. I know I hurt you so much, and it makes me feel terrible now. You were just little boys and deserved so much better. I hope you'll forgive me."

"Of course," Mark and David said in unison.

The entrées were served, with Mark and David eating sole filets, while Dan and Nora had chosen the poached salmon in white wine sauce. It wasn't long before they were enjoying the food and stories about the things they'd been doing since they'd last seen each other.

Dan was impressed with his sons. They were gracious and kind throughout the evening. They seemed to completely forget about the pain Nora had once caused. Dan couldn't help but remember those nights he'd spent with the boys in tears over her departure. It was good to see what God could do to mend the past. In some ways, Dan realized, he needed this in order to move forward with Karen. He'd never really thought about it before this moment, but Nora had been like an unfinished story. There had never been any real closure on their relationship. Now there was.

CHAPTER 9

I've never been here either," Karen told her mother and aunts, "but I won this gift certificate in a raffle, dinner for four at Chez Yasu. It's a highly praised French restaurant, and I think we'll have fun trying it out." She pulled into the parking lot and found a handicapped place to park the Sequoia.

"I don't recall if I've ever had French food," her mother said. "I know I've had French pastries but not regular meals."

"I've eaten French cuisine when Gary and I went abroad and took a Rhine River tour. It was rich and delicious. We both agreed we could be fans of it."

"Seems strange to have French food in the middle of Kansas," Aunt Leticia commented.

"Why so strange? We have Mexican restaurants," Aunt Helen replied.

"Yes, but we also have people of Mexican heritage who live here."

"And you don't think we have any folks of French descent?" Karen's mother asked. "Goodness, I'll bet there are a lot of different kinds of people who live in Topeka."

"I suppose so. I just hope the staff are clean."

"Stop it, Lettie. You're always so critical," Aunt Rachel chided.

"I'm not being critical; I'm just hoping the staff are clean." Aunt Leticia gave a huff and squared her shoulders.

"I'm sure it will be fine," Karen said, adjusting the handicapped placard. "Let's go see for ourselves."

They were greeted at the door and led to a beautifully set table. Karen gazed around to take in the buttery-yellow walls adorned with photos of French scenery and botanical prints. They ordered just water for the time being. None of them drank alcohol, at least Karen didn't think her aunts were given to having a drink. It was just the way they'd been raised and had never really been a big deal. Alcohol was expensive and debilitating and so her grandparents had avoided it. Those reasons carried down in the family, and while they could now afford it, it just held little interest.

Karen looked the menu over and was glad for the gift certificate. She had known she'd have to pay for at least one extra dinner, but the prices were a lot higher than she was used to paying.

"Everything is expensive here," Aunt Leticia said.

"You never did get out much," Aunt Helen countered.

Karen smiled but said nothing. She was determined to have a nice evening with her family. This was the first time she'd been out to eat in a long time, and everyone seemed quite content to join her. It was going to be a great night.

"I don't know why you'd have to charge six dollars for a bowl of soup," Aunt Leticia added.

Helen rolled her eyes. "Goodness, Lettie, you don't know much about fine dining. These are reasonable prices. There's a restaurant we used to eat at in Kansas City that would charge fifteen dollars for a bowl of soup, and in New York it was even higher."

"Outrageous. You could buy a dinner for two for fifteen dollars when we were young. No, I take that back. You could feed the whole family for that."

"Those days are gone now," Karen's mother replied. "I remember the first time we paid over a dollar for a cup of coffee. Curtis said he was going to give it up if that's what he was going to have to pay. He'd be shocked to see the prices in one of those fancy coffee shops."

Karen laughed at the thought of her father strolling into Starbucks or elsewhere and trying to make heads or tails out of the menu, much less the price.

"Well, I need to find the restroom," Aunt Leticia announced. "Karen, come with me in case I get lost."

Karen smiled and placed the white linen napkin she was about to put on her lap back on the table. "Of course."

She got up and went around to help her aunt up from the table. "I'm sure it's nearby. The place isn't that big."

They left the others and had only gone a few feet when Karen happened to see Mark Polk at one of the tables. He didn't see her, but Karen thought she might stop and say hello on her way back. That was, until she saw that his brother and father were with him, as well as a lovely looking woman who was now laughing at something. Karen started to look away, when the woman leaned over and kissed Dan's cheek.

Karen swallowed a growing lump in her throat. The woman was clearly comfortable with him and had no trouble openly showing her affection.

"Here it is," Leticia declared upon finding the ladies' room. "Wait for me." She disappeared inside the room while Karen, still stunned to see Dan with another woman, waited outside.

She didn't know why it bothered her so much. He wasn't

obligated to her in any way. They hadn't even gone on a date together. And while it was obvious that they both liked each other and had made comments about getting to know each other better, Dan owed her no allegiance.

"This is silly," she muttered. She didn't even know who this woman was. She could be Dan's sister for all Karen knew. Did he have a sister?

When her aunt finally returned with her update of what she thought of the bathroom, Karen was more than ready to forget about everything and get back to their table. She didn't want to be jealous of a woman she didn't even know. Dan could date or take to dinner any woman he liked. She had no say over him or his life.

They started back for the table, but this time her aunt spied the party and made a beeline for the table. Karen had no choice but to follow.

"I thought that was you," her aunt said to Dan.

"Hello," Dan said, getting to his feet. His sons did likewise. "Are you out celebrating tonight?"

Karen had caught up to her aunt by then and answered. "I won a gift certificate for dinner for four. None of us have ever been, so we thought it might be fun."

"I've never been either," Dan replied, looking at her for a long moment. "Oh, let me introduce our former governor's wife, Nora Fisher. Nora is an old friend. Nora, this is Karen Jacobs."

Nora smiled. "It's nice to meet you. I understand Dan has been working on your house."

"Yes." Karen wasn't sure why she felt so uncomfortable. She turned to look at the boys to calm her spirit. "I've missed you showing up the last few days, and now the project is all but done."

"We thought we might come out and help you gather the last

of the walnuts. . .if you wanted us to," David offered.

"That would be most helpful. Just let me know when you have in mind, and I'll make sure we're all set up for it." She smiled at the others. "For now, I believe we should let them get back to their dinner, Aunt Leticia." She put her hands on her aunt's shoulders and tried to turn her back.

"Well, I suppose we should. Too bad we didn't know you were coming. We could have sat together," Aunt Leticia said in a firm tone that Karen knew better than to contradict. When her aunt was of an opinion on the way a thing should be done. . .well, that was the way it got done.

"That would have been fun," Nora said graciously.

"It was nice to meet you, Mrs. Fisher," Karen said, this time pushing a little more insistently on her aunt's frame.

"Good evening," Karen's aunt called over her shoulder.

"I'll be out tomorrow, Karen."

She heard Dan call after her but didn't reply. Instead, she gave a little wave over her shoulder and kept moving toward their table in the smaller of the two serving rooms. She helped her aunt back into her seat, and before she could even reach her own, Leticia was telling them all about what had transpired.

"He's here with another woman," Aunt Leticia announced. "She used to be married to the governor of Kansas."

Her aunts all looked at her as if awaiting some comment. Karen unfolded her napkin and placed it on her lap. She had no idea what to say. Part of her felt sad and jealous, yet she knew she had no right to feel that way. But truth was, she was really starting to feel something for Dan.

"What is she to him?" Aunt Rachel asked.

"I don't know, but they seemed quite chummy," Aunt Leticia

replied. "He said she was an old friend."

Karen wished they could just forget about it and talk about something else. She didn't like dwelling on the feelings the encounter had stirred up. Thankfully, the server showed up.

The rest of the evening was a sort of blur for Karen. They all enjoyed the food. Her mother and aunts insisted everyone get something different and then they could sample each other's food. Karen might have been embarrassed had the situation with Dan not already happened. Instead, she did as the others and tasted bites of each dish. When it was time for dessert, however, she was desperate to just leave the restaurant and head home.

"If you want dessert, maybe we could get it to go," she suggested.

"Oh, I'm much too full," her mother answered. Thankfully, the aunts all nodded in agreement.

Saturday morning, Karen was slow to rise. She knew Dan planned to come out, and while she would have looked forward to that before, now she was just hard-pressed to know how to deal with it all.

She pulled on old jeans and a sweatshirt, knowing she'd be working with the messy walnut husks. If she hadn't seen Dan with the fashionable woman, Karen might have tried to dress up her appearance, but it was clear she couldn't compete. Nora Fisher obviously had plenty of money, and while Karen was quite comfortable, she knew she needed to make her money last for her lifetime, unless she wanted to go to work.

The house was quiet by the time she made it to the kitchen. It seemed everyone had had their breakfast and gone back downstairs. With the elevator in place, Dan had encouraged them to use it as much as possible. She wondered if the aunts and her mom had used it that morning.

Coffee sounded like just the thing to take the chill off, so Karen made herself a cup and doctored it up with sugar-free creamers and a little sugar-free syrup...salted caramel. She sipped the concoction and smiled. It was warm and soothing, perfect for her mood and the chilly day. Soon it would be November, and perhaps they'd see some snow. She definitely needed to have the garden completely cleared and the walnuts all gathered and drying before that happened.

She grabbed her fleece-lined jean jacket from the closet and pulled it on. She liked the warmth and snuggled the collar to her face for a moment. Next, she grabbed her work gloves and decided to take the elevator. She had ridden it once before, and it seemed quite nice.

When the door opened on the commons area downstairs, Karen found everyone rather formally assembled. She frowned.

"What's going on? You four look like you're up to something."

Her mother looked away as if embarrassed, but Aunt Leticia spoke right up. "We're concerned about you and Dan. We need to make sure that young man knows how you feel about him."

"Please, don't say anything to him. He doesn't deserve to be picked on."

"But you like him," Aunt Rachel said.

"I do." Karen wasn't going to deny her feelings. "I like him very much."

"Then we need to do whatever we can to see the two of you get together," Aunt Leticia declared. The others nodded. Even Karen's mother.

"If it's meant to be, it will happen," Karen replied. "Don't be pestering him."

"No one intends to pester him," her mother assured her.

"Well, whatever you have planned, maybe forget about it." Karen looked at the foursome and shook her head. "Honestly. I don't need you playing matchmaker. It will be all right."

She headed outside just as Dan drove his truck down the drive and parked not far from the patio. Karen knew she needed to wait and greet him, but a part of her wanted to run away. She wanted to know about Nora, but if he had a close relationship with the woman, Karen really didn't want to hear about it.

"Morning," Dan said, jumping out of the truck.

"Good morning." Karen forced a smile. "My aunts and mother are inside. You might want to ask them about their elevator rides, because they've been practicing."

"I'm glad they aren't afraid of it. I thought at first we were going to have trouble with that."

Karen nodded. "They seem to have adapted." She started toward the pond, but Dan called her back. She turned. "Did you need something?"

"I wanted to talk to you. You brought up the idea of putting grab bars in the upstairs bathroom. I wondered if you still wanted to do that?"

She relaxed a bit. "I think it would be a good idea. They like to eat upstairs sometimes, and it would definitely provide extra help for them. It certainly doesn't hurt anything to have the bars there, so I think we should go ahead with it."

"All right. Maybe come upstairs and show me where you want them and how many."

Karen wanted only to avoid being with him, but she had no choice. "All right."

CHAPTER 10

Dan could tell things weren't right with Karen. She seemed uncomfortable with him and not at all herself. He wondered if it had something to do with seeing him with Nora. At least he could give her an explanation and, if that was the problem, put it to rest.

"Ah, before we go upstairs, I want to talk to you about last night."

She glanced at him and shook her head. "You don't owe me an explanation."

"I know that, but I want to explain. Nora and I used to be together. It was quite a long while ago. I had thought we'd marry."

Karen hadn't been able to hide the surprise in her expression, but she looked away so quickly that Dan knew the entire matter bothered her.

"I got caught up in that whole 'You need a mother for those boys' attitude. People were always after me to remarry for their sake, and when Nora came along seeming to share the idea of wanting to mother them, I started thinking in that direction."

He motioned to the chairs on the patio. "Why don't we sit."

She followed him to the chairs and took one, while Dan did the same. He wasn't exactly sure how much detail to give Karen, but he figured a full disclosure was probably best because he wanted to start a future with her.

"Nora seemed like the right choice for a long time, except for her lack of interest in God. She went to church and made the appearances of being saved, but she wasn't, and she had no idea of becoming a real Christian. I should have let that stop me from pursuing anything more than friendship, but I was starting to feel a little desperate."

"People and their well-meaning advice can be difficult to ignore." She gave him a hint of a smile. "I'm sure that wasn't easy."

"No, it wasn't. Then one day when I had determined I would ask her to marry me, she showed up at the house and told me it was over. She had realized she didn't want children and had already found someone else to be with."

"The governor?"

"Well, he wasn't governor yet, but he was rich and smitten with her."

"She is a beautiful woman."

"A shadow of her old self. I don't know if she'd mind or not, but I'm going to tell you anyway. She's dying. She has cancer and not much time. She had come to me after all these years, and I'm ashamed to tell you I almost threw her out. She'd hurt me so much, more so for what she did to the boys, but I hoped to never see her again."

"That must have been hard." Karen sounded more like herself.

"It was, but then she told me she'd come to know God and knew that she had to make amends and apologize for what she had done to me and to the boys. I could hardly turn her away then."

"No." Karen shook her head.

"She told me how she'd thought having money would solve all of her problems and keep her from harm. Then her husband died and she found out about the cancer, and her world fell apart. Before finding God, she only ever cared about her looks. I can't imagine what that did to her."

He drew a deep breath and shook his head. "Last night at the restaurant was about her asking the boys to forgive her. I had already given my forgiveness, and she wanted to speak to them with me."

"I'm glad you were all able to forgive her. What a burden to carry as you face death."

Dan nodded. "That's exactly what I thought. There was a time, however, when I don't think I would have forgiven her. Even knowing what the Bible says about forgiving so that God will forgive us. I just hated her for the pain she'd caused the boys. They were so deeply wounded by her. Yet when I mentioned meeting up with her and what she wanted, they were okay with it. Neither Mark nor David had any problem with offering her forgiveness."

Karen smiled. "That's because you raised them right. They're wonderful young men."

For a moment Dan said nothing. He couldn't help but wonder how to proceed with what he wanted to say about their future. He whispered a prayer and looked at Karen.

"There's something more. Something I've wanted to say for a while now."

"All right. Go ahead."

He smiled and reached out to take hold of her hand. "Karen, I think you must know that I've developed feelings for you. I haven't been terribly open about it because I wanted to know how you felt. It seems to me that you feel the same. Correct me if I'm wrong."

"You're not." Her voice was barely audible.

"Good. At least we have that out of the way. I honestly feel like a little kid trying to ask someone out for the first time."

She laughed. "I know exactly what you mean."

"I guess what I want to say is that I'd like to go out with you. I'd like to spend more time together—time that would focus on the future. I don't want to just date for the fun of it. I'm not looking for a Friday-night companion."

"That's a relief. I have no desire to peruse the dating pool either."

"I'm glad you feel the same way. Since Geena, I've never felt about anyone else the way I'm feeling about you, Karen. I'm thinking this is it, but we haven't even gone out together."

"No, but we've spent a lot of time here working together and talking. I don't need dinner and a movie to know I enjoy your company."

"I enjoy your company too. More than I ever thought would be possible."

"I have to say, I felt jealous when I saw you with Nora. My aunt Leticia had just been giving me a hard time about you, and it actually hurt to think you belonged to someone else. I guess that's when I realized just how dear you had become to me."

"I'm glad to hear you say it. I hated the situation last night. I felt like I had somehow betrayed your trust."

"But you hadn't. We had no claim on each other."

"But we do now—right?"

She seemed to consider his question for a moment. "Right." She let go a sigh. "I never thought this would happen. I thought I'd be alone for the rest of my life."

"I thought so too. After Nora, I wasn't about to lay my heart on the line, but here I am again. . .falling for love."

Karen laughed. "That's a good way to put it. I'm falling for love."

~⁀

"So what happened after that?" Karen's mother asked as they shared lunch together.

Karen shrugged. "We went upstairs, and I showed him where I wanted the grab bars in the bathroom."

"Did you set up a date?" Aunt Rachel asked.

"We did. We're going out tonight, in fact."

Aunt Leticia leaned forward. "Where are you going?"

"I'm not sure. I left it in Dan's hands. I just want you all to know, however, that we're not looking at this as a casual thing. Neither one of us want to date a bunch of people. We're looking toward a future together."

"It's courtship," Aunt Leticia said with a single nod of her head. "That's what we called it. There wasn't any time or interest in seeing a lot of people. We were determined to find that one person and make a life together."

Aunt Helen nodded. "We used to run around together—all of us girls—and the boys would come along and eventually we just started pairing off, but no one wanted to run willy-nilly with a lot of different folks. I swear the way kids are today they don't even care about one person. They just want to experience everything with everyone."

"Well, Dan and I agree we are smitten enough with each other that we only want to focus on each other." Karen got up to go to the stove, where she ladled more soup into her bowl. "Can I get anyone some more potato soup?"

"I'll take a little," her mother replied, but the aunts had all had enough.

"I love soups for cold weather. I do hope we'll have a lot of soup," Aunt Leticia said.

"And fresh bread," Aunt Rachel added.

"And butter," Helen threw in.

They all laughed. They'd been together less than a full month, but the arrangement worked so well it seemed they'd always been together.

"So what's the plan when you two marry?" Aunt Leticia asked. "Will you live here or at his place?"

Aunt Rachel shook her index finger in the air at no one in particular. "Maybe you should just get a new place. Sometimes folks have problems when it's her place or his place. They just don't feel they can share."

Karen got her mother's soup and returned to the table with her bowl as well. "I don't think we're at the place to worry about all of this just yet. But never fear. I will make sure you're all taken good care of and have what you need."

"You don't need to worry about us," Aunt Leticia said, buttering her bread. "We'll be just fine. We four have always been able to arrange for ourselves. Just look at where we are."

They all chuckled, but Karen wondered if maybe her mother and aunts had gotten together to plan out this new living arrangement before anyone even mentioned it to Karen. It wouldn't have surprised her in the least. They were all very good at planning and maneuvering things to go their way.

She looked at each of them, and her smile broadened. She kind of liked to think they had planned out this entire thing. She could imagine her mother calling them and telling them how lonely

Karen was and how they needed to do something. She laughed and everyone at the table looked at her.

Karen shrugged. "I just thought of something funny."

"Well, share it with us," Mother encouraged.

Shaking her head, Karen picked up her spoon. "Maybe later. My soup is getting cold."

Dan arrived to pick up Karen at precisely six o'clock. He had made reservations at a less expensive restaurant and was looking forward to having Karen all to himself. He liked her mom and aunts, but he liked Karen by herself all the more.

She answered the door dressed in a coral-colored turtleneck and black slacks. She'd fluffed out her curls a bit more than usual and wore gold earrings.

"Well, don't you look nice," Karen said, glancing him over.

"I was just going to say the same about you. Are you ready?"

"I am. Let me grab my jacket and purse."

Moments later they were in Dan's truck heading to town, and he couldn't wait to hear what Karen's family had to say about this new arrangement.

"So what did Leticia say about us going out?"

Karen laughed. "They were all quite thrilled. What you don't understand is that Aunt Leticia has been trying for weeks to throw us together. She was quite determined that we belonged together."

"I'm glad. I'd sure hate to have to win over those four women before I could move forward."

"You're not going to have any trouble from them. They already adore you."

"And what about your boys? Will they be uncomfortable with

you being with someone other than their dad?"

"No. Apparently they've been concerned that I was too young to be alone. I never knew they felt that way. They certainly never said anything to me about it."

"Well, you know how my boys feel. They adore you. I never knew how much you meant to them. Not long after we started the job, Mark even confessed that you had prayed with him when he was at a particularly bad place. Your kindness and promise to keep praying for him was what got him through."

Karen smiled. "We sometimes never know how we touch the life of someone. I'm glad to know that he was blessed. It seemed such a little thing to do."

Traffic was light and it wasn't long before they'd reached the restaurant Dan had chosen. He hoped Karen wouldn't be put off by it. It didn't look like much on the outside, but the food was incredible BBQ. His favorite.

"I hope you'll like this."

"I love it. Stan and I used to come here from time to time. Best BBQ in Topeka."

Dan laughed. "And here I was worried that you wouldn't care for it."

"Worry no more. I have a feeling that we're going to see eye to eye on quite a bit."

He chuckled. "I've got that same feeling. Looks like we're in for a great time—a great future."

EPILOGUE

The following September, Karen and Dan married in an afternoon ceremony by the pond. With their sons to stand up with them and Karen's aunts and mother to bear witness, Karen felt that they had more than enough people. But Dan had wanted to invite a few people from church, and Mom had invited some extended family, and soon the affair was quite large.

Thankfully, the day was beautiful, and the outdoor picnic reception came off without a hitch. Dan and his boys had arranged to build some simple picnic tables, and they rented folding chairs for the guests. A smorgasbord was laid out with a vast selection of food that had been created and brought by the guests. Mom and the aunts had also contributed to the fare, having whipped up some of Karen's all-time favorites. They proved to be Dan's favorites too.

By the time Karen and Dan needed to leave to catch a plane in Kansas City, Karen was happier than she'd been in a long time. She couldn't have asked for anything to be better.

"I hope you know that we're so happy to have you as our new mom," Mark told her as he came to kiss Karen goodbye.

"We even prayed for you to be our mom," David added. "Of

course, then we found out you were already married and had two boys. We were rather jealous of them."

"You have to be careful what you wish for," Karen's son Rod declared. "She wasn't always this sweet and nice."

Karen looked at him. "I wasn't? I thought I was pretty understanding about the time you brought snakes into the house. Then there was the time you snuck off with your grandpa's truck and—"

"Okay, okay. Don't give away all of our secrets," Stan Jr. protested. He looked at Dan's sons and grinned. "I'm sure we probably all have our stories."

Mark and David nudged each other and laughed.

"What did I miss?" Dan asked as he came to join them.

"We were just contemplating our escapades as young men," Mark said with a smile.

"You're still all young men as far as I'm concerned," Karen said. "But old enough to know what's expected. I'm glad you'll be here to help with your grandmother and the aunts."

"Just go and enjoy your honeymoon," Mark said. "We'll keep an eye on Stan and Rod and make sure they don't get out of hand."

"Oh, you will, will you?" Rod said, shaking his head. "I don't think that's how it's going to work."

Everyone laughed, and Dan slipped his arm around Karen. "We need to go if we're going to catch that flight."

She nodded and kissed all four boys. "I love you all."

"Love you too," they said in unison.

Dan laughed. "Ditto for me."

Karen quickly said goodbye to her mother and aunts and waited while they chided Dan to drive carefully and watch out for deer on the turnpike.

"They're bad this time of year," Karen's mother said. "I remember once—"

"That's a story for another time, Meredith," Aunt Leticia declared. "Now get on, you two, before someone else has a story they want to tell." She winked, and Karen could only laugh.

When they reached Dan's truck, Karen waited while he opened the door. She wasn't expecting his next move, however, as he lifted her into his arms.

"I figure I won't have a threshold to carry you across for a while, so this will have to do."

She snuggled against him and kissed his cheek. "I don't mind at all."

He sought her lips and kissed her for a long moment. "I don't seem to mind either. Falling for love seems to suit me just fine."

Winter

SILENT NIGHTS

Chapter 1

"Wait a minute," Lynn Murphy said, hands on hips. "Do you mean to tell me that you're going to leave me on Christmas? That's just great; why am I not surprised?"

"Now don't take that tone with me," Frank countered his wife's angry retort. "This wasn't my idea. Mr. Bridgeton needs me to handle the case."

"And there isn't another lawyer at Bridgeton National Life, one preferably who isn't about to celebrate his tenth wedding anniversary, who can handle the case?"

"No," Frank said flatly, pulling a suitcase down from the bedroom closet. "There isn't."

Lynn felt an overwhelming urge to grab the suitcase and hurl it out the window, but instead she remained fixed in her spot. This kind of scene was happening more and more, and now only weeks away from Christmas, they were fighting again. Only this time, Lynn wasn't sure she even cared about the outcome. Frank was gone more than he was home, and when he was home, he kept himself wrapped up in a cocoon of work and business issues.

Dejected and totally discouraged, Lynn plopped down on a chair as her husband swung the suitcase up onto the bed. He apparently noticed or sensed her mood, because his expression softened.

"Look, Lynn," he said, sitting down opposite her on the bed. "I know we have the plans for the trip, but we can just reschedule them."

"We can't reschedule our anniversary," Lynn replied. Deep within, her heart ached at memories of other special events rescheduled.

Frank sighed. "You know this job is important. It's our ticket to the future. I've worked hard to get where I am, and unfortunately that has often required my traveling on days when I'd rather be home."

"I don't believe you," Lynn answered flatly. "I don't believe you'd rather be home." She knew she sounded like a harpy, but she didn't care. "I married you for better or worse, but I'm beginning to think that I'm getting nothing but the negative end of that arrangement."

"It isn't always a bowl of cherries for me, either," Frank replied. "What about my desires for a family? You agreed once I finished law school and got myself established in a good job, you'd quit your job and start having children. I don't see you sticking with your promise."

The words stung Lynn. He had spoken the truth, but the circumstances and reasons were so complicated that she hesitated to even comment on his statement. "You wouldn't begin to understand my feelings on the matter, because you're never home long enough to find out what they are."

Frank frowned. "You'd made your feelings clear when we were dating. I didn't realize they'd changed."

Lynn got up, hands raised in the air. "Look, why don't you just go back to packing. We're obviously not going to get anywhere this way. We never do."

She started to walk away, wishing he would call after her and apologize, but he didn't. So she turned at the door to their bedroom and looked back at him. Already in her mind she'd decided to leave him. She'd given up on their marriage. *I don't even know you anymore,* she thought. It hurt so much to even think the words. She loved this man. Loved him more than she'd ever loved any other person. How could she just walk away?

In the living room, Lynn paced nervously as Frank finished his packing. Christmas was in little over two weeks, and she'd done nothing to prepare for it. She hadn't even bothered to go out and get a Christmas tree. She kept putting it off, hoping Frank might actually spend an entire weekend with her and they'd make a day of searching for just the right tree. But Frank had only been home for three days since Thanksgiving, and his exhaustion and devotion to that stupid job kept him from being even decent company, much less creative or productive in thoughts of Christmas.

She went to the window and stared out on the Chicago skyline. They'd lived in Chicago for nearly four years, and in all that time, Lynn had never gotten used to the view. She had grown up in Kansas, Council Grove to be exact, and it wasn't until she went to college at the University of Kansas in Lawrence that she began to explore anything else of the United States.

She'd met Frank when they were in college. He was in his third year, and she was barely eighteen and into her first semester. He was everything Lynn respected in a man. He kept himself busy with serious ambitions toward his future, and he made and worked toward real goals—something Lynn never felt good at.

After a lifetime of parents who seemed to take nothing

seriously, not even raising Lynn and her sister Monica, Frank was like a breath of spring air. Not only that, but Lynn had never seen any man who filled her thoughts the way Frank Murphy had. He was only of medium height and build, but he had a face that drew her immediate attention. He always wore a serious expression, but his eyes seemed to be alive with a depth of spirit that she found most attractive.

"I have to leave if I'm going to catch the early flight."

Lynn turned to see Frank setting his suitcase by the door. She stared at him and he returned her gaze, discomfort apparent in his expression.

"Look, you know I hate to leave while you're mad at me. When I get back, we'll talk this all out. I promise."

"You always promise," Lynn replied, her voice low.

Frank's expression contorted. "I suppose by that you mean that I promise, then fail to carry through. Is that it?"

"You said it, not me."

"You say it," Frank replied. "You may not use words, but you've made it very clear what you think of my word. I'd like you to reconsider what I said earlier, however. We made certain promises to each other when we married. I've fulfilled my end of the arrangement."

"Is that all our marriage is to you? An arrangement? Maybe I should arrange to become one of your clients. At least I'd see more of you."

"When you act like this, is it any wonder I dread coming home?" Frank threw out.

Lynn felt as though he'd dealt her a hard blow. "So you admit it." She bit her lip to keep from crying.

He shook his head. "Admit what?"

"That you dread coming home."

"I didn't mean it that way. You always twist what I say and use it against me."

Lynn felt ill. She knew their marriage was hopeless, but deep inside she didn't know what to do. She wanted to save it, but how? She didn't believe in divorce; the Bible made it clear that God hated the institution, and she certainly didn't want to participate in what God hated. Yet, how could she continue to live with a man who was obviously very unhappy with her whenever he was around?

"All we ever do is fight, Lynn," Frank said, his voice registering concern. "I don't want to fight with you. I don't want to leave with you angry at me. It's hard enough to go away, but knowing that you're mad at me is even worse."

Lynn shook her head. "It isn't hard for you to go away. You enjoy what you do; you've told me as much. You probably look forward to the next trip and plan it out in your mind, even when you have a few days to be at home. I just don't think I know you anymore, Frank. You used to be exactly what I wanted and needed in a man, but now I feel like we're strangers."

"Don't say that," he said, taking a step toward her. "You're just saying these things because I've ruined your anniversary plans. Look, it's just a date. What matters is that we fell in love and married. We can celebrate our marriage every day—in our hearts, in our actions, whatever."

He reached out to touch her and Lynn stiffened. "It's not just a date. It's important to me. December 29th is the date I gave myself over to the job of being your wife and partner. It's the day I re-evaluate the year and see what has gone before me, and what I might do to make the next year better. It's not just a date on the calendar to me."

"I was only implying that we shouldn't set it aside as the only time we can celebrate our relationship." He rubbed her arms gently, gazing steadily into her eyes. "I love you, Lynnie. Don't let me leave here without telling me that you love me too."

She wanted to burst into tears, but instead she forced herself to lean up on tiptoes and kiss his lips. "I do love you, Frank. Whatever else happens. I'll always love you."

Frank smiled. "Good. Why don't you pick out a Christmas tree and have it delivered. I should be home by Thursday and we can decorate it together. Okay?"

"I'll see," Lynn replied. She already knew she wouldn't be here when he came back to Chicago. She didn't want to lie and tell him she'd be ready for some sort of homecoming celebration, when she knew she wouldn't be around to join in the festivities.

"That's my girl." He went to the hall closet and pulled out his coat. "I'll be back before you know it," he called out, then grabbed up his suitcase and was gone.

Lynn went to the sofa and sat down in an almost stunned silence. Switching on the radio, she heard violins playing a haunting rendition of "Silent Night."

In her typical fashion, Lynn began to play at the words. She usually did this with pop songs on the radio, making up her own lyrics to the tunes. Even as a child, she had played at this, personalizing every song she heard.

"Silent night, lonely night," she sang in time with the music. "You're gone again and nothing's right."

Tears came to her eyes and she began to cry in earnest. Her marriage was over. There seemed no hope of reviving the dying embers of Frank's love for her. Her own love for Frank still burned hot, which was why she found it so hard to see him go off every week—to give his life to a job, rather than to her.

"Oh, God," she prayed aloud, "nothing is the way I'd hoped it would be. I had such high expectations for our marriage. I just knew that everything would be wonderful, but so far, it's been so very hard. I don't know where to go or what to do, but I know I can't stay here. I can't live like this anymore." She pulled a pillow into her arms and cradled it while she cried. "I've become a shrew and a nag, and please forgive me, God, but I think I hate myself."

A jazzy version of "Jingle Bells" came on the radio and soon an announcer was telling her how she could get her horseless sleigh cleaned for the holiday season. Snapping the radio off, Lynn tossed the pillow aside.

"I'm not accomplishing anything by sitting here feeling sorry for myself. God expects us to be people of action, not of reaction," she reminded herself. This morning's sermon had touched on this matter, and it had made a deep impression on her.

"There isn't a whole lot that's useful about reactions," her minister had said. "We react to things every day. We react to the red light, when we wanted a green one. We react to our favorite shoes going on sale. We react to our car not starting. We react to the news that someone we love is going to die. Reactions can be bad or good, productive or destructive, but reactions in and of themselves will never accomplish the fullness of God's plan for us. Actions truly speak louder than words or reactions."

Lynn almost smiled at the memory. She seriously doubted Pastor Gates would have figured his words would lead her to separate from her husband. But they were useful in figuring that something needed to be done. She needed action in her life. She needed to do something that would result in something else. And, at this point, anything else was preferable to the pain she was enduring within her marriage.

Picking up the telephone, Lynn dialed the number for her boss.

"Dr. Madison," the female voice announced on the other end of the line.

"Hi, Cindy, it's Lynn."

"Well this is a surprise."

"More than you realize," Lynn countered. "Look, Cindy, I have some personal problems, and I want to take an emergency leave of absence."

There was a pause. "No problem. I hope this won't interfere with your anniversary trip."

"There is no anniversary trip. Frank canceled on me. I just found out about it."

"Oh, Lynn, I'm so sorry. I know how disappointed you must be."

Lynn frowned at the telephone. "No, I don't think you do. Look, I've decided to separate from Frank for a time. That's why I need the leave. I want to take at least a month and isolate myself somewhere and decide what's to be done. I just needed to know that I could take the time. I want it to start as of tomorrow."

"That's fine, Lynn. I'm really sorry about you and Frank though. Do you want to talk about it? I mean, I might be a health clinic MD, but I'm also a married woman who's trying to juggle career and family."

"No, I don't really want to talk about it. . .at least not just now," Lynn replied, hoping Cindy's feelings wouldn't be hurt. "Are you sure you can spare me from the clinic?"

"I'm absolutely positive. It won't be easy; you're the best office manager I've ever had. But we'll manage. I want you to go and work through this. I'd hate to see you and Frank call it quits."

"Me too, Cindy. Me too."

Lynn hung up the telephone without any idea of what to do next. She wondered where she should go. Her parents were in Europe, and her sister Monica's busy life and family in San Francisco would never allow Lynn a moment's peace. Then, like a phoenix rising from her past, a thought came to Lynn. There was only one place to go.

Picking up the telephone once again, she dialed the Council Grove telephone number.

"Hello?" came a gravelly male voice.

"Gramps, it's Lynn."

"Well, Lynnie, what do I owe this pleasure to? It ain't my birthday, and Christmas is a few weeks away."

Lynn couldn't keep the tears from coming anew. "Oh, Gramps, my life is a mess. Can I come for a visit? For a very long visit?"

"You know you're always welcome. Frank coming too?"

"No, you might say I'm running away from home."

Gramps laughed. "You're a little old for that, aren't you, darling?"

"Maybe," Lynn admitted, "but I'm coming nevertheless."

"When?"

She breathed a sigh of relief. He'd just accepted things as they were without asking a bunch of prying questions. "I'm going to pack and leave tonight. I'll drive until I get sleepy, then stay the night somewhere. I should be able to get in by late tomorrow."

"Just don't take any chances," the old man replied. "I'm not going anywhere."

Lynn gave her word to be careful, then hung up the phone. She glanced around the apartment as if seeing it for the last time. "This is the only way," she whispered to the air.

Chapter 2

Lynn pulled her car onto the long dirt and gravel drive to the Lewiston farm and uttered a sigh of relief. She was a bit more road-weary than she'd thought she'd be. The long, lonely drive had lent itself to nothing but stark, barren fields and boring interstates. Coming into Kansas was rather like taking a step back in time from Chicago. Where things moved at a nonstop pace in the big city, Lynn knew Kansas life moved much slower. People were inclined to chitchat with each other, as was evidenced when she'd stopped for gasoline in Junction City. She'd thought herself to be safe at one of the self-service pumps, but she'd no sooner stepped up to the pump than an older woman smiled from the opposite side and bid her good day. People in Chicago learned to keep their thoughts to themselves and not even make eye contact. It was amazing what could be taken the wrong way.

The two-story white farmhouse came into view as Lynn cleared a small grove of leafless trees. She had found this place a haven for as long as she had memory. Of course, Grammie Ketta wouldn't be there. She had died three years ago and it had nearly broken Lynn's heart. Grammie had always given Lynn a listening ear and a sympathetic nod whenever there were problems to be discussed.

Grammie never pretended to have the answers; she simply offered the kindness of truly caring about what Lynn might have to say.

Lynn had just pulled the car into the space beside Gramps' ancient Chevy pickup when she spied the old man coming around the house. He hadn't changed much in the three years since Grammie's funeral. He stooped a bit more from his eighty-one years, and his gait seemed a bit slower, but he was the same old Gramps.

Jumping out of the car, Lynn raced to the old man. He embraced her with a bear hug that suggested his strength was as great as ever. Tears came to Lynn's eyes as she held on to the old man.

"You're liken to squeeze the tar out of me girl," Omar Lewiston said with a chuckle. "What's that Frank feeding you these days?"

Lynn pulled away and tried to smile. "I'm just so happy to be here."

"Happy, eh?" He seemed slightly embarrassed by her tears. "Then what's all this about?"

Lynn sniffed and wiped at her eyes. "I'll tell you after supper. How about I take you out?"

"No need for that. I figured you'd be coming in about supper-time and fixed us a bite. How's the car running?"

He was referring to the cause of her extra day on the road. She'd had car trouble near Columbia, Missouri, and ended up spending an extra night and part of the next day getting it fixed.

"It was the water pump," she told him. "Never knew they could make that much noise going out."

Omar nodded. "Let's get your stuff in the house, then we can eat. It's supposed to blow up a snow tonight."

"I know. I heard them mention that this same storm system dumped a foot of snow on Denver. Sure hope we don't get that much."

They chatted amicably about the weather and the look of the sky while Lynn unlocked the trunk of her car. Inside were three large suitcases.

"Planning to move in?" Gramps asked with a grin.

"I just might need to do that," Lynn replied soberly. "But for now, I was hoping you'd tolerate an extended visit."

Gramps nodded. "Sure. Sure. Whatever you need. You know that."

Lynn smiled. "Thanks, Gramps."

Later they sat at the kitchen table, white ceramic bowls filled to the brim with homemade potato soup. The women of Gramps' church tried to look after him and kept his freezer stocked so that all he had to do was heat up a meal from time to time.

"This is very good," Lynn said, warming up from the inside out.

"Isadora Blackman makes the best soup in the county, but Lizzy Jenkins runs a short second."

"Is this Isadora's or Lizzy's?" Lynn asked with a smile.

"Neither one. It's your grammie's recipe and my handiwork."

"It's wonderful. Tomorrow, I'll cook for you," Lynn told him. "After all, I'd hate two years of gourmet cooking classes to go to waste."

With Frank continuing to put in longer and longer hours, Lynn had taken up a number of hobbies to keep herself busy. Cooking classes were only one of a variety of classes that had taken her time and energy. There had also been piano lessons, quilting, sewing, aerobics, and even bowling. The lessons and subjects had been too numerous to remember.

"So, you gonna get around to telling me what's going on with you and Frank?" Omar asked, not even trying to disguise his interest in the matter.

Lynn shrugged. "What's to tell? He's never around. He's always breaking promises and he works outrageously long hours. I don't even feel like I know him anymore. Maybe I've never known him. We got married so young, and after such a short time of dating. Frank was already consumed with college and then law school, and I kept telling myself he would change as soon as he graduated and got a job. But he didn't."

"Nothing wrong with working hard, Lynnie."

"Don't you dare take his side," Lynn said half mocking, half serious. "Frank's a bona fide workaholic. He never takes time off and he never keeps his promises. We were supposed to go on a trip to Mexico. Just Frank and me and the sun and the sand. We were going to celebrate our tenth wedding anniversary, but he canceled on me."

"And that's worth leaving the man over?" Gramps asked seriously.

Lynn shook her head. "No, and if it were just that simple, I wouldn't be here. There's so much going on and so many reasons for why I'm here. All I ask is that you give me a few days to sort it all out in my head. I just need time."

"I sure like Frank. I think you two are good together."

"Whenever we're actually together," Lynn muttered between spoonfuls of soup.

They ate in silence for several minutes, then as if she'd never made the request for time, Omar asked, "Why do you suppose it's so all-fired important to the boy to spend all his time working?"

Lynn knew he didn't mean to torment her with the question. "I guess because he wants to be rich. Money has always been important to him. I don't know why, but it is."

"You've been married ten years to the man and you don't know why he works as hard as he does? You two ever think of talking your problems through? Maybe ask him why he has to work like that?"

Lynn sighed. If only it were that simple. "I've asked him to slow down, but he insists on being practical. He says it's important to plan for the future. We have a nice nest egg, a beautiful home, and everything we could ever want, but it's still not enough for Frank."

"What about a family?" Gramps asked innocently.

Lynn swallowed hard. "We both want one, but—"

"But what?"

She got up from the table. "Please, Gramps, just give me some time to think. I'm going to go for a short walk, if you don't mind."

"Go ahead, but it's already starting to snow. I wouldn't stay out there too long. Sun's going down and it won't be light for long."

"I promise not to stay past sunset."

Donning her coat and gloves, Lynn stepped back out onto the porch and exhaled loudly. She had hoped Gramps would understand her need to remain silent. How could she explain the situation to him when she was so confused herself that there didn't seem to be any answers?

Fat, wet flakes of snow covered her head and shoulders as she walked down the porch steps and headed toward the machinery sheds. Uncle Kent used to farm this land when it had become too much for his father, but Gramps had told her that her cousin Gary, Kent's oldest son, had long ago taken over. Kent and his wife had wanted to do a bit of traveling before old age set in and so they now spent their winters in Texas and their summers wherever the urge took them.

She pushed at one of the shed doors and found it locked. This was something new. Gramps never used to lock up anything. She supposed, however, that crime was possible everywhere and that small-town Kansas was just as vulnerable to theft as Chicago.

Deciding to go to a favorite spot, Lynn retraced the path that she'd so often taken as a child. The only time she'd been truly happy was here on the Lewiston farm. Her mother and father were so seldom around, always traveling with one symphony or another. They were musicians, and their lives were spent in whirlwinds that seldom slowed enough to take notice of the two daughters they'd brought into the world.

Lynn and her sister had grown up with nannies and babysitters during the school year and Grammie and Gramps in the summer. Summers were always better. Nannies and sitters changed with the years, but Grammie and Gramps were always the same. They filled the need for security and consistency that Lynn could not otherwise find.

Coming to the end of the path, Lynn picked her way up a rock pile that had been there as long as she could remember. Gramps planned to use the rocks to build a smokehouse but had never gotten around to it. Now they sat, much the same as they had for thirty years. At the top, Lynn had a view of the snowy valley. Winter had painted the sky a dull, gunmetal gray. It seemed to match her spirit.

"What do I do, Lord?" Both she and Frank were Christians. They believed in honoring God and living their lives in accordance with the Bible. And because of that, Lynn was uncomfortable with her contemplation of leaving her marriage. Divorce was out of the question. Frank hadn't cheated on her or beat her or done anything but work himself half to death. He wanted children and pressured her on a regular basis to give him some as she had promised she would, but memories of her own disappointing childhood left Lynn reluctant. Her parents were never there for her. How would it be with Frank? Would their child or children suffer because of his long absences? Would they sit at the window and wait for a father who had to delay one more day in Pittsburgh in order to satisfy his client? Or would they grow resentful and bitter as she had?

The cold evening air chilled Lynn to the bone. Hugging her arms to her body, she wondered how she could ever sort through the mess of her marriage.

Hours later, Lynn prepared for bed in the same room she'd shared with Monica when they were children. This was their summer room, their dream room. Here they had helped Grammie hang new curtains every summer. Here, Lynn and Monica had shared their innermost secrets about what life would be like if Mom and Dad would give up the symphony and come home for good.

Lynn smiled at the books on the bookcase shelves. *Little Women*, *Eight Cousins*, *Pride and Prejudice*, among others, greeted her like old, dear friends. These were the books she'd dreamed her dreams upon. Books of good families and wonderful homes where people were more important than things.

With a sigh, she sat down on the iron-framed bed and smiled at the same old squeaky springs. She bounced up and down just a bit, to remind herself of the times when she and Monica had bouncing competitions. Tears came to her eyes. She almost wished she could be ten years old again. Wished she could go back in time and plead with her parents to change their lives before they grew up and apart.

What would she say to them, if she could go back and make things different? What would she say to Frank? How could she explain to him that her own haunted memories of childhood kept her from wanting to have children of her own?

She bristled at this thought. She'd never so much as allowed the idea to be spoken into words. Even thinking of it caused her to look around the room in a panic. She had never told Frank how she felt. He had first met her when he found her working in a rescue shelter's day-care center. She had been knee-deep in toddlers, loving every minute of it. She adored kids and they seemed drawn to her, but how could she bring a child into the world only to allow him or her to suffer the things Lynn herself had suffered?

She thought back to the missed birthdays and to holidays spent waiting for parents who never showed up until well after the celebration had passed. She thought of waiting all week to tell her mother about the scores on her sixth-grade mastery test, only to have that year's nanny extend the message that her parents were off to perform for a last-minute charity benefit.

The pain still gnawed at her like a sore that refused to heal. She had spent so many disappointing hours watching, waiting, and wondering when her parents would arrive home—hoping against all of the odds that they'd surprise her and pop in unexpectedly. But they never came home early or unexpectedly. Instead, they were often absent and predictably late.

Crawling into bed, Lynn allowed herself to cry freely. She thought of the loneliness she endured in her marriage. She knew Frank loved working for Bridgeton National Life, but couldn't he see that his constant traveling was tearing their marriage apart? Didn't he ever wonder how she felt about the situation? How hard it was to go to bed alone, wondering where he was and if he missed her.

"How can I bring children into this world if this is all I have to offer them? How do I dry their tears when their father never comes home except to get caught up on laundry?"

Would it be worth trying to explain the situation to Frank?

"It won't change anything," she muttered. Frank would never understand her anxiety over the matter. She just knew he'd laugh it off. *He'd call me silly and tell me I was borrowing trouble. Well, maybe he won't see my leaving as silly, although I've probably borrowed myself plenty of trouble by coming here without leaving him so much as a note.*

For a moment she felt a guilty twinge. She'd left in such a hurry that she'd actually forgotten to leave Frank a note as to her whereabouts. But after she'd driven as far as Bloomington, her first stop for the night, Lynn was actually glad she'd forgotten.

"Let him see how it is to worry," she told herself.

But now she felt even worse. No one deserved to fret and worry in that manner. In this day and age of people disappearing due to serial killers or simply being in the wrong place at the right time, Lynn knew it would be horribly unfeeling to leave Frank without any word at all.

But would he even care? Maybe he'd come home and find her gone and celebrate. At least she wouldn't be there to nag or condemn him. He'd not have to dread being there. Tears streamed down her cheeks. He actually dreaded coming home to her. It was just too much to bear.

CHAPTER 3

"You've reached the Murphy residence," came Lynn's voice over the telephone. "We're unable to come to the phone right now, but if you'll leave a number and a brief message, we'll get back to you as soon as possible." *Beep.*

Frank scowled. "Lynn, if you're there, pick up the phone. This is the third time I've called and you haven't bothered to answer any of my messages."

He waited for several seconds, hoping she'd pick up the phone, but she never did.

Slamming the receiver down, Frank wondered what to do next. He'd hoped to catch her at home in order to properly apologize for the callous way he'd treated her dreams of a proper anniversary celebration.

She deserved to have her special day, and he'd made the mistake of implying that it was the same as any other date. That they could celebrate anytime. Well, obviously she didn't feel that way, and he should have respected her feelings.

Glancing at his watch, Frank figured the only thing he could do was try Lynn at work. She wasn't supposed to be there for another hour, but it was always possible she'd gone in early.

Dialing the number, Frank waited expectantly for Lynn to answer.

"Dr. Madison's office," a female voice, clearly not belonging to his wife, answered.

"Ah, I'm calling for Lynn Murphy."

"I'm sorry, she won't be in the office today."

"Did she call in sick?"

"I'm sorry, sir, I'm not allowed to give out that information."

"Look, this is her husband and I'm out of town. I've been trying to reach her for three days. Let me talk to Dr. Madison."

"Just a minute," the woman replied.

"Frank?" Cindy Madison's voice reassured him.

"Cindy, where's Lynn?"

"You mean she didn't tell you?"

"What are you talking about?" Frank questioned, a sickening feeling twisting his stomach in knots. "Tell me what?"

"Frank, she's taken a month off. She called me Sunday at home and asked for an emergency leave."

"Lynn never takes time off unless it's important. Did something happen with her grandfather?"

"No, Frank," Cindy replied flatly. "She left because of you."

"What!" he replied, more loudly than he'd intended.

"Look, I can't hang on here. I'm not sure where she went, but she asked for the time off. She was pretty upset, Frank, and I think she's trying to figure out what to do about it."

Long after Frank had ended his conversation with Cindy Madison, her final words rang in his ears. *She's trying to figure out what to do about it.*

Frank caught a cab at O'Hare International Airport and headed for his apartment. He still found it hard to believe that

Lynn had actually left him. He knew there were problems with their marriage, but to suggest their problems were insurmountable was ridiculous. He paid the cab driver and greeted the doorman.

"Good evening, Mr. Murphy."

"Evening," Frank murmured, inserting a key into his mailbox.

"Hope the missus is having a pleasant trip."

"What?" Frank questioned, now giving the man his full attention.

"I helped Mrs. Murphy bring her suitcases downstairs. Is she having a good trip?"

"I hope so," Frank replied, not liking this confirmation one bit. "I've been out of town, so I haven't had much of a chance to talk to her." He added the latter to keep the building staff from speculating on the status of his marriage.

He caught the elevator and while thumbing through his mail, waited for the floors to click by. She couldn't be gone. She just couldn't be gone.

Yet, by the time he'd opened the door to their apartment, he knew she was very clearly absent. Silence greeted him as it had on several other occasions when Lynn had been off to one class or another, but this was different. This silence seemed very final.

Setting his flight bag aside, Frank tossed the mail on the coffee table and went to search the bedroom. Flipping on the light, he found a perfectly ordered room. The bed was made; the clothes were all put away. There wasn't a single sign to suggest anyone had been around for days.

Going to the closet, Frank's suspicions and fears were confirmed again. Most of Lynn's clothes were gone. Empty hangers seemed to taunt him. Going to the bed, he checked underneath and then sat down in a dejected manner. Her suitcases were gone.

"What did you expect?" he asked himself. "Cindy told you she'd taken time off. She never takes time off unless it's an emergency."

A feeling of hopelessness washed over him. Reaching for the telephone, he dialed the one person who could offer him comfort at a time like this. Perhaps, too, she would have insight into Lynn's actions and have suggestions for her son.

"Mom?"

"Frank, is that you?" Cissy Murphy questioned.

"Yes, it's me. Look, something's going on here and I need some advice."

"Are you okay?"

He heard the concern in her voice and desired only to put her mind at ease. "Yes and no. I mean, physically, I'm fine. Mentally and emotionally, I'm a mess. Lynn's left me."

"What? Is this a joke, Frank?" Cissy questioned in disbelief.

"I wish it were that simple. But it's not. Lynn left while I was away on business."

"Why?"

"I wish I knew," Frank replied. Then stopped. "No, that's not true. I have my ideas."

"Did you fight?"

"Yes. We argued before I left, because I canceled our anniversary trip to Mexico."

"Why did you do that?"

"Bridgeton needs me to oversee a meeting with one of our clients. I've been on the case all along and I figured I'd better be the one to handle the job."

"You let work take precedence over celebrating your anniversary with Lynn?"

"I wouldn't have considered it if it had been another case,"

Frank said, but even as he spoke he knew it was a lie. "Well, maybe that's not exactly true."

"Frank, I've talked to Lynn many times on the telephone. Usually when I call, you're off on one business trip or another. Don't you realize how lonely she gets? She tells me about all the different classes she's taking, and she's only doing it to fill the emptiness in her life. An emptiness that you've helped to create."

"My job is important. I've worked hard to get where I am, and I don't want to do anything that might jeopardize it. I saw how you and Pop struggled, and I don't want that for my family."

"Frank, you won't have any family if you can't find a way to have time for both your job and your wife."

"I know. That's part of the problem. I want to start our family now, but Lynn is against it. We both agreed that once I finished college and found a good job, she'd quit her job and start having kids. But every time I bring up the idea, she refuses."

"On what grounds?" Cissy questioned softly.

"She never says much. She always brings up my job and how much I'm gone and how hard I work."

"I don't blame her."

"But can't you see, Mom? I know what it is to be poor. I saw the way you had to make do with so little. I saw Pop go off to a job he hated, and he still never made enough money to do much more than put a roof over our heads."

"Is that why you drive yourself so hard?"

Frank could hear the disbelief in his mother's tone. "Well, it certainly plays a part. I want a better life for my family."

"A better life? But Frank, I thought you had a happy childhood."

"I did. That's why I want a family of my own."

"But you make it sound as though we lived in poverty."

"Well, we did. We didn't have much in the way of material possessions and there were never any extras. I remember how hard you worked to get material to make a dress for Irene's prom," he replied, remembering his older sister's desire for a full-length gown of green velvet.

"Frank, we certainly weren't rich in possessions, but we had a great deal that kept us happy. When you think about your childhood, what are the memories that make you feel good? What are the things that made you say, 'Yes, I had a wonderful childhood'? Think on those things and tell me what you see."

"That's easy. I remember the security in knowing that you and Pop loved me. I remember your encouragement and counsel. I remember that you always took time out for me."

"None of those things have anything to do with money, Frank."

"Yes, I know, but I also remember worrying about you and Pop. I would overhear you talking about the finances. Wondering how we were going to get through from one month to the next. It worried me. I knew then that I would find a job that paid a lot of money, and I would never put my family through that same concern."

"I'm sorry you worried. Your father and I never intended for you kids to ever concern yourself with such matters. I know you didn't have every material possession you ever desired, but you had our love and trust."

"I know that, and it means the world to me."

"So why do you imagine that your family would want anything less? Lynn probably doesn't even know you feel this way. If your attitude towards work is as much a mystery to her as it always has been to me, then I can't say as I blame her for leaving. As the saying goes, money can't buy happiness."

"Yes, but it buys all the things that help to make life better. Money provides the extras in life. Money sees to it that you have what you need, when you need it."

"And here all this time, I thought God did that," Cissy replied sarcastically.

"Mom, you know what I mean."

"No, Frank, I don't think I do. Look, you were raised to put your trust in God. I was there when you made a public acceptance of Jesus as your Savior. You can't serve both God and money. The Bible makes that real clear. You'll only come to hate one or the other."

"I'm not serving money," Frank protested.

"No? You told me a few minutes ago that 'Money provides. . .' that 'Money sees to it. . .' Sounds to me like money has taken the place of God. You trust money to get you through. You trust money to make your way easy and clear. You give yourself over to a job that consumes all your time and energy, and then wonder why your wife would walk out on you."

"You aren't much help here, Mom. I suppose you're saying this is all my fault?"

Cissy laughed softly. "I'm sorry for laughing, but you sound so much like a little boy again. Remember the time you accidentally broke the back window? You were playing baseball with your brothers and some of the neighborhood kids."

"I remember."

"You said much the same thing then. 'I suppose you're saying this is all my fault,' you told me. Then you reminded me that Brian had pitched the ball and Terry hadn't been able to catch your pop fly. You said it was as much their fault that the window was broken."

"I remember," Frank replied, easily seeing what his mother was suggesting.

"Frank, it doesn't matter who broke what. Placing blame isn't going to fix the problem. You need to make some tough choices here. Either you serve God or you serve money. Either you want a life with Lynn, or you don't. It sounds overly simplified, I know, but that's about as clear as it gets."

"I have to work for a living," Frank protested.

"Yes, but you also need to take some time out to live," Cissy countered. "You need to work to pay the rent and buy the groceries. That much is true. But hoarding money in case something happens, losing sleep over all the what-ifs, and losing a wife because you're never home is hardly worth working toward. You're going to have to decide on your priorities, Frank. Either you give yourself completely to your job, or you find a way to compromise and be there for Lynn as well."

"I thought I was here for her."

"Not when you consider that since Thanksgiving you've only been home three days, and none of those were consecutive days. And now you've canceled the one thing she was most looking forward to?"

"I suppose you're right, but it doesn't make it any easier. I don't know where she's gone. I don't even know where to start."

"Search your heart, Frank. Think of all that Lynn needs right now. She's lonely. She's going to search for that place that makes her feel secure and whole. She's going to look for where she can find love."

"I thought she found that here."

"I know, honey, but you're going to have to look beyond what you thought to be true. Pray about it. I will too. I know God will show you the answer."

Frank ended the conversation and sat staring at the wall for several minutes before actually hanging up the telephone receiver. What his mother said had hurt him deeply, but not because she had dared to say the words. No, it hurt because they were true, and Frank didn't know what to do about it.

Taking up his Bible, Frank searched for the verses his mother had spoken of. The sixth chapter of 1 Timothy loomed up to accuse him.

"Those who want to get rich fall into temptation and a trap and into many foolish and harmful desires that plunge people into ruin and destruction. For the love of money is a root of all kinds of evil. Some people, eager for money, have wandered from the faith and pierced themselves with many griefs," Frank read aloud.

"But I don't love money. I simply see it as a necessity and to keep my family comfortable and happy—" He fell silent remembering his mother's words. He had grown up happy, and yet their father's wages had never come near a fourth of what Frank made. They were happy because of their commitment to one another. They were happy because of the love they shared, not because of the security they had in their financial status.

Leaning back on the bed, Frank closed his eyes in complete exhaustion. "God, have I been serving money? Is that what this is all about?" He knew the answer but still found it impossible to admit to himself. Just as he found it impossible to believe that Lynn wouldn't suddenly appear in the bedroom to welcome him home once again.

CHAPTER 4

Frank awoke the next morning feeling strangely refreshed. He had an energy about him that gave him the strength to go forward. His first task was to figure out where Lynn had gone. His mother said he should think about a place where Lynn felt safe and secure—where she knew happiness and love. The only thought that came to mind was the farm her grandfather owned near Council Grove, Kansas.

Frank remembered when he'd first met Lynn. She had spoken with fondness of summers spent with her grandparents and of the happiness she had known with them. He thought back to the funeral of her beloved grandmother. A funeral he'd had to send her to alone. She'd come home saddened by the loss of her grandmother but strangely at peace from the time she'd spent with her grandfather.

Reaching for the telephone, Frank called directory assistance and asked to place a call to Omar Lewiston.

"Hello?" It was clearly the voice of an old man.

"Omar? This is Frank Murphy."

"Kind of figured I might be hearing from you sometime soon."

"Does that mean Lynn is with you?"

"She's here all right. Not too happy and not at all her talkative self, but she's here."

"Do you think she'd be willing to talk to me on the phone?"

"I don't know," Omar admitted. "She didn't say that she wouldn't. Let me go get her."

Frank waited in silence while Omar went in search of Lynn. He prayed that she'd come to the phone and at least let him explain how important she was to him. Maybe he could offer to rearrange the trip plans. Maybe they could go to Mexico after New Year's.

"Hello, Frank." Her words were clipped, her tone devoid of emotion.

"I'm so glad you're safe. I was so worried," Frank began. "Why didn't you at least leave me a note telling me where you'd gone?"

"I didn't think you'd even notice I was gone," Lynn said flatly.

"Lynnie, that's not fair. You know I love you. I was frantic when I couldn't reach you, and then I called Cindy and found out you'd taken a leave of absence. Why didn't you wait to talk this over with me when I got home?"

"Who could ever say when that might be?" Lynn countered angrily. "I've sat at home many a night waiting for you, and you might say I'm done waiting around."

"What do you mean by that?" Frank asked, fearing he already knew her meaning.

"I mean that I'm here with Gramps and I'm thinking hard about what's to become of our marriage."

"I see."

"No, Frank, I don't think you do." She paused and Frank wondered if she was working to control her temper or her emotions. "I'm considering a divorce, or at the very least a permanent separation."

"No!" Frank couldn't stand to even hear the words. Running a hand through his sandy-brown hair, he shook his head. "You can't mean that."

"Oh, but I do. I've tried to make it work, but you know, Frank, it's hard to make a marriage of two people when one is never around."

"I know and I'm sorry. That's one of the things I want to talk to you about. I know my schedule caused all this, and I'm going to do what I can to put things into proper order."

"It's too late for that."

"No, it's not. Don't say that."

"Look, I know we see things differently. Probably so much so that it's impossible to make a marriage together. I don't believe in divorce, and I know God hates it, but I can hardly ask you to stay in a marriage when I don't plan to be around to be a wife to you. I'm here to think things through and figure out what's to be done."

"Don't you suppose that's something we ought to work on together?"

"There were a lot of things I figured we were supposed to do together," Lynn replied. "You apparently had other thoughts."

Frank didn't know what to say. They were getting nowhere at this rate, and he hated trying to resolve anything over the telephone.

"Please just come home and work on this with me. I'll take a few days off from work and—"

"That'll be the day!" Lynn retorted angrily. "You couldn't take a few days off to go on a long-planned anniversary vacation, why would you take time off for this? After all, money's not involved."

Frank felt his own anger stirred at this. The problem was her words hit too close to the truth of the matter. "Look, I want to save this marriage."

"Well, I'm not sure I do," Lynn countered.

"I don't believe you. I know you love me."

"Yes," she replied, her voice softening. "That much is true. I can't deny my love for you. It's the only thing that's kept me there this long." She said nothing for several seconds, then added, "I think you've made a choice in your life that doesn't include me."

"That isn't true, and if you'd get off your high horse and come home, you'd see it for yourself. I love you, Lynnie. You have to know that."

"Well, I don't think I do," Lynn replied, her voice once again taking on a tone of defensiveness. "You're seldom home, and when you are there, your mind is clearly given over to your job. You badger me about having a family, yet you cannot begin to imagine what it is to grow up without a father. Now, why don't you just leave me alone and give me the space I need? I'm happy here, which is something I can't say for our place in Chicago." With that, she slammed down the phone, never giving Frank a chance to reply.

Rage coursed through him like a wildfire, but even as Frank slammed down his own receiver, he knew Lynn had some very valid points. Her feelings were completely justifiable, but he couldn't bear that she was happier away from him than with him.

Remembering that his boss George Bridgeton had no idea he was back in town, Frank showered and dressed and made his way over to the office. He'd already decided that if it took taking time off from work to prove his devotion to Lynn, then he'd simply have to make it happen. No doubt Ray Wagner, his newest protégé, could handle his caseload until he was able to return.

"Frank!" George exclaimed in greeting. "I didn't expect you back until tomorrow."

"I know, but something has happened," Frank explained,

unfastening the bottom button of his suit coat.

"With the case?"

Frank shook his head and took a seat. He watched as the older man's expression changed from worry to curiosity.

"Then what?"

"I'm having some problems at home. I need some time off."

George nodded. "Well, I know you had planned to take those two weeks off over the holidays, but the Greigs' case came up and—"

"I know, but I want Ray to handle it," Frank replied, still unable to believe he was actually saying the words. It had come to dawn on him as he'd made the drive to the office that he was actually fearful of anyone else stealing his thunder. His mother's words had caused him to do some heavy-duty soul-searching, and Frank didn't like the things that kept coming into view.

"May I ask why?"

Frank took pity on the man. George had been a good friend as well as a boss. They were going on four years of working together and Frank knew George respected him. "There are some personal problems that need my attention. I'd rather not say anything more about it just now. Suffice it to say, I need to leave today and I'm not sure how much time I'll need."

"I see," George said, shuffling the papers in his hands. "Will we be able to reach you for troubleshooting?"

Frank sighed. "I suppose if matters were critical, but otherwise, I'd prefer to be completely out of the loop. I don't want to have the conflict of my attention being divided between two issues."

Frank watched as George seemed to consider the matter for a moment. "All right, Frank. You've been a valuable asset to this company, and I know you wouldn't leave if it weren't of the utmost importance. Call me periodically to touch base, but otherwise, we'll try to leave you alone."

"Thank you," Frank said, extending a piece of paper. "Here's where you can reach me, but only if it's critical."

George took the paper and studied for a moment. "Are you sure there's nothing else I can do?"

Frank smiled. "You could pray. I've known that to work miracles, and right now I need one of major proportions."

George nodded. "I'll do that, Frank."

Two hours later Frank was packed and headed down the interstate. His thoughts were consumed with images of Lynn. Lynn, when he'd first met her. Lynn, when she'd walked down the aisle to marry him. Lynn.

He could see her soft, blond hair feathered around her face and cut to the shoulder. He imagined her blue eyes gazing with longing into his own. He remembered her laugh and the way she always made him take things less seriously. But this time he couldn't take things less seriously. This time his entire future was on the line.

He picked up speed as he cleared the downtown traffic and headed out of town. He almost reconsidered driving to Kansas in favor of flying. A flight could have him to Kansas City in a few hours, and from there he could take a commuter flight to Topeka and rent a car to drive down to Council Grove. He could be there in time for supper. It sounded very appealing.

But in his heart, Frank knew he needed to take the time to reconsider his life and what he'd done. He needed to think through the way he'd allowed memories of poverty to direct his course. His mother was right. He'd allowed money to run the show—to rule him, in a way.

Lynn must have picked up on that fact long ago, so why hadn't she said something?

But hadn't she?

Frank was reminded of conversations they'd shared in the past. Conversations where Lynn had begged him to take time off to be home more. He remembered not only the canceled anniversary trip but other trips they had canceled because of Frank's schedule.

He remembered, too, that Lynn had taken up a variety of activities, which at first Frank had seen as a blessing. But now he realized she was only trying to fill the void he'd created. She was a married woman with an absentee husband. Who could blame her for her discontentment?

He pounded the steering wheel. "What a fool I've been," he declared. "I thought I could build her contentment out of financial security and material possessions, and instead, I drove her away."

But is it too late? he wondered. Could he find a way to win her back?

"Please God, tell me it's not too late."

CHAPTER 5

I can't believe he expects me to just drop everything and come running back home," Lynn told her grandfather.

Omar smiled and rubbed his balding head. "Could be he expected you to take your marriage vows seriously. You know, 'till death do us part'?"

Lynn turned back to give her attention to the frying pan where chicken sizzled and popped. "You would say that. You and Grammie had sixty good years of marriage. It would be easy to stay until death if you were married to the right person."

"I never said it was easy," Omar replied.

Lynn looked over her shoulder to see the grin on the old man's wrinkled face. "What do you mean?"

"You think your grammie and I didn't have our problems? I'm telling you, girl, life with that woman was like being on one of those amusement park roller coasters. We were up one minute and down the next. Life's like that, don't you know."

Lynn turned the heat down on the chicken and came to take a seat opposite her grandfather. "But you two never fought, right?"

Omar laughed heartily at this. "We had some horrible fights. Grammie made me sleep on the couch more than once."

Lynn knew her expression registered shock. She couldn't help the fact that her mouth had dropped open, and this only made Omar laugh all the harder. "I can't believe you and Grammie ever had problems."

"Oh, Lynnie, everybody has problems. Marriage is hard work. People are individuals, and you can't put two individuals together and not expect to have two different opinions and two different solutions for everything. Your grammie and I had to learn to work through our differences, just as you and Frank will have to do. That is, unless you plan to divorce him."

Lynn shuddered. "No, I know that's wrong. But at the same time, I just can't imagine waltzing back into the same situation without resolving some of the problems. Frank just doesn't understand my feelings."

"Have you ever tried to explain them to him?" Omar asked.

Lynn opened her mouth to readily admit she had, but she knew it wasn't true and instantly shut it again.

"I thought not. Why is that, Lynnie?"

Lynn shrugged. "I suppose it's because I've always figured if he cared about me, he'd try to find out these things on his own. Besides, he's never around to talk to for more than a few minutes."

"So your main problem is that Frank is gone all the time?" Omar questioned. "Is that how you see it?"

"Well, it certainly hasn't helped things. Frank talks constantly about having a family and yet he's never there to see how things are. First of all, we certainly couldn't raise a family in that apartment. So what does Frank expect me to do? Am I supposed to go out and find a house or a bigger apartment while he's off on yet another of his business trips?" She barely paused for breath before continuing. "And if we did have children, who would end up raising them?

I would. I would be alone most of the time. Frank would be an absentee father, and I know how it feels to be on the receiving end of one of those."

Omar nodded. "And it scares you to death to think you might have to relive those memories."

Lynn felt her defenses rise. "Of course I find it frightening. Those were horrible times, Gramps. Mom and Dad were always gone, always playing one concert or another, always sending sweet little cards with lovely messages and balloons and flowers, but never themselves."

They both fell silent for a moment and then Omar reached out and patted her arm. "But it's in the past."

"But it will be the future if I go back to Frank and start having babies!" Lynn exclaimed. "Don't you see? Frank is going to have to change his ways. This whole situation is his fault."

Omar shook his head. "Takes two to make a marriage and it takes two to break one up. What's your fault in all of this?"

"My fault?" Lynn questioned indignantly. "I'm sure I don't understand what you mean. I'm not the one on the road all the time. I'm there at the apartment, faithfully waiting for Frank to return from conquering the dragons of the insurance world."

"Think about it a minute, Lynnie. You must have played some part in this."

Lynn settled back against the dinette chair. "If you call it a fault that I refuse to have children until I'm sure about becoming a parent, then I guess that's my fault in all of this."

Omar chuckled. "Maybe you could also point to a bit of pride and stubbornness, as well."

Lynn let out a sigh. "I thought you would be on my side."

"I am on your side. But I'm also on Frank's side. You two are one, now. Don't you see that? What affects the one equally affects the other. You can't just walk away from your marriage and say, 'Well, that didn't work, so I'm off to live with Gramps.' Lynnie, it doesn't work that way."

Her shoulders sagged dejectedly. "I just don't have the energy to try and make it work anymore. I'm lonely, Gramps. I'm lonely and sad so much of the time that I don't even like myself anymore."

"That could certainly be a big part of the problem," Omar suggested. "How can Frank like you if you don't even like yourself? I went through a spell like that with my Ketta. She gained a whole bunch of weight after having your mother and she wasn't very happy about it. Said she looked horrible and that she'd just as soon hide in a cave. At first it wasn't that big of a deal. I'd tease her a little, console her a little, do whatever I could to make her feel better. But things just got worse and worse. Pretty soon she didn't want to go anywhere with me, so I had to go to functions by myself. Then I'd get home and she'd rant and rave because I left her alone. I didn't know what to do. I tried to reason with her that some things just had to be done and some events couldn't be avoided, but when she even stopped going to church on Sunday, I knew we'd come as far as we could."

"What did you do?" Lynn questioned, absolutely fascinated that her grammie had ever worried about things like weight and appearance.

"For a time I didn't do anything. We didn't talk about it, and I stopped trying to help her see reason. The weight stayed on, and she might have even added to it, but it didn't matter to me. I loved her and she looked just fine to me. Then one day, Ketta's good friend Mary came to call. Mary wasn't at all sympathetic like I had been. Mary told Ketta that she was a vain and prideful woman and that both were sinful traits for a woman of God. I was just outside the house, painting the windowsill, but I could see your grandma's face through the window. She looked like Mary had punched her in the nose. Here she had expected a sympathetic and compassionate ear, but Mary told her to stop feeling sorry for herself and either do something about the weight or accept that she was who she was."

"What did Grammie say?"

"For a time, she said nothing. Then she started to cry. She told Mary she couldn't stand the way she'd been acting, but that she seemed hard-pressed to figure out how to change things around. She apologized and promised Mary to do better, but Mary stood her ground. She told Ketta apologies and guilt and promises and so forth were all well and fine, but she wouldn't feel better until she accepted things for what they were. She took your grandma to the mirror in the hall. I had to move to painting the front door jamb, which I hadn't planned to paint, in order to hear what she had to say."

Lynn grinned. "I can just see you there with your ear straining to catch every sound."

"Yes sir, I was pretty good at eavesdropping. Anyway, Mary told your grandma to take a good look at herself and tell her what she saw. Ketta said, 'I see a fat woman.' Mary just nodded and said, 'What else?' Well, Ketta was kind of stumped for a minute, so Mary started talking for her. 'You're also a tall woman. You're an attractive woman with beautiful blond hair that doesn't bear a hint of gray. You're a wife and mother and a Sunday school teacher. You're a godly woman who loves her family and has shown great acts of kindness to those around her. At least, you were that woman—are you still?'"

"Well, by this time, Ketta started crying and she could see what Mary was trying to say. The weight was just one aspect of her physical makeup, but it had very little to do with why people loved and needed her. That was an important turning point for her. You'll have to find that important turning point for yourself. You'll have to see beyond the physical and the things that seem so apparent. You need to dig down deep inside and see what's truly motivating your heart. Ketta felt her weight made her unworthy, and she focused so much on that one thing that the things that had made her worthy to so many people were forfeited. Well, at least for the time being. She found her way back. Learned to be content with herself, and pretty soon the weight wasn't an issue anymore. She started getting involved again and doing all the things she'd done before, and pretty soon she realized the weight had dropped off on its own accord."

"But how does that help me?" Lynn asked.

Omar patted her arm again. "You're afraid of a great many things right now. You feel unloved and unworthy for whatever reasons you want to choose. You need to look into your heart and figure out what the real problem is, Lynnie. I seriously doubt that either you or Frank are truly dealing with the real problem. Frank obviously is worried about having enough money for his family. Has he ever told you why? Did he grow up without a great many of the things he needed?"

"I don't know," Lynn said, shaking her head. "He's never really talked about it. All I do know is that he had a happy childhood and that's why he wants lots of kids. He wants to relive those moments, I guess."

"I'd talk to him," Omar told her seriously. "I'd tell him why you're so afraid. How painful your own memories are, and how you fear your children will grow up under someone else's care like you did."

Lynn got up to turn the chicken, all the time thinking about what Gramps had said. Maybe there was something to it. Maybe she was only seeing the surface problem as the issue, instead of the real, underlying cause.

"Mom and Dad were never there for me," she said all of a sudden. "They missed my high school graduation and very nearly missed my wedding. They were gone when I had school programs." She paused for a moment remembering a particularly painful memory. "Even when I had the lead in the school play when I was a freshman in high school, they were on the road somewhere performing."

"And your point is?" Gramps coaxed.

Lynn put the turning fork down and rejoined Omar at the table. She didn't sit, however, but stood staring down at him. "My point is they were gone more than they were there. They missed most every important moment in my life. They were never there, Gramps, and I really resent that."

"So, you going to keep carrying the bitterness around with you all of your life?" he asked softly.

Lynn studied the balding head and wrinkled face for a moment. His glasses and bulbous nose made him look even older than his eighty-one years, but Lynn didn't care. She loved this man more than anyone in the world, and he was the only one who could ask such a question of her and not have Lynn retaliate in anger.

"I suppose you have a point, Gramps."

"Doesn't solve the problem, but it sure sheds some light on things, don't you think?"

Lynn nodded. "Yes, I guess it does. I suppose I have a great deal to think about."

"You can't ever help the future by carrying the mistakes of the past into it. We need to learn from our mistakes, and the mistakes of others. Your mom and dad were wrong to leave you so much. They probably should have never had children, just as you feel you shouldn't have them. But I know I would have regretted that choice. I loved having you around. I loved, maybe selfishly so, having you girls spend the summer with us. I'm sorry it wasn't enough."

Lynn instantly felt remorse for her words. She'd never meant to make Gramps feel bad. "You and Grammie were my life. You were the only ones who got me through the bad times. Don't ever think you weren't enough," she said, hugging the man around the neck. She kissed his bald head and added, "You were, and still are, everything a girl could want in a grandfather. I wouldn't change anything about you."

Omar laughed. "If your grammie were here, she'd give you a long list of things she'd like to have seen me change."

"Then I would certainly have to question her sanity," Lynn replied. "Because I think you're perfect."

CHAPTER 6

Frank wasn't sure what kind of greeting he'd get when he reached the Lewiston farm, but he held on to his determination to force Lynn's hand. If she wanted to play a game of bluff or otherwise, he was going to stand his ground and see the thing through. There was no way he could allow his marriage to just fall apart, and whatever he needed to do, he would do.

At least, this was his resolve as he parked his car in the Lewiston driveway. Without worrying about his things, Frank made his way to the house and drew a deep breath. "Help me through this, Lord," he whispered, then knocked loudly on the screen door.

The cold air chilled him as he waited for someone to answer. He'd passed through snow and sleet on his way from Chicago to Council Grove, but his desire to see Lynn and figure a way to make things work had been all the encouragement he'd needed. Even when the road advisory on the radio had suggested all nonessential vehicles stay off the roads, Frank had pushed on. Now, as the snow came down in earnest and the lead-gray sky seemed darker than ever, he wondered if he'd be allowed to stay.

The door finally opened, and Frank came face-to-face with Lynn. He smiled kind of sheepishly, hoping she would see it as a gesture of his willingness to work on their problem.

"Hi," he said softly.

"What are you doing here?" Lynn questioned. Then look-ing beyond him at the snow, she added, "We're due for at least six inches of snow. Didn't you think about that before heading down here?"

"I thought maybe you'd be at least a little glad to see me. I thought maybe we could talk through our problems."

Lynn seemed to consider this before stepping aside for Frank to come into the house. "I suppose since you're here and since the weather is turning bad, I have no other choice but to let you stay."

Frank laughed. "At least you still care enough to take pity on me."

Lynn had turned to precede him down the hall, but at this she stopped and her expression looked so pained that Frank immediately wanted to comfort her. "I never said I didn't care, Frank. It wouldn't hurt this much if I didn't care."

He immediately felt sorry that he'd laughed and made a joke of the situation. "I didn't mean it that way. I was just hoping to lighten up the situation."

Lynn said nothing more but led him into the kitchen. "Do you want some coffee?"

"Sure, that sounds great," Frank replied, wondering how to get her to open up and discuss the issues at hand. "Will you have some too?"

Lynn looked at him blankly for a moment, then nodded. "All right." She brought two cups of black coffee, then sat down at the small dinette set.

Frank looked at the set and smiled. "You know, reproductions of these are selling like hotcakes up in Chicago. That 1950s chrome and Formica seems to appeal to a lot of folks."

"Probably reminds them of what they used to know," Lynn replied softly.

Frank took the seat opposite her and nodded. "Probably. Say, where's Omar?"

"He's gone out to take care of some things around the yard. He says when the weather folks say six inches it's more likely to be twelve. Snow is very hard to predict."

"I see." He sipped the coffee, then decided to get right to the point. "Look, I know you're hurting, but I'm hurting too. We can't just let this thing come between us. I've always known that we'd have our ups and downs; I just never expected you to run away at the first threat of trouble."

"It wasn't the first threat of trouble that sent me running," Lynn replied, her eyes never quite meeting his.

"All right, then why don't you tell me what this is all about?"

Lynn drew a deep breath and nodded. "I suppose I should. Gramps would say it was only right." She looked down at her cup and sighed. "I love you, Frank. There's no doubt about that. I've loved you since I was eighteen years old. I wouldn't have married you otherwise. I loved you for your serious, take-charge attitude and for the drive and motivation that I knew would see us through the problems to come."

"But?" Frank interjected, knowing beyond a doubt that there was more to come.

"But I can't go on like we've been living. You're never home. You care more about your job than you do about me." She held up her hand as Frank started to protest. "No, hear me out. You drove all this way; now the least you can do is listen."

"All right."

"It isn't just the trip being canceled or the fact that you're seldom around to go places with me. It's that even when you are home, you aren't there. Your mind is on your clients and the problems you have to resolve in order to remain top dog at Bridgeton National Life. You know more about your clients' needs and concerns than you do mine.

"I've tried to make it work. I've tried to fill the void, but it just isn't any good anymore. I feel like I'm tap-dancing on top of a moving train and sooner or later I'm going to fall off or crash up against a tunnel or something else. I'm tired, and I'm not sure I have the energy to go on trying."

"I didn't know you felt this way," Frank said softly. He felt confused by her words, wondering how things could have gotten to this point without him realizing that something was amiss.

"I suppose my fall or my tunnel came in the form of your desire to have a baby," Lynn said. This time she raised her face to meet Frank's gaze.

He could see the pain. Her anguish and sorrow cut him like a knife. She wasn't just being testy or selfish. Lynn appeared completely consumed by her misery.

"It isn't that I don't want to have children, Frank. I think you know that full well. I've always wanted kids. I even wanted the big family you dreamed of. But what I don't want is to raise those children alone. My mother and father were never around when I was growing up. The symphony consumed all their time and took them on the road nearly as much as Bridgeton Life takes you.

"I had nannies and babysitters and in the summer I had Grammie and Gramps, but it wasn't enough. I needed my mother and father. I needed them both and they were always gone or too busy. I remember once when I tried to tell my father about a difficult test I had managed to ace. He was busy going through sheet music at the time, and I figured I only had half of his attention. But in truth, I didn't have any of it. When I told him about the test, he said, 'Well, try harder next time.' If he'd slapped me in the face it would have hurt less."

"Lynn, I'm so sorry," Frank told her. He'd had no idea that she was harboring this hurt from the past. "Why didn't you ever tell me about your childhood?"

Lynn shrugged. "I didn't want anyone to know how painful it had been. I thought I could leave it in the past, but when I saw you becoming the same man my father had been, I knew it had followed me right into the future."

"I'm not like that," Frank replied.

"Yes, you are," Lynn said indignantly.

"How can you say that?" Now Frank was starting to get mad. This accusation was far from the truth. He was like his own father, gentle and caring. He would be the same kind of father to his children. He certainly wouldn't resemble the kind of man Lynn had just described.

Lynn looked at him sadly. "I can say it because I've seen it in play. Do you remember when we had Chinese food when you got back from that post-Thanksgiving trip?"

"Sure. It was great."

"You asked me then if it came from the Red Dragon Restaurant," Lynn continued. "I told you no, that I had made it. It was a recipe I learned in cooking class. Do you remember what you said?"

Frank scanned his memory, but it was blank. He didn't remember Lynn saying she had made the meal. "No," he finally replied.

"You went on with your conversation as though I'd said, 'Yes.' You said, 'I've never had a bad meal from the Red Dragon and this one is no exception.' Then you proceeded to compliment their seasonings and the tenderness of the pork."

"I can't believe that I did that," Frank said defensively. He couldn't remember any of it and this alone bothered him as much as her words. "I'll bet you just misunderstood what I meant."

"Like I've misunderstood spending 360 days of the year by myself?" she retorted angrily.

"That's not fair. I haven't been gone that much. Look, I know I travel a lot, but that's what my job required."

"And the job of parenting requires a mother and a father. And while I realize a great many children grow up without one or the other, and sometimes without both, I will not raise a child by myself."

"Who said you'd have to?" Frank countered, stunned by her supposition.

Lynn slammed her hands down on the table. "Who did you plan to have help me? You're never there. Were you going to hire a man to play your part?"

"That's hardly fair, Lynnie."

"Maybe not, but it is accurate."

"No, it's not."

"Then tell me," Lynn began, her voice much calmer, "what did you plan to do? Were you going to quit your job? Were you going to cut back your hours? How were you going to ensure that I didn't raise our baby alone?"

Frank ran his hand back through his sandy-brown hair. It was a nervous habit he'd picked up whenever tough issues gave him cause to stop and rethink his strategy. He realized he would have to come clean with Lynn about his own past. He would have to explain his fear of poverty and the fear he had for his family.

"I have to…tell you something," Frank said hesitantly. "Just as you have fears from your childhood, I have my own." Lynn looked at him oddly but said nothing, so Frank continued. "I grew up in a big family, which you knew. There were a total of seven people living in one house, my four brothers and sisters and my mom and dad and me. My dad had a low-paying factory job, and while he did his best to see that we had what we needed, sometimes that just wasn't possible.

"I can still remember my mom and dad praying about the finances—giving their worries over to God because they had no idea where the next meal was going to come from. Once, my mom told us kids we were having a contest and that the person who came up with the most creative way to use her homemade ketchup and bread for a meal would win a prize. We kids thought it great fun. We made ketchup sandwiches and soup from ketchup and water. My sister even tore up chunks of bread and blended them in ketchup and sugar and baked it in the oven. We ate and laughed and joked about what was best. My sister won the prize, a much coveted candy bar, which she promptly allowed my mother to cut into five equal pieces. I never knew until I was older that the game had come because there was nothing else to eat. Mom had nothing but bread and homemade ketchup to feed her five children. The candy bar had been a gift from the lady next door who thought my mom was starting to look a bit on the thin side. Of course, Mom never had any of it, and we kids were too excited to worry or wonder where it came from."

Lynn's expression seemed to soften. "I can't even imagine. We never worried about our food."

Frank nodded. "That's why money concerns me so much. My mother admonished me that I was making money my god. And

I think she just might be right. I figured if we had a good nest egg and all the material things my folks lacked, then I could relax and bring children into the world and they would never have to suffer like I did."

"But I thought you said you were happy."

"I was," Frank answered.

"Then this attitude is foolish."

"No more so than yours. You figure because your parents were always gone that I would be that way with my children."

"Well, isn't that how it will have to be? If you're going to worry about whether or not we have enough to eat, you'll just keep on working at that ridiculous pace you've set and the kids and I will be left to fend for ourselves."

"That's not true!" Frank declared, his anger getting the better of him.

"It is true!"

"No more so than—"

"You know," Omar said, coming in through the back door and shaking off snow, "I could hear you arguing as I came up the walk. I don't think I've ever known two bigger ninnies."

"Don't you dare take his side," Lynn said, getting to her feet. "I won't have you both ganging up on me." With that, she stormed from the room, leaving Frank and Omar to stare at each other.

"What was that all about?" Frank questioned.

"Oh, we've been discussing this situation," Omar said, going to the coffeemaker to pour himself a cup of coffee.

"And did you come to any conclusions?"

Omar smiled. "I'll tell you the same thing I told her."

"Which is?"

"You've shared ten years together and it's downright foolish to throw that away. You both need to decide what's important and what isn't and you'd better do so in a hurry."

"Family is important to me," Frank replied flatly. "I want children, and Lynn's afraid I'll never be around long enough to help raise them and be a real father to them."

"You suppose your long hours and traveling has anything to do with her fears?" Omar questioned, taking the chair Lynn had vacated.

"I suppose it does, but a man has to work. I can't just up and quit a good job in order to be home all the time. I don't know what Lynn expects from me, but when we married, we both agreed that I would work and she would stay home and take care of our children. She used to like the idea."

"Maybe she liked the idea of family. You know, her own was kind of taken from her at an early age."

"She told me about her parents. She said that's why she was afraid of having kids. I think she's way off base here. I see nothing wrong with having children and still maintaining my job. I probably wouldn't travel as much, but—"

"You'd better get you a mighty fine picture album," Omar interjected.

"Huh?" Frank was taken totally aback by this.

"You'd better get a picture album. One with lots of pages," Omar answered. "You'll need it if you plan to keep up with your traveling and long hours and still want to see those kids. Course, it won't be the same as being there with them, seeing them do things for the first time, speak their first words. Photographs aren't the same as making your own memories."

The old man finished his coffee and got up. "You can have the room at the top of the stairs. I'd suggest with the way that snow is coming down, you'd best be bringing your things in right away."

Frank could only stare and nod. His mind was still on Omar's words. Reluctantly, he got to his feet and made his way out to the car. He had no reason to doubt Omar knew what he was talking about, but the truth bothered Frank in a major way. A lot of men raise good families and don't necessarily work an eight-to-five job, he told himself. He thought of his friend Mike and how happy Mike seemed with his family, in spite of his traveling position. Then just as quickly, Frank remembered a conversation he'd had with Mike. Mike had spoken of missing his oldest son's birthday. It was a meeting that couldn't be avoided, and Mike had bought the child an outrageously expensive gift to make up for it, but his son wanted nothing to do with it or him.

Would my kids feel that way? Frank wondered as he pulled his suitcases from the trunk. The ordeal had really hurt Mike. Glancing back at the house, Frank realized he hadn't begun to think this thing completely through. Lynn was angry and hurt, and Omar was stuck in the middle. With a sigh, he headed back to the house. He had a tough road ahead of him, if he was going to figure out a way to save his marriage.

CHAPTER 7

By the time Lynn came down to breakfast the next morning, both Omar and Frank were wrestling a Christmas tree into the house through the back door.

"Good morning," Frank called enthusiastically.

"Morning," Lynn answered, trying hard not to look directly at him. She'd cried most of the night and now her eyes were red and swollen. There was no hope Frank wouldn't realize what had taken place, but nevertheless, she tried to conceal her face.

"Omar suggested we get us a Christmas tree. I thought it sounded like a smart idea."

"Figured you two could decorate it while I go to town," Omar added.

Lynn poured herself a cup of coffee. "What about the snow, Gramps? Do you think it's wise to drive by yourself? I could take you wherever you needed to go."

"I wouldn't hear of it. Don't go figuring me for an old man who can't take care of himself," Omar told her. He and Frank maneuvered the tree past Lynn and into the living room.

Lynn followed at a conservative pace. She had no heart to tell her beloved Gramps that her heart wasn't into celebrating

Christmas. She was confused by her feelings and this just wasn't helping matters at all.

She watched silently as the men arranged the tree and stood back to admire their handiwork. Frank looked so good to her, and all she really wanted to do was run and throw her arms around him. He looked much like he had the first time she'd laid eyes on him. He had come down to do community service at the local homeless shelter. Lynn was working in the day-care center and playing with about half a dozen toddlers when he'd popped into the room. He'd worn blue jeans, just as he did now, and a sweatshirt that very nearly resembled the one he wore today. His hair was tousled and windblown, and his blue eyes studied her with such intensity that he had made her blush.

Pulling her thoughts back into the present, she realized Frank was studying her now, just as he had studied her then. Only this time he didn't smile.

"You kids have a good time with this. You'll find the box of decorations over there on the piano bench," Omar said, pointing. "I'll be gone for a couple of hours, so don't look for me until after lunch."

Lynn wanted to say something, but her throat constricted the words. Frank walked with Omar to the door, said something that she couldn't hear, then laughed and patted the old man on the back. They seemed conspiratorially chummy. Too chummy, as far as Lynn was concerned. This was her haven and sanctuary and Frank had invaded it.

Frank closed the door and turned to give her a sympathetic nod. "I see by your face, you've spent most of the night crying. I won't say I did the same, but I sure didn't sleep."

Lynn hadn't expected him to admit to being just as troubled

over the situation as she was. "I don't suppose either of us will sleep much until we get past this."

Frank shook his head. "I don't want to get past it if it means losing you. Lynn, I don't want to give up on our marriage. It's that simple. I'll do whatever I can to make it work."

"I wish I could believe that," Lynn replied, walking absent-mindedly over to the box of Christmas decorations.

"You can," Frank assured her, coming to stand beside her. "Look, we've got some issues to sort through. Just tell me what you want me to do, and I'll do my best to see it through."

Lynn shook her head. "I don't want to run your life. As much as you might think that's the case, it isn't."

"What do you want, Lynn?"

"I don't know." She pulled out a string of lights and let Frank take them from her. "It just doesn't seem like we're cut out to be married to each other."

Frank had just started to wrap the lights around the spindly spruce. At Lynn's words he stopped. "Do you really believe that? After ten years of marriage?"

Lynn picked up a crocheted snowflake ornament and shrugged. "I don't know what I believe anymore. I thought I knew. I thought I understood it very clearly. But last night I prayed and prayed and nothing seems very clear."

"What about our love? Isn't that clear?"

Lynn looked up and allowed her gaze to lock with his. "My love is."

"But mine isn't? Is that it?"

"I don't feel very loved," she barely whispered.

Just then the telephone rang, and Lynn moved to picked it up. "Lewiston residence." She glanced to where Frank stood trying to adjust the string of lights. "Yes, he's here."

Frank looked up as if surprised. "It's for me?"

Lynn nodded and put down the receiver. "Why am I not surprised?"

Frank went to the phone, while Lynn forced herself to focus on decorating the tree. George Bridgeton himself was calling for her husband. It would be important and it would no doubt require Frank's utmost attention. It might even necessitate his return to Chicago.

Her heart ached at the thought. Surely he wouldn't just up and leave. Not when so much was at stake. Lynn tried not to listen to Frank's animated conversation, but she couldn't help it.

"If there's another way to do this, I'd rather not," Frank said firmly.

He glanced at her, but Lynn looked quickly away. She didn't want him to feel pressured by her stares. If he stayed, she wanted him to do so because he wanted to. Because he knew how much it would mean to her if just once he told Bridgeton National Life, "No."

"All right, where?" Frank asked, running a hand through his hair.

Lynn could always tell his degree of frustration by this move. Things weren't going well, and suddenly she knew she'd lost another round.

"Yes. I understand," Frank replied. "But you owe me." He hung up the phone and looked at Lynn with such a pained expression that she almost forgot to be hurt. Almost.

"I have to fly up to Chicago."

"I figured as much."

"I tried to get out of it. You must have heard me," Frank said, coming toward her.

"I tried not to listen," Lynn replied, turning away from him on the pretense of hanging another ornament.

"George said the case is falling apart. It could cost Bridgeton millions."

"Sorry to hear that." She knew her tone left him little doubt as to her mood over this latest development.

"I have to drive to Topeka. I'm supposed to catch a hop to Kansas City and then to Chicago. I'll be back as soon as possible."

"Whatever," Lynn replied, trying hard not to cry. He was leaving her again. Leaving her for his job and making it very clear that she could never hope to count on him being there solely for her.

"Lynn," he said, barely whispering her name. He'd come to stand directly behind her and put his hands on her shoulders. "We can get through this, but we have to be willing to work together. We'll have to compromise a few places, but I know we can work this out."

Lynn refused to turn and let him see the tears that had come to her eyes. "I'm glad you're so certain."

Frank turned her very gently and lifted her face to meet his. "Please don't cry. I love you, Lynnie. I love you more than you will ever know." He traced a tear with his finger. "I promise to make this as short as possible."

"Just go," Lynn told him, trying to pull away.

He wouldn't let her go and instead encircled her with his arms and held her tightly against him. "I don't want to go," he whispered.

"But you will," she countered, growing completely still in his arms. "You will."

And a half an hour later, he did just that. Lynn listened to the echo of the door latching and forced herself to keep from running after him. *I have to be strong,* she told herself. *I can't fall apart.*

She heard his car start up and felt her resolve waver. Almost running to the radio, she switched it on and turned up the volume. A rich baritone voice was just concluding "O Holy Night," and the DJ was segueing right into a choral version of "O Christmas Tree."

"O Christmas tree," Lynn joined in rather bitterly. "O Christmas tree, guess once again it's just you and me."

Frank sat opposite George Bridgeton and handed him a stack of signed papers. "It's finalized and both parties have agreed to the settlement."

George smiled broadly. "A job well done. I can't thank you enough."

"I'm glad I could help, but I'm sorry to say, it will probably be the last time."

George's smile faded. "What are you saying, Frank?"

Frank had given the matter much consideration. For as long as the negotiations had taken between the two parties, he could hardly think of anything but Lynn's sorrowful expression upon the news that he was leaving.

"I suppose I'm resigning my position," he replied. "I know it sounds crazy, but this job has taken a huge toll on my marriage, and I can't go on without making significant changes."

"Such as?" George asked softly.

"Such as an eight-to-five schedule where I can be fairly certain of going home each night at a regular time."

"What else?"

Frank sighed. "That's pretty much it. I need to stop traveling so much. In fact, for a time, I probably need to stop traveling altogether."

"And if I told you I had a position that would allow all of this and result in an increase in salary, would you stay?"

Frank looked at George for a moment before answering. "Are you saying such a position exists?"

George grinned. "I am."

Frank swallowed hard. He hadn't dared to allow himself to even believe such a thing was possible. He'd prayed for practically the entire flight home, begging God to give him the strength to forget his worries over money. He wanted to prove once and for all to Lynn that she meant more to him than the job. Now it appeared God had honored his faith—faith that hadn't come easy given the details of his past.

"I can't begin to explain what I've been through," Frank replied. "I've been praying constantly about the situation and it seemed my only hope was to quit my job. Lynn feels I've put my career ahead of her, and I can't say as I blame her. I'm gone more than I'm home, and lately I've been bugging her about having a family. She put her foot down and told me she wasn't about to start having kids if there wasn't going to be a father around to help raise them."

"Smart woman," George said, quite seriously. "And just so you know it, Frank, I've been praying too. Ray told me what happened and how you found out that Lynn had gone without a word. I just started adding everything up and figured a change of pace was probably in order for you. However, I didn't want to force it on you."

"So what did you have in mind?" Frank asked, almost afraid to know.

"I'd like you to be my vice president. My wife would kind of like to see me take more time off too." He laughed. "Sounds like our wives could probably become good friends. We'll have to get them together sometime."

Frank laughed for the first time in days. It felt as though a tremendous weight had been lifted from his shoulders. "This is almost too good to be true."

"It's answered prayer for both of us. We can discuss the details of the position later, but I have a feeling that like Dorothy in *The Wizard of Oz*, you're just itching to get back to Kansas."

"Yes, sir," Frank admitted, "I am."

"Then go. There's a ticket waiting for you at O'Hare and a commuter will take you from Kansas City to Topeka. The rest is up to you," George said with a smile.

"You can't imagine what this means to me," Frank replied, getting to his feet.

"I was once young like you. I missed out on a great deal that related to my family, and I've always regretted it. I hope to keep you from doing the same thing."

"Me too."

~⁀

"Now, aren't you glad I talked you into Christmas shopping?" Omar asked Lynn.

Lynn smiled up at him. "Yes, it was a good idea." She continued glancing into the shop windows of Main Street Council Grove. "I still haven't figured out something for Frank. Not that he probably wants anything from me."

"A photo album," Omar said without any explanation.

"What?"

"Trust me. Get the man a photo album. They've got some real pretty ones in here," Omar said, pulling Lynn into one of the stores.

She shrugged and let Omar lead her to where the photograph supplies were stashed rather sloppily on a shelf near the back of the store. Omar looked through the meager supply, then waved over a store clerk.

"Where's that real nice album you had here last week? The one with the silver plating on the front—makes it look like a picture frame."

The girl smiled. "Oh, I know the one you mean. I think we still have one of those in the back. Hold on a minute." She took off down the aisle and Omar smiled.

Lynn had no idea what the big deal was with a photograph album, but at least it was something to give Frank—just in case he came back in time for Christmas. She felt completely empty inside. Frank meant the world to her. She'd spent most of the time since he'd gone praying and thinking, and the conclusion she'd come to was to go home.

She walked a few steps away and toyed with a selection of wallets while Omar conducted business with the salesgirl. Home. That's all she really wanted. Staying with Gramps had been a blessing, but when Frank had come to her there, she realized how empty even this haven had been. She belonged with Frank. She loved Frank. And somewhere in her silent nights she had decided that even if she couldn't have him on a full-time basis, she would take whatever she could get. She would go home to her husband and raise the family they both wanted, and whether or not he ever understood her need, well, she'd live with the consequences.

"You going to stand there staring off into space all day?" Omar questioned.

Lynn looked up and realized he'd finished with the selection of the album and now stood at her side. "Sorry," she said, smiling sheepishly.

"Come on," he said, acting as though it wasn't important. "I have the album. You'd better pick out some wrapping paper."

Lynn nodded and followed, but her thoughts were of her marriage and of all the complications she had created by running away from her problems. God had come to her in a very real fashion in His Word—encouraging her to let loose of her worries about the future.

Overhead the store intercom played Christmas carols. Lynn smiled as the singers joyfully exclaimed, "Let it snow, let it snow, let it snow."

"Let it go, let it go, let it go," she murmured to the tune.

"What was that?" Omar questioned, looking at her curiously.

"Oh, nothing," Lynn countered. "I was just singing."

CHAPTER 8

Lynn and Omar returned from the Christmas Eve services, neither one saying much about Frank's obvious absence. Lynn could tell Gramps wanted to comfort her, but he said nothing, choosing instead to concentrate on the snowy road.

"I'm going home," Lynn finally said.

Gramps nodded. "Thought it through, did you?"

"Yes. I've decided that having Frank part of the time is better than not having him at all. I love him, Gramps."

"I know you do, and you know what else?"

"No, what?"

"He loves you too. I had a nice long talk with that boy when we were scouting out a Christmas tree. He's going through a hard time, but he knows what's right and wrong and he knows what he needs to do. I think if you give him half a chance, he'll make this work out for the both of you."

Just then, as they rounded the bend to the Lewiston farm, the truck's headlights beamed out across Frank's car.

"I hope you're right, Gramps," Lynn said softly. "I pray you're right."

Omar parked his truck beside the cars, the tires sliding ever so slightly in the packed snow. Omar handled it without any noticeable concern. "Not bad for an old man, eh?"

"No," Lynn replied, leaning over to give him a kiss on the cheek. "Not bad at all. In fact, I'd say you're something pretty special, Gramps."

Just then, Frank switched on the porch light and emerged from the house. He pushed his hands deep into his pockets. "I let myself in," he called out as Omar and Lynn got out of the truck. "Hope you don't mind."

"You're family," Omar replied. "I would hope you'd have sense enough to let yourself in out of the cold."

"We went to church," Lynn offered as explanation.

Frank looked at her and smiled. It warmed her through to the bone. How she loved this man. When he looked at her the way he was just now, Lynn could very easily forget there was ever any problem. She missed him. Missed his touch and his kiss. Missed his teasing and his long speeches on the injustices of the court system. She just missed him.

"I thought you might have. I tried to get here earlier, but the commuter flight was delayed in Kansas City."

"Lynnie, I'm going up to my room. I kind of figure on getting to bed early tonight," Gramps told her as they climbed the porch steps. He gave her a wink, then kissed her lightly on the head. "If you need me, you'll know where I am."

He walked into the house, letting the screen door bang against the jamb. Lynn stared after him for a moment, then turned her attention to Frank. *Please God,* she prayed, *let us work this out so that we both feel good about going home together.*

"I'm glad you're here," she finally said.

"You are?" Frank asked hopefully.

Lynn nodded. "Yes. Come on inside. I think we should talk."

They settled themselves on Omar's well-worn couch. Everything in the house looked like it had been purchased in the 1950s, and the couch was certainly no exception with its rectangular straight-backed style and orange-rust upholstery.

Lynn turned slightly so she could see Frank's face. She drew a deep breath and nervously smoothed down the edges of her pink angora sweater. "I've been thinking."

"Me too."

"Things aren't perfect, but they're even worse now that we're completely apart."

"Yes," Frank agreed, his blue-eyed gaze piercing her heart.

"Oh, Frank," she murmured his name. "I've been so lonely. I thought it was bad at home, but it's worse here. I came to Gramps' house, remembering how I always felt secure and happy here, but that was before I met you and fell in love."

"I'm sorry you were lonely at home." His voice was soft and warm, the sincerity of his heart quite evident. "I never meant it to be that way."

"I know."

Silence filled the room for several seconds before she continued. "I know you have to work, and now I guess I can better understand why your job is so important to you."

"I quit my job."

"What!" Lynn nearly jumped up from the couch. "You what?"

Frank grinned mischievously at her. "That's what you wanted, isn't it?"

"Well. . .no. . .I mean. . .maybe," she sputtered. "What are we going to do? Did you really quit?"

Frank laughed and rubbed the palm of his hands against his

jean-clad thighs. "In a sense. I went to George as soon as the case was settled. I told him I couldn't continue to travel and work all the crazy hours I was giving him. I told him it was destroying the only really important thing in my life. You."

Lynn felt tears come to her eyes. "Oh, Frank. I can't believe it."

"Well, it's true," he said. "George was very understanding. Said he'd been praying about it and he knew I needed a change. He accepted my resignation and offered me another position."

"Another position?"

"Yes. You're now looking at Bridgeton National's newest vice president."

"And you won't be gone so much of the time?"

"Nope," Frank said, smiling. "I'm going to be an eight-to-fiver and I'll leave traveling to Ray. There might come the need for an occasional trip or a few overtime hours, but George assured me it would be minimal. He even gave us a Christmas present."

"This was gift enough," Lynn said, barely able to speak.

Frank held up two airline tickets. "Our trip to Mexico."

"What?" Lynn could hardly believe what she was seeing or hearing. "Our anniversary trip?"

"Yes ma'am." Frank held them out to her, but Lynn pushed them aside and slowly came across the couch to put herself in Frank's arms.

"Last night, I told God that if I could only have you part of the time, even a few days out of the year, it was better than never having you at all." She inhaled deeply and smiled at the scent of his cologne. There was a great deal of happiness in familiar things, she decided.

"I told God that even if most of my nights were silent nights,

I'd be all right, so long as you came back to me once in a while. I told Him I'd go home and live with whatever time you could give me."

"Oh, honey," Frank murmured, pulling her tightly against him. "I'm so sorry for the lost time. I'm so sorry I allowed money and fear to control me. I'm not saying there won't be any future problems, but I am assuring you that this issue won't be one of them. I see the error of my ways. I know what it nearly cost me."

"Thank you, Frank. Thank you for the best Christmas of my life. Say, I have an idea." She scooted away from him and went to the Christmas tree. "Let's open our presents. I have something for you, but I have to admit, it was Gramps' idea."

"Why should we open our presents now?" Frank questioned curiously. "I kind of liked the snuggling we were doing."

Lynn cocked her head and grinned. "If we open our presents now, we won't be in any hurry to get up in the morning."

Frank jumped up from the couch so quickly he made Lynn squeal in surprise. "Then open mine first," he declared, reaching for a rectangular gift box.

Lynn laughed. "I'll open mine while you open yours." She handed him the wrapped present and took the box.

"It's a deal."

They opened their gifts, and Lynn couldn't help but gasp at the contents of her gift box. "Oh, Frank. It's exquisite." Inside was an antique jewelry box.

"Lift the lid," he encouraged.

She did so and listened to the music box rendition of "Silent Night." "I love it," she whispered.

"I hoped you would," he said, reaching out to take hold of her hand. "I have something else for you at home, but this just seemed to speak your name."

"What do you think of your present?" Lynn asked, straining to control her emotions.

Frank finished unwrapping the paper and laughed out loud.

"What?" Lynn questioned. "Gramps said it would be perfect."

"It is," Frank replied.

"Then why are you laughing?"

"Omar told me I'd better set my priorities straight if I planned to have a family. He said I'd need to get a good photograph album if I insisted on keeping my job and seeing anything of my family."

Lynn stiffened slightly at the mention of children. She wanted to bring the subject up herself. Wanted to tell him that she'd decided to have a baby as soon as God allowed them to conceive. It seemed such a delicate subject, however, that she'd just not gotten around to it yet, and now Frank was speaking of it and she didn't know what to say.

Frank sensed her mood and put the album aside. Reaching out, he took the music box from her hands and put it with the album. Pulling her with him to the couch, Frank drew her into his arms. "There's something else I want to say," he told her, pushing her back just far enough so he could see her face. "You don't have to have a baby—if you don't want to. I was wrong to badger you about a family. Children should come into a home where they are wanted by both parents. I would never force you to have my baby, and I just want you to know that, here and now."

Lynn smiled, knowing what it had cost him to say those words. "Frank, I want to have your baby. I want to have lots of your babies. I just wanted to have them with you."

He reached up to touch her face and Lynn felt her pulse quicken. "I think that's a workable situation."

"You think so, eh?" Lynn teased.

"It would make a rather nice Christmas present, don't you think?"

Lynn laughed out loud, then realized Omar was just upstairs. "Perhaps, we should take this to my room."

Frank had her up on her feet before she could say another word. Pulling her against him, he kissed her passionately. Lynn melted against him, relishing the feelings of desire that washed over her. No one else existed in the whole world. There was no one but this man—this moment—this love.

Before she knew it, Frank had started walking her toward the stairs. His embrace remained tight, however, and before she could protest, he'd swept her up into his arms.

She giggled out loud.

"Well, it looks like I got my Christmas wish," Omar said from the top of the stairs.

Lynn felt her face grow hot and Frank just laughed. "Guess we got a little noisy, huh?"

"Sorry, Gramps," Lynn added.

"I'm not," Omar said with a laugh. "I couldn't be happier. Looks like we all get a merry Christmas."

"Yes," Lynn replied. "And no more silent nights."

EPILOGUE

After two years of acting as Bridgeton National Life's vice president, Frank came to realize just how much he'd missed out on during his years of travel. He was content in a way he could never hope to put into words. God had blessed him over and over, and when all had seemed hopeless, God had seen him through the worst of it and had given him more than he could have ever imagined possible.

Stacking firewood into a sling, Frank whistled a Christmas tune and headed back into his new house. He heard Lynn's voice coming from the living room and laughed to hear her rearranging the words of yet another yuletide carol.

"O Christmas tree, O Christmas tree, instead of one baby, I got three."

Frank laughed and looked from where Lynn danced around throwing tinsel on the Christmas tree to where his triplet daughters sat clapping and laughing at their mother's antics.

To say they had been surprised by the arrival of triplets was putting it mildly. To say they'd been blessed far beyond comprehension was also an understatement.

"So how are the Murphy women?" Frank questioned, unloading

the wood beside the fireplace.

"We are all just fine," Lynn replied. "The girls think they completely understand this tree business and have decided that next year they will handle the decorating themselves."

Frank laughed and came to embrace his wife. "I'm sure they will give us plenty of help throughout the season. After all, they are starting to walk with rapid agility."

Lynn nodded. "They are something else, aren't they?"

"I'm amazed at this thing which you have done, Mrs. Murphy," Frank told her, giving her a light kiss on the lips. "I never fail to be amazed, even now over a year after their birth."

Lynn pulled back, a mischievous grin on her face. "You think this is something, wait until you see what I do next time."

About the Author

Tracie Peterson, often called the "Queen of Historical Christian fiction," is an ECPA, CBA, and *USA Today* bestselling author of over 130 books, most of those historical novels. Her work in historical fiction earned her the Lifetime Achievement Award from American Christian Fiction Writers in 2011 and the Career Achievement Award in 2007 from *Romantic Times*, as well as multiple best-book awards. Throughout her career, Tracie has also worked as a managing editor of Heartsong Presents under Barbour Publishing, speaker of various events, and teacher of writing workshops. She was a cofounding member of the American Christian Fiction Writers organization and has worked throughout her career to encourage new authors. Tracie, a Kansas native, now makes her home in the mountains of Montana with her husband of over forty years.

JOIN US ONLINE!

Christian Fiction for Women

Christian Fiction for Women is your online home for the latest in Christian fiction.

Check us out online for:

- Giveaways
- Recipes
- Info about Upcoming Releases
- Book Trailers
- News and More!

Find Christian Fiction for Women at Your Favorite Social Media Site:

 Search "Christian Fiction for Women"

 @fictionforwomen
